A BAND OF
ANGELS

Also by
JULIAN F. THOMPSON

Discontinued
Facing It
A Question of Survival
The Grounding of Group 6

A BAND OF ANGELS

JULIAN F. THOMPSON

**SCHOLASTIC
HARDCOVER**

Scholastic Inc.
New York

Library of Congress Cataloging-in-Publication Data

Thompson, Julian F.
A band of angels.

Summary: While traveling across the country, a group of teenagers decide to launch a kids' campaign against nuclear war unaware
that they are being pursued by government agents determined to
kill each of them.
[1. Antinuclear movement — Fiction]   I. Title.
PZ7.T371596Ban 1986   [Fic]   85-24984

ISBN 0-590-33780-7

12 11 10 9 8 7 6 5 4 3 2 1   4   6 7 8 9/8 0 1/9

Printed in the U.S.A.   12

In loving memory of Sarah,
for Jason and Darien and Rebeccah,
and two billion other children.
And for Polly, more than ever.

PROLOGUE — 1971

For more than a week, they'd been shredding up their old lab notes, and taking the shreds out of the building in their pockets, and releasing them out of the car window on the drive home. She'd written up some new notes in their place, and from time to time she'd read what she'd written to him, and he'd actually laugh.

During that time they'd also poured the various solutions they'd been using into different sinks, replacing the tightly stoppered test tubes on their racks, loaded now with different colored waters.

When they did the pouring and the shredding, they always had the door locked.

That was an extra precaution. He believed they'd fooled the man from HEW, the Department of Health, Education, and Welfare — the man who'd carefully explained to them why it was that if they got "it," the government must have "it." Not his "people," of course, but the Defense Department. That would be "just in case" the Russians ever succeeded in concocting a supervirus of their own, he'd said; "it" would be "our check and balance," so to speak — a chip to bargain with, if need be. Of course, he said, we'd *never* use it. There'd be no winner in a supervirus war. He'd said he would be back in two weeks' time.

They both had listened to the man, both with their minds racing, both praying that the other one would keep his cool, or hers. They both had nodded, said they understood, "of course." He'd been afraid the man might see his heart beat through his lab coat, and she had smiled and clenched her teeth against the sentences she would have liked to scream: that they were doctors, healers, interested in saving human lives, not taking them; interested in general disarmament, not weapons. They both had told the man that what he'd learned was true. Preliminary tests *were* "promising," but the final product — "it" — was still a good ways up the road.

That wasn't true. Even as they spoke those words, they had "it" in the room, right there.

It took them days to talk the whole thing through. It was insane that they had gotten in a mess like this. The reason they had gone into research at all was . . . *pressure*, you could say. They both had been the same, although some years apart, in med school:

always on the edge of screaming, even dropping out. Although they both got A's, they never had the *time*, they felt, to really learn; to do a proper job. Internship was even worse; both of them — in different cases, places, times — blamed themselves for patient pains and even patient deaths. They cared so much, perhaps too much. Too much for their own good, for sure. They often said to one another that they were twins as well as lovers.

And so they'd, separately, decided on research: the quiet of the lab, a different kind of competition; no exhausting sense of guilt. Who would have ever thought that knowledge of their work would somehow reach *those* people? And that now, that now. . . .

The problem wasn't the work; they could always destroy the work. They *would* destroy the work, their notes, and so on. The problem was the knowledge in their minds. They knew how to do it. And so, the knowledge was accessible.

For one thing, they believed there were chemical ways of forcing them to give up what they knew. It wasn't their field, but they'd heard stories. An injection, a trained questioner, and the facts would just flow out of them.

But there was an even easier way than that. All the government would have to do would be to take their baby, and threaten him with any sort of harm. A bad *pinching* would be all the threat to him she'd need, she told her husband; she'd tell them anything.

So what was left for them to do was very simple, really; there wasn't any other way. They'd kept their money — savings and inheritance — in several different high-yield, accessible investment accounts, so it had been easy enough to get a lot of cash together in one place. The night before The Day, they'd told the entire story to their closest friend, telling her about the money — even showing her the suitcase, where it was — and how they planned to take it and the baby, and to simply disappear. Plan A, they called it, talking to each other. If *she* — an outside person — saw the thing the way that they did, it'd mean they weren't being paranoid. It'd mean they had to go ahead. They counted on her clarity, her outsideness.

She had agreed with them; it seemed the only thing to do, she'd said. She'd cried. It meant she'd lose her three best friends, she told them. She'd been there at the baby's birth and loved him, in her way, as much as they did.

They both were sure she'd do as she was asked, when the moment came. In a way, it was totally unfair — immoral, even — to put that sort of burden on a person; but they'd convinced themselves they didn't have a choice. She loved the baby, and she'd understand. If she could understand Plan A, she'd have to see Plan B was even better.

Plan B would mean that "it" was gone forever. Or at least until the time some other researchers had the skill and luck it took to find "it." Plan B would solve the problem. Though neither of them said it to the other, Plan B had been, for many, many years . . . familiar to them both.

Before they made the phone call, having drunk the solution, they laid out on a lab bench some writings that they wanted to be found with them. There wouldn't be a note, just those.

She smiled and gestured at the racks of test tubes holding only colored water, and the lab notes full of jokes, and the pamphlets and the open books in front of them. And she said to him, "Except for us, perhaps, they'll find a very peaceful scene."

They knew exactly where she'd be that day: at their house, working, caring for the baby. She did that twice a week. He made the phone call, talking through her protestations on the other end, giving her the facts: that what they'd done already was a fact, and irreversible. He thought that she was very near hysteria, but then, who wouldn't be?

The custodian who came to clean the lab found them with their arms around each other.

PART ONE

1

THE ACCIDENT —
1985

Riley actually saw it happen. She'd been on the other side of the street, right on the corner, with her toes hooked over the edge of the curbstone as if that piece of granite was a starting block and she was on her mark. It was the twentieth of June, and she was — merchants, grit your teeth and shake your heads — boldly and entirely barefoot. All the way to slightly past the middle of her thighs, to give you still another horrifying fact.

The woman who stepped off the curb across the street from her had never looked where she was going. In a way, of course, she couldn't; it can't be seen from here. One moment, the woman was stepping off the curb and looking back, talking to the boy who'd stopped and hunkered down to tie his tennis shoe. The next moment, with the light still showing amber, she was hit and tossed and rag-doll-floppy: broken, dead.

If the boy, who was about her age, had had no shoes on (so thought Riley Roux, peculiarly) that woman might be still alive right now. She stood there frozen on the curbstone, with her toes still hooked and holding it.

The next events were slightly less peculiar. A man ran from the other corner, the one to Riley's right, to kneel beside the woman sprawled out in the intersection. The car that hit her was long gone. The man knelt just the way a priest might kneel at his devotions, on both knees; he touched the woman here and there. The man was not a priest, he was a doctor, Dr. Illuzzi. He'd thought of becoming a priest when he was a freshman in college and was having all kinds of trouble getting dates with any of the girls he thought were worth his while, and a moment or two after he kneeled down next to the woman, he wished a priest *was* there that minute, a priest or *anyone*, instead of him. The woman was dead and he was a doctor, overqualified for kneeling in the street, and with a lifeboat-load of patients on his calendar.

A cop came out of City Hall, took in the scene, and shouted something back inside the door before it closed behind him. Then he hustled to the place the woman lay and stood beside the doctor, looking down, and speaking. Riley saw the doctor shake his head. The policeman gave *himself* a little shake and

10

raised his eyes. He might have wanted to tell somebody to step back or move along, but there wasn't
anyone that close, yet.

She saw the ambulance arrive, and guys rush out
of it and listen to the kneeling man, and then slow
down and start with their routine. As a matter of
fact, one of the guys was a woman, Riley noticed.

All the time, she also watched the boy. She might
have anyway. He was shaped like Michael Jackson,
only taller: slender with a lot of curly black hair and
a smooth, unwhiskered, mocha-colored face. The
face, of course, was completely different from Michael's. This boy had much more of a nose, equally
enormous eyes with thick black brows, a pointed
chin.

Probably he'd been squatting down and looking
at his shoe when the woman was hit, and by the
time he'd straightened up and taken everything in,
the doctor was already kneeling there beside her,
and the cop was running down the street in their
direction. Four kids coming out of the arcade on the
corner diagonally across from Riley walked over and
stared, soon joined by an older man and woman
carrying plastic shopping bags half full of empty beer
and soda cans and bottles.

The boy became a part of this small group; these
other six, who stood and watched the ambulance
people pile the woman on a stretcher and put her
into their van. There wasn't any blood. The cop had
taken out a notebook and, as Riley crossed the street
in his direction, he asked the people there if anyone
had seen the accident; had seen the car that hit the
woman. Riley saw that everyone, the boy included,

shook his head or hers, or shrugged.

As the ambulance pulled away, the four kids from the arcade headed back in the direction of the arcade. The man and the woman collecting empties were drawn toward the big green trash barrel by the steps of City Hall. The boy just turned and started walking back up the street, the one he must have just come down. He didn't weave or stumble, but neither did he stride along. It was hard to tell from the back, but he looked kind of spacey, to Riley. She followed him.

He walked slowly up the street, with his arms swinging. Riley thought of the word *shambled*. He had on straight-leg jeans above the tennis shoes — no socks, at least — and above the jeans he wore a loose, knit, cotton crew-neck sweater, with the sleeves pushed halfway up his forearms, which were tan. The sweater was a nice light aqua. Riley thought that was a good color for a black-haired, dark-com-plected person.

The boy kept on going for three blocks. He didn't look in any of the shop windows, he just shambled along. But when he came to the Unitarian Church, he wandered off the sidewalk and onto the big lawn that surrounded the church, and he walked across it until he came to a smooth, young birch tree. He turned around and put his back to the birch tree, and then he more or less slid down it, until he was sitting on the ground at the base of the tree, with his back and the back of his head against the trunk of it, and his knees drawn up, and his hands flat on the ground on either side of his butt.

Once the boy was seated, Riley Roux stepped off the sidewalk, too, and went across the lawn in his direction. As she got closer, she could see his eyes were closed, and tears were running down his cheeks.

2

JORDAN PARADISE

Being barefoot, and wearing just a dark blue T-shirt with her pure white shorts, Riley Roux had moved without a sound. When she was very near the boy she crossed her feet and sat straight down, folding her body quietly and neatly, the way an athlete is able to. She sat there, tailor-fashion, on the ground and waited.

In a while the boy reached down behind him, eyes still closed. He fished a red bandanna from his right back pocket. He blew his nose and opened his eyes, and there was Riley.

"Hello," she said. "I saw what happened and I'm very, very sorry. I wondered . . . well, if maybe I could help some way. My name is Riley. I live right here in Northfield."

The boy first wadded up his bandanna and pushed it in the same back pocket.

"I don't know," he said. "I just don't know." His voice was soft and husky. Spacey. He slowly put his right hand out, in her direction.

My God, she thought, this kid wants to shake hands.

"My name is Jordan Paradise," he said. "Maybe you can tell me what I ought to do."

She took his hand and looked in his big dark eyes. What she saw in them was mostly sweetness and confusion, swimming in a sort of emptiness. Just like outer space, she thought, mysterious and deep. Pure spacey-ness. Of course, she didn't rule out drugs.

"Let's start by going to my house," Riley said.

3

RILEY ROUX

The next surprise for Riley was: The boy had wheels, a car, a station wagon, yet — big, dark blue, complete with plates from out of state. He also had a driver's license that he'd gotten somewhere else, a third state altogether, way down south, he said. Riley would have liked to see that license. *Jordan Paradise?* She knew she'd never seen the guy before, or heard that name.

He drove all right, followed her directions calmly, without question. Left just past that Texaco; bear right now, at the blinker; keep on going straight for half a mile, until you see. . . . She said to him, "The woman who was killed, was she . . . a relative?"

"No, no," he said. "She used to be my mother's closest friend. A good friend of my father's, too." He paused. "And mine, of course." His voice had trouble saying that, the last part.

She didn't ask him anything else, on the way. At one point he started to whistle, but stopped before she recognized the tune.

Riley's parents' house was huge and modern; fairly new, not understated. If anything, outspoken. Here is what it said: Look at me. I cost a lot of money. It sat off the road a ways and had a lovely view; before it was built and landscaped, there had been a lovely view from the road.

Jordan drove the car between the white brick posts with frosted light globes on the top of them, then up the white-topped, crunchy driveway. As they approached the house, he slowed way down, until the car was barely moving.

"You can leave it here," she told him. "Right in front. My parents are away at fat camp."

He cocked his head and looked at her, one eyebrow pulled way down. Riley puffed her cheeks and raised and bent her arms in front of her, as if she had a barrel on. *She* wasn't fat, no way; she wasn't skinny either. Riley had a swimmer's body, or at least a body shaped by training for that sport, both in and out of water. She had strong, broad shoulders, small breasts, a flat belly, and long-muscled, powerful legs. She also had frizzy brown hair, parted five-and-a-half feet off the floor (a little long and growing wild, since it was June, and out of season), a big mouth, and both a tan and freckles. She'd long since given up on "glamorous," and knew she wasn't

17

even known as "lotsa fun." That bothered her, at times, because it seemed unfair. She was — could be, might be — more fun than they realized, given the right set of circumstances. She knew she was a very . . . *female* person.

"They go to this place twice a year: to get ready for summer, and to get ready for winter. Can you imagine? It's their big fitness thing. But what it amounts to, of course, is paying someone to make them do what they won't do on their own for the rest of the year. The program lasts three weeks and Daddy almost always makes the pound-a-day club. One year, he got this little sterling silver dingus, kind of like a trophy. He said it was called the Slender Reed award." She laughed. "You should see Daddy." Then she thought that maybe she was being too much fun, considering.

The boy just nodded, with a tiny, fleeting smile, but he didn't speak. He opened the car door and got out, and looked back down the driveway. Riley got out, too.

There were lots of suitcases in the back of the wagon. "Grab your bag and come on in," she said. "You are going to stay, aren't you? It's perfectly all right. You can meet Thalia, and I'll tell her you're staying. Thalia's our housekeeper. She's neat. And don't worry" — she cleared her throat — "we'll figure something out. Maybe I'll call my friend Michael and ask him to come over. He really knows all sorts of different stuff and he loves to tell *me* what to do."

Riley knew that she was being pushy; she also knew that she was nervous, very slightly nervous. "May I ask you," asked her father, once, "just when you were appointed keeper of the strays for Dennis County?" But even if her parents had been there, she still would have brought this boy back to the house, and might also have invited him to stay there. Her father probably would have made some noises but, she thought, he'd also have approved. He liked his kids to show initiative, take charge. In their absence, though, she decided it'd be good to get Michael to come and stay over, too; that'd be natural enough. There was something important they had to talk over anyway. She concentrated on relaxing, took a nice deep breath. This boy certainly didn't look even remotely dangerous, actually. He'd had a terrible, terrible shock; of course that'd make him seem a little different. Well, that was okay: Some people thought she was different, too.

Now he was standing by the back of the car.

"Well, I don't know," he said, not opening the tailgate, not reaching for a suitcase. "I'm not sure I ought to . . . you know?"

Riley *didn't* know, and so she said, "Well, anyway, why don't you just come in and use the phone? You probably have some calls you want to make, and — "

She stopped because the boy was shaking his head.

"No," he said. "There's no one I should call that I can think of. But — I don't know — what happens now, to her? To Karen. Her . . . body, I mean."

"Well," said Riley again, "I don't know exactly. But I imagine that what they do is try to . . . well, *identify* her, first. Look in her wallet, or something. And then, once they've done that, found her home address and all, they probably try to get in touch

19

with someone who lives there. Or if they can't, maybe the police in that town so's to find a friend or relative, who could make the arrangements about the funeral, or burial, or whatever they wanted."

The boy, Jordan Paradise, listened to all that with an expression of great interest, concentration, on his face. Riley couldn't remember ever being listened to so hard, even by Michael, who was pretty intense himself. But when she was finished, he looked down the driveway again and shook his head some more.

"That won't work," he said flatly. "They won't be able to find anyone. She has some relatives — a brother and some others — but she wasn't that friendly. . . . And besides, they won't be able to find them. Not going by what's in her wallet, anyway."

"Hmmm," said Riley Roux. "How about your parents, then? If your mother's her closest friend, I'm sure she'd want to know. Maybe your parents'd be the ones to do that stuff." His parents were who she thought he'd like to call, when she'd suggested that, of course. People always called their parents *in extremis*. Even people like herself, who didn't have a lot in common with the loins from which they'd sprung — or slid, whatever.

"No," the boy said. "My parents are dead."

He was looking right past her ear when he said that, and Riley had the feeling that one of three things was true: Either Jordan Paradise had not cared about his parents at all, or they'd been dead a real long time, or he was lying.

"Boy," she said, "I'm sorry. That makes this whole thing even — that much worse for you, I guess. I can't imagine. . . ." She drew a circle in the gravel with her big toe. "Listen," she said. "I'm sure we'll be able to figure out something. Maybe *you* could make the arrangements." Of course he started shaking his head right away, and Riley began to wonder if she could say *anything* ("The situation in the Middle East is dangerous." "Atomic weapons are destructive.") he'd agree with, ever.

"I mean," she went on, gamely, "without actually going to the hospital, maybe, or even *seeing* anyone, if you didn't want to. We could figure something out, I'll bet, and I'm sure Michael would be a big help with that." She paused before she got too carried away; there was a practical side to this. "Of course, whatever it is would cost some money, but maybe we can — "

"Oh, I have *money*," Jordan Paradise said. "*I* have money, some money, that'd be all right. But — I don't know — your friend. . . . I don't know him, or anything, and ordinarily I wouldn't be speaking to you even, except for . . . *I* don't know. I've just got to figure out what to *do*." And he got in a few more shakes, maybe just out of habit, Riley thought.

"Look," she said, "Michael's a lot like me. I mean, we're not all that much alike, actually. But we do a lot of the same things, and neither one of us is the sort of person who's big on hanging out, and blabbing things to people, if that's what you're worried about. I guess you could say we're not all that sociable, either of us. He doesn't even have a girl friend, right now."

She felt ridiculous after she'd said that last thing; oh hell no, she wasn't *much* of a blabber, was she?

The boy was looking at her fixedly again, but not saying anything. And he wasn't even shaking his head.

"All right," the boy said suddenly. "All right, I will." He opened the back of the station wagon. "I have to decide things," he said firmly. "You are being very kind to me, coming up to me like that, inviting me to stay. I'd hate to be alone right now. And I'm sure your friend will help me also . . . Riley." And, with that, he smiled at her — a real smile, this time.

It took her by surprise — its absolute and total friendliness, and innocence. He doesn't smile like any guy my age, she thought.

4

MICHAEL GORDON

Given all the shocks, excitement, *weirdness* of that afternoon, it surely wasn't odd that Riley hadn't mentioned Allison to Jordan Paradise. And so, of course, (it figured) there *was* Allison, coming down the staircase, just the very moment they went in. She was heading for the pool, presumably.

Allie was her sister; she was twelve, and the greatest kid in the world as far as Riley was concerned. And if that wasn't enough, she also had hair the color of maple sugar, so straight it looked as if it had been melted and poured through a strainer; blue eyes; the definite beginnings of a Fido-fetching body (as in, "Down, boy! Down!"); and at that moment, over it (just here and there) a bikini so small that her mother had forbidden her to wear it outside of her own *bathroom* ("for God's sake").

"Hi," she said to Jordan Paradise, and tossed her hair. "Hi, Kanga," to her sister. Only as practiced an Allie watcher as Riley would have noticed that her sister sort of hitched and stumbled on the bottom step, and snuck a little nibble on a thumbnail. Allison didn't know if she should stop and meet this boy — this *beautiful* new boy! — or run to get a bathrobe on. She definitely didn't know what else to say.

"We'll see you out there in a little bit," said Riley, taking over, being cool and casual — walking, pirouetting toward the dining room. "Oh, this is Jordan Paradise; he's going to stay a day or so. And Michael's probably coming over, too. We're just going to meet Thalia and get him organized. Jordan, sister Allie. Follow me."

"Hello," said Jordan Paradise. He was staring fixedly at the two crystal swans in the middle of the dining room table, and at Riley's words he trotted past her for a closer look at them, or that's the way it seemed.

"Later, then," said Allie to the label on his Levi's, recovering her poise. She even gave a little wave in their direction, then skipped lightly through the tall French doors. She had a tank suit inside the cabana by the pool, and it wouldn't seem unusual, self-conscious, *childish* — would it? — if she changed

. . . to swim some laps. Anyway, she wasn't about
to give any cheap thrills to Riley's couthless, curly-
headed friends; she'd just decided that.

Jordan Paradise met Thalia in the place she called
"my kitchen."

"All the warning that she gives me," Thalia said,
scolding Riley with a wooden spoon, "there's barely
time to thaw a TV dinner." She winked at Jordan.
"Not to say we're having that."

Jordan swallowed, bit his lip, and said that anything was wonderful. That he liked every kind of
food, and hated to be trouble.

"You're not from here," said Thalia.

"Oh, no," he said, at once. "I'm from — " He
stopped. His head went down, and his eyes went
back and forth. Riley was afraid that he was
going to cry. At last his eyes came up to Thalia's.
" —from Manchester," he said.

She nodded, looking back at him, taking him in.
"That's real nice," she finally said, and smiled.
"Manchester is *fine*."

It was after four o'clock, already.

Michael came over at five. Wild horses wouldn't
have stopped him. When he heard about the way
that Riley'd met this Jordan Paradise, he almost
flipped.

"You're sure that he was *with* the woman? I mean,
you think the two of them were *traveling* together?"
he asked her on the phone. She said that yes, she
did.

"*Peculiar*," he insisted. She told him what the boy had asked and said, about the funeral arrangements. Michael said he'd be right over.

Jordan Paradise was formal, on his best behavior, when Riley introduced them.

"Hello," he said to Michael. "I'm very pleased to meet you." They shook hands.

"Jordan?" Michael asked, typically. He looked the boy over. "Is that what you like to be called? There's a song called 'Geordie,' but I think that's short for George, in Scotland." Michael liked to have the facts on line.

Jordan said, "Jordy is also fine. Or Jordan. It doesn't matter. Anything." He gave a little laugh.

"Riley told me what happened to your friend," said Michael. "That's really rough."

And that was Michael, too; he was never one to mince words. There were kids at school who didn't go for Michael's style at all, who thought him too intense, too undiplomatic, too pushy — and a show-off, even. Riley thought that it was just the way his motor ran: no neutral or reverse, just on or off. His last name was Gordon and he'd never had a nick-name.

Michael was short, closer to Riley's height than Jordan's. If it had been just the two of them, he and Riley would have gone down to the pool before supper and swum underwater races, hacked around with Allison, played some ball tag, practiced funny dives. He was a freestyle swimmer on the high school team. The trunk of his body was shaped like an inverted triangle, and he could get it up on top of the water, the way the coaches loved him to, and really churn his way along, with his round head buried in his bow wave. At sixteen-and-a-half he had a heavy beard already, and a hairy chest, too; except at the year-end meets, when he shaved his body down to marble smoothness. He never cut his hair completely off, but he wore it very short, the year round. Riley liked his hair that way, on him; any other style, given the rest of the way he was, could easily have been too much.

Swimming was one of the things that he and Riley had in common, not just the sport but their approach to it, the weights and everything. The girl's team had to work out with the boys' at their school, and teammates sometimes found this pair "fanatical."

Michael was also founder and president of the Junior Futurists of America. He hated the Junior in the name of the organization, which was dedicated to the anticipation of, and preparation for, the changes that the human race would have to cope with and be a part of, ten or twenty years from the present time. That was his other intense interest, in addition to his swimming and his schoolwork, ranking just ahead of both of them, in fact.

Weekends, he sold all manner of appliances at a local factory-direct discount outlet owned by a cousin of his. In the family, Michael was considered a born salesman. Many people would have said — and the cousin *did* say, meaning it as flattery — that Michael sold so many microwaves and other big appliances because he liked — *believed in* — what he sold so much. Michael didn't contradict his boss but, as Riley knew, he did it for the money, his commissions. Money was a ticket to the future, he believed. To cope, one needed capital.

Earlier in the spring, he'd told Riley he was thinking of moving out of Northfield. He'd just come up to her and said that.

"Look," he'd said. "I can't believe that there aren't a lot of people who live over geological faults who *know* they have a real good chance — statistically, a *likelihood*, almost — of dying in an earthquake. Okay. So why don't they move? They don't move because it's too much trouble, or too expensive, or because they've hypnotized themselves with some non-argument like: You gotta die sometime, doncha? But the biggest reason they don't move — *I* think — is that they see a lot of other people who they think are smarter than themselves who're also staying there, not moving. Priests, geologists, and bankers — politicians, generals. They feed on one another's ostrich-headedness. *I* call it the reverse lemming effect.

"Well, I'm a futurist," he'd gone on. "Which means I mean to be there when it happens. By which I mean the future. And where it happens, too. Which, conceivably, may not be here."

It wasn't until a month later that he told Riley that in the event of a nuclear war, the Northfield area was one of about eight places in the country that doubtless had a big damn bull's-eye on it, on all the Russians' maps.

Jordan Paradise just nodded and looked away when Michael said that it was "rough" about his friend. Riley got iced tea from the refrigerator and poured them all a glass. The pitcher had some sprigs of mint in it, which Jordan asked about; she crushed a leaf and held it to his nose so he could smell it.

Carrying their glasses, they went wandering outside, and down the sloping lawn to where the pool was set, with its cabana. Allison was cruising up and down it (in her Lycra-Spandex swimsuit; not exactly streetwear, either). She'd been in age-group swimming for three years, and Riley knew that she'd be very good, if she decided that she wanted to. So far, she hadn't. Riley had suspicions Allie was afraid she'd break *her* records, trespass on her older sister's "thing." Riley was her idol, but also vice versa, which many people would have said was odd, if they'd known it.

Michael had a plan all ready in his mind. They sat around a metal table, in woven metal chairs, and he explained it. If you wore a bathing suit, those chairs left little diamonds on your thighs and fanny; but they, that night, were fully dressed. And with their glasses partway full of ice and amber-colored liquid, they looked, in that respect, a lot like Riley's parents looked, that time of day, all summer long.

"You have to have an undertaker," Michael said. "The law insists. Gilson's is the best one, here in town. You could give them any name; just make one up, and say. . . ."

Riley looked at Jordan as Michael explained it all. He was staring at the table top, his hand around the bottom of his glass — but he is concentrating hard, she thought. At least he wasn't shaking his head, so that was progress.

Michael had gone and gotten a scoring pad from

the cabana, the kind that Riley's parents used when they were playing gin. He jotted down the different things — coffin, gravestone, flowers, transportation, and so on — that Jordan would be billed for and, unsurprisingly, he offered his "best guestimate" on cost, as well.

" . . . two, three thousand, minimum. And the minimum is perfectly okay, I understand: dignified and decent — you know what I mean. Obviously, the sky's the limit on the other end. Carrera marble, mahogany — all that."

Jordan stared at *him*, then.

"Karen would like it very simple," he said. "I wish that I could bury her myself, somewhere. Without a lot of strangers having anything to do with it." He shook his head. Michael was shaking *his* head, too.

"But if that isn't possible — " He sighed. "— Three thousand dollars would be fine. I imagine I could send them cash?" he said to Michael.

Riley had her eyes on Michael, so she saw him blink before he nodded.

"Sure, no problem," he said. He licked his lips. He'd have to *see* the cash before he swallowed though, she knew.

5

DINNER

Allison went up and down the pool for more than
half an hour, flipping one turn out of four, keeping
to the same strong, steady pace. It looked completely
effortless. But when she'd finished and had ottered
out of the water smoothly, onto land — the pool
deck — she lay there for a minute in the slant-
ing sunlight, glistening and breathing deeply,
with her arms above her head. Then she rose,
and bent, and shook her hair, and went and got
a thick white terry wrapper from the cabana
before joining the other three for the walk back
up the lawn toward dinner. When they reached
the house, Riley went upstairs with her, and

so she got the word, such as it was, on Jordan Paradise.

"Wow," said Allison, wide-eyed, open-mouthed . . . *agog*. "Kanga, that's *amazing*. And mysterious. Poor *guy*." She had her sister's tendencies; Jordan was forgiven his peculiar inattentiveness — poor, curly-headed orphan boy.

Riley thought that Jordan Paradise was glad to have them back, when she and Allie came downstairs again. Michael had been asking questions. Clearly.

"Well, I'm not completely sure of that," Jordan Paradise was saying, softly. He pushed both sweater sleeves back up above his elbows. "Maybe west some more, or south. I've got to do a lot of thinking, still. Make some fresh decisions." He floated a hand up to about head height and fluttered it around, as if to circulate the possibilities.

"Is that your car out there?" asked Allison, getting down to basics. "The big blue wagon? What a boat!" She was smiling at the boy and wiggling her toes.

"Well, I guess it is" — he shook his head — "although of course, it's registered in Karen's name. I . . . I know she'd want me to just keep it. We picked it out together." And when no one spoke, he added, "It was gray."

"How come you had it painted blue?" asked Michael, as of course he would.

"We thought that would be better, maybe," Jordan said, and smiled. "Just for a change." Riley almost had the feeling he had tried to make a little joke.

They went into the dining room just as Thalia was starting to put things out on the sideboard.

"Yummy — Stroganoff," said Allison. And Riley said to her, "Why don't you lead the way?"

Then she watched Jordan Paradise watch what Allie did: Collect a plate, put down a bed of noodles first, then spoon meat and gravy onto it, crowning all of *that* with peas. This was vintage Allison; whenever possible, she liked her foods mixed up, together. Riley motioned Jordan Paradise to follow and he did, doing everything the same as Allie, right down to his portion's size. But when they'd all sat down, and he noticed that she and Michael had put their peas *next* to the other stuff, he quickly ate a forkful of his own and nudged the rest of them onto the plate, beside his other food. Riley thought she'd seen conformists in her life (the word was not a compliment, as used by her), but this was ridiculous. Yet when he looked up from his plate and caught her eye, his smile had so much gratefulness in it she once again felt touched by him, disarmed.

"What does everybody think?" said Riley to the table. "Maybe we should have some wine." She hoped she wasn't laying on the hostess bit too thick, or would *seem* to be doing so, to Michael. It wasn't that she thought Jordan was so extra cute, or nice, or even pathetic. It was just . . . she felt like having wine.

"Oh, yay," said Allison, jumping up. She didn't

much like wine, but thought she needed practice drinking it. "I'll get it, Kay. Red, right?" She disappeared into the pantry.

"Your sister doesn't call you *Riley*," Jordan Paradise observed.

"No," said Riley. "Once Allison met Winnie the Pooh, I became Kanga for life. Or Kay for short, sometimes. Kanga . . . and *Roo*?" she said. "I told you our last name was Roux, didn't I? R-O-U-X?" And she laughed.

He laughed then, too. But it reminded Riley of the way the people at Estoril, on the Portuguese coast, had laughed when she spoke to them in high-school Spanish.

"Kangaroo," he said. "Of course."

Allison came back with a bottle of wine and a corkscrew, holding them up, one in each hand, and turning back and forth between Michael and Jordan.

"Okay, gents," she said, "who does the honors?"

"Michael," Jordan Paradise replied at once. "I'm all thumbs with things like that. I always spill, too. He should be the one." And he watched while Michael turned the top of the corkscrew so that the two arms rose from its sides up to the horizontal, and how he pressed them down again to pull the cork.

The conversation during dinner didn't touch on funerals or cars — or Jordan Paradise. Not for very long at least; Riley saw to that, with help from him. It wasn't that he wouldn't answer questions at all; he dodged, slip-slided, generalized: "Oh, I don't know." "I hate to ever think about that kind of stuff." "It seems a hundred years ago." "Pretty much around the New York area." He finished off his wine and Michael filled his glass twice more.

With the dessert, the conversation turned to getting into schools and colleges. Allison was going — "being sent" — to boarding school, come fall.

"Luckily," said Riley, "she had a lot of choices. Besides being such an all-around ace of a kid, Allie really slew the test — the S-S-S-S-SAT's," she stuttered.

"SSAT's," corrected Allison, "the Secondary School Admissions Test." And Michael, a National Merit semifinalist himself, went into his usual harangue about objective testing.

"I, myself," he concluded, "would never have taken either the PSAT's *or* the SAT's, if they hadn't as good as forced me to. You'll never convince me they're a fair measure of a person's intelligence *or* aptitude — whatever they want to say — or that you can't be coached for them. But the schools still treat them like the holy of holies," he said to Jordan Paradise. "I mean, isn't that the way it is where you go?"

Jordan Paradise blinked. He looked significantly bombed, to Riley.

"I don't have any idea what you're talking about," he said to Michael, and blinked again when everybody laughed.

6

FREAKED

After dinner, Allison announced she had business with the tube: a movie she had had to miss the last three times around. She headed for the study. The other three went back outside to the terrace off the living room; there was a lot of daylight left.

Riley, feeling like her mother, took the chaise; her mother also had good-looking legs and always got to sit there. She turned at once toward Michael.

"Well?" she said. "Did you ask your parents? Talk to them, I mean?" She swiveled to her other side, now facing Jordan Paradise. "Sorry to be rude." That *was* her mother. She touched his arm, but up above his elbow, on the aqua cotton sweater. "But I had to ask him right away. A *most* important question. It's about our summer plans." Then back to Michael. "Well?"

Michael grinned at her. Jordan Paradise stood up and walked to the edge of the terrace. He looked down the lawn, back toward the pool. Beyond it there were trees, a little wood.

"Of course I did," said Michael. "I said I would. It went all right. Pretty much the way I expected. My father said he thought I was crazy, but it was my money if I wanted to blow it like that. My mother wanted to know if your family had 'given their permission.' She made it sound as if we were getting married. So I guess as far as I'm concerned we're all set."

"Fan*tastic*," Riley said.

Jordan Paradise had cupped his hands in front of his mouth, and now he made some sounds.

"Coah — cooo-cooo-coo," he went. And then once more, "Coah — cooo-cooo-coo," and once again, "Coah — cooo-cooo-coo."

It was a sweet and lonely sound, and from a distance, part of it came back: "Cooo — cooo-coo."

"Hey!" said Michael. "Hey, Jordy! How about that? You got one to answer, didn't you? You fooled a real-live mourning dove." He sounded impressed.

Jordan turned and walked back to his chair. "Yes," he said, "a real-live mourning dove. Did you know they only make that call on days a war is going on somewhere?"

There was a moment's silence after he said that.

Riley felt the way she'd felt the week before, when a friend of hers had said she might be pregnant, at a party.

"Come on." She wanted to say *something*. "They always sound like that." And then, to Jordan's smile and shrug she said, "Oh, yeah. I guess that's right. Incredible. Or *unbearable*, more like it. That has to do with what we're planning" — she waggled a finger back and forth between Michael and herself — "him and me. Planning for the summer." Absurdly, she was feeling nervous again.

"You're going to start a war?" said Jordan Paradise.

Riley laughed. "No, no," she said. "The opposite. Or not that really, either. I don't know why I said that."

"She likes to be dramatic," Michael said. "We're going to do some traveling, is all. Try to see some other places, talk to different people. You know — have a change of scene. This town — " He hinged one hand at the wrist and flipped it forward; so much for Northfield. He was sounding pretty lofty, Riley thought.

"We're hoping we can organize our lives a little," Michael said. "Maybe make some plans. Decide where we want to be a year from now, let's say — or at least where we want to be heading. Everyone assumes we're going to get through high school — like, next June — and then go on to college in the fall. Well, maybe we will. . . . *I* don't know. We'd like to understand why we're doing all this stuff."

"So you hope to find out this summer?" Jordan said. "Traveling around?"

"I know," said Riley. And, "It sounds ridiculous; I realize that. Self-dramatizing, right? As if we're setting out to find our destiny, or the meaning of life, or something." She'd made her voice real deep and fake-o to say that, which gave her a flash of anger at herself. "Even if we were — as soon as you say it, you feel like some kind of an asshole."

Jordan Paradise quickly dropped his eyes. He licked his lips and took a sideways glance at Michael. It was hard to tell in that light, but Riley thought he could be blushing.

"One thing you've got to realize," Michael said to him, "is that Riley and I — in certain ways — are a lot more freaked than most of the kids around here."

"Freaked," repeated Jordan. "Meaning scared." It was halfway between a statement and a question.

"Beyond scared — *freaked*," insisted Michael. "Oh, scared's part of it, I guess — but also horrified, in-credulous, disgusted."

He was sitting forward in his striped upholstered outdoor chair, his feet drawn in and under him, heels touching, his elbows on his thighs. Riley thought *he* might be feeling the wine a little bit, too.

"Ever since I was in the eighth grade," he said, speaking quickly, earnestly — the supersalesman, getting into it, "the future's been a sort of hobby of mine. You know, trying to read about and think about the different trends and developments going on in the world. How the changes going on right now are going to lead to other changes in the future." His eyes widened. "It absolutely blows my mind to think of all the money waiting to be made." Jordan raised his eyebrows. "All a person has to do is pay attention. Realize that everything's connected. For instance, having the smarts to see that changes in the family — you know, both parents working, that crap — created a need for fast foods everywhere: Pizza Huts, Kentucky Frieds, McEverythings."

Jordan Paradise was blinking again, but he was also smiling — more relaxed, thought Riley.

"I think I understand," he said. "Sort of. But your study of the future, that's not the thing that's . . . freaking you. Or is it?"

"Only indirectly," Michael said. "Only in the sense that maybe the future won't be there, when we're old enough to . . . well, enjoy it. You see" — he leaned back in his chair and stretched, arms up over his head, trying to look casual, Riley thought — "all that depends on something else." He pursed his lips in a little embarrassed smile. "So, yeah, it's nuclear war. That's what we're freaked by. The possibility of them having one without all the rest of us ever having been consulted, for God's sake."

"What happens," Riley said, "is that you start thinking about that — about how easily it could happen, and how nobody seems to be doing anything about preventing it — and you start to go a little crazy. I know *I* do, don't you?" Jordan Paradise didn't answer; he was just staring at her.

"So then my parents go into their big, reasonable routine," she went on. "If I'll *only* get through school and college — maybe law school, too — *then* I'll have the learning and the 'leverage' (a favorite word of Daddy's) to do *all* the things their generation hasn't done: end starvation, stop pollution, bring about disarmament — the works. Or maybe find it isn't all that easy. They tell me this: '*Every*body wants to save the world when she's sixteen.' And then they look at each other. And *then* they chuckle." She took a big deep breath.

"Why?" said Jordan Paradise. "That doesn't seem so funny." But he smiled.

"That's what I ask myself," said Riley. "Why are these people laughing? And the answer I get is maybe they know, or *think* they know, that I'm going to end up just like they are. Namely, part of the establishment: smug, self-satisfied, and a total ostrich." She looked right in his eyes and said, "And you know something? I think they may be right. And that scares the shit out of me. Not that I don't love them — I do. But I can't let that happen. So, for me, this trip is my big chance to try to get organized, like Michael said. Figure out what's best to do, somehow. Maybe things'll get clearer if we're in a completely different setting, with a lot of new people around. Or maybe what we ought to do at some point is each of us go off alone, and meditate or something. Just for forty days or so." She laughed. "Examining our navels." She waved a hand. "I know that sounds crazy."

Jordan Paradise had stopped smiling and was staring at Riley with great intensity again. But now he was nodding.

"Like I said, it's perfectly possible," said Michael, making with a little condescending chuckle, "that we'll discover college and all that crap *is* exactly what we want after all. And in that case we'll come home, and grin and tell everyone what a great trip we had, and just do it. Or at the opposite extreme, who knows? We may find a beach somewhere and cover ourselves with cod liver oil and let the sea gulls peck us to death." He smirked. "I'm joking, obviously. But what I'm saying is: We could decide, like, anything."

Riley thought, He isn't very good at jokes. But she said, "Right," to be supportive, and then she shrugged, feeling herself start to come down. How urgent was she, *really*; how dedicated? Maybe she was just a phoney and a dilettante, just bullshitting — looking for a good time, like the "change of pace" her parents always said they needed, as they left for Barbados. Maybe she'd already turned into her parents.

Jordan Paradise got up and went once more to the place on the edge of the terrace where he'd stood before. Again, he cupped his palms and made that sound inside them.

"Coah — cooo-cooo-coo." The call of the mourning dove.

And once again he got it back. "Cooo — cooo-coo." There was still a war going on, somewhere.

He turned around and faced them. "How do you plan to travel? Do you have a car?" he asked.

"No," said Michael. "Neither of us has a license; you can't get one at sixteen here. What we thought we'd do is take the bus a lot, and hitch, sometimes. Riley's mother goes bananas at the thought of her hitching, so it'll be up to her how much of that we do. I think there's, like, a Greyhound student bus pass you can get. What you do is pay this one flat fee, and that's it. A friend told us his brother got one."

42

"Maybe," — Jordan Paradise both shrugged *and* raised his eyebrows as he spoke the word — "maybe you could come with me a ways. I don't know if you'd *want* to, of course. I'd have to tell you . . . some things, first. And if you decided you'd *rather* take the bus, I'd certainly understand. I can see how that might be — well, a lot of fun."

Riley looked at Michael, who looked back at her. He did a little something with his eyes, which came to her as: Whoa. What is this, anyway?

Riley switched her own eyes back to Jordan, and smiled at him. He was still standing a few steps away, and he'd sunk his fingers into the pockets of his jeans and was moving his head around a little. He gave no sign of having seen the way that Michael looked at her.

"Well," she said to him, to be saying something, "what sorts of things would you have to tell us first? That you flunked drivers' ed at seven different schools you've been kicked out of, and you don't really have a license after all?"

"No," he said. "I've got a license, all right. I can show it to you. But you're almost close on the school part. I've never been to school, to any school, in my entire life. All I've done since I was two years old is move around. From one place to another, all the time. I guess that I've been trying to hide from someone." He twisted up his mouth, like in disgust. "Someone dangerous, I suppose. But just to me, specifically. Not to you guys, I don't think. And, maybe not to me, anymore. The thing is: I don't know exactly."

7

SEEKERS

"So Karen Archibald is Dorothy," Sweets said again. He had the folder open on his lap. "Hit and run down dead. Assuming that the *po*-lice" — he used his "Comic Negro" accent — "up in North-field, there, are competent to take and match a set of fingerprints. But even if they ain't, it *sounds* like her, the physical description, right? Which changes things around some. You think that this one's Dorothy? I do."

Eric grunted, and out of the corner of his eye he watched Sweets take the cellophane off one of those mentholyptus cough drops of his and pop it into his mouth. It wouldn't take the hoarseness out of Sweets's voice; more than likely, nothing could do that. But it was still something Sweets *did* — "a payback for the aggravation, you might say," he'd explained to Eric once, and chuckled. Sweets smoked a few yards of king-sized cigarettes a day — *had* done, ever since Vietnam, he'd said — and pacified his throat with cough dope. And every night, wherever he was staying, he'd wash the ashtrays carefully — get rid of all the ground-in ash and tar and crap — and start clean in the morning. When they were driving, like now, he'd also wash the ashtray from the car.

"Of course it's her," said Eric, when Sweets did not go on. "Dietetic Dotty. Her prints, the things they said about the body type, the facial features — all that foxiness. . . ."

Eric was driving; he almost always drove. It was up to him who drove (you *could* say, if anyone wanted to get technical about it), in that he was basically in charge of who did anything and everything. He could have *made* Sweets drive, but he didn't. Being driven around by an older black guy — Sweets was thirty-nine, exactly nine years older — would have made Eric feel less professional, more like in a cab. And besides, he preferred to have something to do on a trip, in addition to talking with Sweets.

He thought this . . . *event* was the first good thing to happen since he'd come on the case. They'd heard about, and even gone to look at, other bodies — boys' bodies, three of them, and one woman who'd been burned a lot — but never with a lot of optimism. The actual *live* sightings, five or six of them, had all occurred before; when it was just Sweets and what's-his-name — the guy in charge before him,

45

Donahue — looking for two missing persons, you could say. Dorothy Simon had been twenty-five when Donahue and a bunch of others had started looking, and Amos Goodspeed, Junior, had been two. Donahue had bugged around for seven years, and then Sweets took over; by then there was just the one man on it. Sweets and Donahue were two big, easy-going, untrained bloodhounds, Eric thought. Not that it was their fault. They were investigators for Cousin Huey, the Department of Health and Human Services. Pussy guys who carried an attaché case and, at the worst, a big Swiss-army knife, the kind with *tweezers*, just in case they got a splinter somewhere. Eric's ID said he worked for Cousin Huey, too. That wasn't true. He was a member of the family, sure enough, but the cousin that he really worked for didn't have a name the public was familiar with.

Originally, of course, the point had been to find the two of them — the woman and the boy — because we *wanted* them, because they might be valuable. Or — better — because they might *have* something valuable, a formula the woman might have gotten from her friends, the scientists, before they drank that final cocktail. A formula quite valuable to *us*, the people of this country.

At first, nobody knew for sure that the woman had taken the boy. Or if she had taken him that she'd kept him; people can get tired of kids. But pretty soon reports came in. People saw the posters, with Dorothy Simon's picture on them, and they called in. It was interesting (to Eric) to learn that all the reports, the live sightings, had been made by

46

women, and that in each case the women had waited a day or two after they saw Dorothy Simon before they made the calls. All the women said there was a boy with Dorothy: early on, a tiny little boy, and then a bigger one.

"She had a lot of fake ID," said Eric, going on when Sweets kept up the silence. "A home address that looks exactly like a shoe store, a next-of-kin that never *has* been born yet, far as they can tell. No credit cards, no keys, no checkbook. How many honest, law-abiding women with nothing to hide are going to ride around equipped like that?"

"Not too many, I'd say," rasped Sweets. "No more'n three or four, I bet you, in the en-tire country. Three or four, *tops*." He laughed. His full christened name was Sweetwater Clifton Reid, and when he started in, he'd introduced himself as "Cliff" and signed reports "S. Clifton Reid." That worked about a month, until somebody came across — detected — the Sweetwater part, which made it byebye Cliffie-baby.

Eric had been added to the case because things change . . . *had* changed. We didn't need a brand-new supervirus anymore. Some other doctors, working for the government — Department of Defense — this time, had formulated one that was, apparently, a *beauty*. So anything the woman had, and might have given to, or told, the boy would not be needed anymore. The only thing we needed — had to do — was to make damn absolutely certain that the Russians didn't get it.

"Yessir," Sweets kept right on talking, "I agree. In more or less one hour's time, you and I will gaze upon the face of Amos Goodspeed's late companion. Late companion, friend — presumably — and once upon a time, his snatcher."

Eric nodded. Sweets had not been told that things had changed. He didn't have to be. He also didn't have to know what Eric's orders were; not yet, at least. Maybe not until the time it happened.

"One down and one to go," said Eric. Sometimes he really didn't give a damn.

8

REVELATIONS

Michael and Riley both stared at Jordan Paradise, but neither of them spoke. So what he did was give a kind of shrug — maybe still trying to be cool, Riley thought — and then take a hold of the back of his chair and turn it around so he was facing them. After that, he sat down and just looked at them in silence for maybe half a minute, before he licked his lips and started on his story. And as he talked along, Riley got the feeling he wasn't just telling them this story, he was *entrusting* them with it, trusting that they wouldn't laugh or doubt or make remarks. And trusting them — and this was really weird — to care about this stuff, and him.

To say the story was peculiar was the understatement of the decade — make that *century*, thought Riley.

Jordan Paradise (which was not his name) had been on the move with Karen Archibald (and that was not *her* name) since he was two years old. Those names? She'd made them up, apparently.

He couldn't remember anything or any*one* . . . before. ("Karen says — said — everyone remembers everything," he told them, "and if that's right, what I should say is I can't *recall* my parents. I used to try to, very hard. I'd imagine I was lying in a crib, and two sweet people — a man and a woman — they were leaning over me, and smiling, reaching down and lifting me up. . . ," he paused, ". . . and *hugging* me. But I couldn't recall their *faces*. I never have been able to. Maybe one of them was black; I just don't know. Karen wouldn't tell me.")

So everything that Jordan knew about his history, and it was mighty little, he'd got from Karen Archibald, who he'd thought was his mother, up until the age of ten. Here is what she told him, at that time, and since.

His parents were her bosom friends (although she was younger); she'd even been there at his birth, assisting, rubbing his mother's back. They both had died — she wouldn't tell him where or how; they were wonderful, intelligent ("She said 'brilliant,' " Jordan said.), and beautiful and good. She wouldn't tell him either of their first names, even.

He and Karen lived this transient life for fourteen years — moving, moving, moving all the time — "for safety's sake," he had been told. Who or what was *un*safe for them she would never say, of course. But she was very sure that they were being looked for. Karen said if any stranger asked, his answer was that he was Billy Wright, or Jerry Green, or Jimmy Johnson — any name — and she was his Aunt Anything, who was taking care of him while his mother "got an operation."

Karen said when he was old enough to live alone (at the age of eighteen, nineteen, twenty — they'd decide, she said), they'd both be able to settle down and lead a normal life. Be Karen Archibald and Jordan Paradise to anyone. But they'd have to split up then, and live apart. Once they weren't together, they'd both be safe, she told him — though even then he should never tell the true story of his early life to anyone. What they'd planned to do was make up a life for him, sometime before they split. ("And one other thing she told me once," Jordan said. "She told me to try not to get fingerprinted. She laughed when she said it. I didn't know if she was joking or not.")

As far back as Jordan could remember, he and Karen had camped out, all over the country, in all four seasons; although from time to time they stayed in a motel, and for part of every summer they'd rent a little place, a cottage or a bungalow. Karen had said it was good for him to get to know some kids his age, and that was when he did, the summers. She was an expert outdoorsperson ("She taught me self-sufficiency," he said.), but also had a lot of formal education. ("Math," he said, and made a face. "And I bet I've read a book or two a week since I was four. One winter we did everything in French.")

51

Schools meant records, papers, staying in one place, so of course he'd never gone to one.

Late in the telling of his story, Jordan looked at Michael, then at Riley. "One thing that may be hard to understand about those years is this," he said to both of them. "I *liked* the life I had with Karen better than the lives I saw the other kids were having." They both smiled at that; he gave a little laugh. "Maybe I've just fooled myself, but I don't think so. I saw what normal was, like on TV, and heard about it from the kids I met. We even ate different food. But what I had seemed good to me. I didn't want to change."

"One thing," Michael said. Riley shot a look at him. Michael had that . . . tactless side. "If Karen told you all this time never to tell anyone that stuff about her and you, and your life, how come you just told us?"

Michael smiled then, a big wide, friendly salesman's one. The way Michael's mind worked (Riley knew), the smile made everything he said all right, completely inoffensive.

Jordan looked at him, his face as mild as usual.

"Well" — he shook his head — "it seems this way to me. Everything has changed, with Karen being . . . dead. She *said* that I'd be safer by myself, so I suppose I am. But I'm also still sixteen and still . . . dependent in a lot of ways. I'm not ready to be on my own quite yet." He gave one quick bark of laughter. "I can build a yurt and net a salmon, but think of all I *don't* know about college, and jobs, and . . . Stroganoff." He licked his lips and turned from Michael back to Riley. "Sure I don't know you, either, but I know you've been completely kind — you both have. And I also know you're kids, like me. I'm not — unsafe with you."

Riley nodded, agreeing with that. For sure.

"Besides," he said, "although I don't *expect* you'll want to drive with me, to take your trip, you might. And just in case you do — decide to — you have to know this stuff. It's only fair."

"I can see that," Michael said. Riley couldn't tell if he was being sarcastic or not.

Jordan just looked back and forth at both of them and gave another little shrug.

Riley stared into the dusk, on down the lawn. My head is full of stuff (she thought) that slightly scares me. I am impressed (she thought) and also attracted, and also excited. There's a part of this (she thought) that's not totally unlike the feeling that I get before a swimming race, a big one in a major meet: What am I doing here?

"And before you make up your minds," said Jordan Paradise, "remember this: I'm also very rich." And he laughed, and Michael laughed, and she laughed with them. He'd said they had this suitcase with a lot of money in it all along; Karen had told him it had been his parents' money. What Riley wanted to do at this point (which had nothing to do with his being rich) was throw an arm around his neck and hug him. Of course she didn't, though.

"Right," she said, instead. "Maybe that's what whoever-they-are are after." She smiled. "And I can sure see why you liked the life you had with her so much. Traveling all over. Learning lots of stuff without having to go to school, even school-type stuff, from what you say. Except for maybe some of the science stuff, you could learn everything worthwhile that we've been fed, and more."

"Yes," he said, "and Karen was very interested in ESP. She thought it was a science of the future."

Michael cocked an eyebrow at that information.

"Interesting," he said. "I assume you mean telepathy, psychokinesis, precognition — all that stuff? Some futurists believe that simple intuition, for example, is going to play a bigger and bigger part in decision-making. Isn't that amazing? I mean on the management level, of course. They think that by the year 2000 — "

"Okay, Michael, yes, all right," said Riley, leaning over, patting him on the shoulder. It was, by then, quite dark outside. "We mustn't get him started," she said to Jordan Paradise. She also swung her legs down, off the chaise. "Not that it isn't fascinating, Michael, but . . . I'm getting chilly and I need something to drink. Let's go inside, okay?"

As far as she was concerned, the last five or six hours had definitely been the strangest in her life, so far. It was like a movie, what she'd seen: a violent death; a handsome boy involved with the victim, who apparently had a suitcase with a whole real lot of money in it. But what she'd heard was even stranger: a story of a boy who'd come from nowhere (that he knew of), and who really didn't know, at age sixteen, a single other person in the world. E.T. was not a whole lot more of an alien than this kid was, she thought.

And what did she think of the whole story? She guessed she believed him. Whether she believed the woman, the late Karen Archibald, was something else again. *She* could have been crazy, just a little crazy: setting 50 meter records in a 40 meter pool. Paranoid. But Riley didn't see any way of checking out Karen Archibald's information, or noninformation, really. She'd have to talk with Michael, privately, and see what he thought. His first reaction had been negative, but that was not surprising. Why add a perfect stranger to their summer plan?

Michael was a lot more *rational* than she was, she supposed.

If it was up to her, alone, she'd be much more apt to make the decision the same way those people in the year 2000 would, the ones on the management level ("of course") — assuming there *were* management and people then, still.

By *intuition*, sure.

9

DECIDING

It took three days to get it all worked out. Riley used that time not only to confer with Michael, but also to examine Jordan Paradise from lots of different angles. To activate her intuition — try to, anyway.

"I want to get more of a *feel* for the guy," she said to Allie, thoughtlessly. That, of course, set off an episode of eye-rolling, face-making, gesturing, convulsive giggles, and the like. Allison's opinion — though shakily and hurriedly constructed the night before ("cute" as its foundation, trimmed in sympathy) — was absolutely positive: Riley and Michael must definitely take Jordan up on his offer. They'd save a bundle *and* have a *much* more "interesting" time — that was how she argued it. Allison liked Michael fine, but not without a reservation here and there. He was "too much of an intellectual," she said. And also, which she didn't say, too hairy.

Jordan was a very easy guy to have around, Riley discovered, in the course of those three days, almost unnaturally — make that *scarily* — easy. She wondered if his strange, disordered life had made him more adaptable. Or maybe it was because he'd been hanging with a woman all that time, and only with a woman, almost. Riley hadn't had a real good look at her, but Karen Archibald had appeared attractive: slender build, curly dark-brown hair. For fourteen years Jordan had been with her, shared space with her; real close quarters at times, tents; eating all his meals across from her, beside her. She'd been his mom, and she'd also been his teacher and his playmate and his pal. Riley supposed this *could* have turned him into a mama's boy, real easily.

But yet (she saw) he wasn't. True, he made his bed and picked up his room before going down to breakfast (you bet she peeked), and he seemed to like to talk with Thalia, and he didn't holler, "All Riiight!" all the time, and clap his hands and laugh too loud for no reason at all. Nor did he throw a ball that great, and when he tried to swim fast, he looked like a person under shark attack. And from time to time he'd sort of drift away, sometimes physically and sometimes just in his head. But still, he didn't act the least bit spoiled, or dainty. Riley realized he must be missing Karen Archibald a lot, just dreadfully, and trying not to show it. That was pretty tough of him, she thought. She tried to let him know she knew what he was going through, and cared. More with looks and smiles than anything.

She wasn't a hundred percent certain what he thought of her. Whenever the four of them were together, and he had anything to say, like an opinion or an emotion that really mattered to him, he'd usually pitch it at her, rather than either of the others. She noticed that. He'd ask Michael for information, but he'd tell *her* stuff, sometimes with a funny little smile that made his statements sort of questions, too. Can I think this and be your friend? he'd seem to ask her. And she'd nod encouragement and feel they were getting close already, in a way.

But he also kept his distance, you could say, in that he didn't flirt or get involved in any of the fantastically casual physical contact that guys his age seemed to specialize in. Except for honest accidents, he pretty much kept his hands off her (and Allison), even once he'd seen the kind of liberties that Michael took, which themselves weren't all that Patrick Henry-ish as a matter of fact.

She couldn't help but wonder how experienced he was. That's, like, "experienced," and roll your eyes around. The possibilities that jumped to mind were quite extreme — from "not at all" right up to . . . well, she decided not to dwell on that. There wouldn't be anything sick or perverted about two healthy people, who weren't related, having. . . . She supposed it didn't make much difference, really.

Riley also considered, fleetingly, the possibility that Jordan had fixed on her as Karen Archibald's successor, in the "mother" sense, rather than the other one — seeing as she was the first person to be nice to him after Karen was killed. She remembered hearing about some experiments with monkeys, where these young monkeys "adopted" all sorts of weird replacements for their missing moms. Riley faced the fact that *her* basic reaction to Jordan Paradise was a lot more carnal than maternal. She definitely liked his looks, and not just the big dark eyes and curly hair and that zitless coffee-ice-cream skin. She liked his body, too, what her mother would have called his "physique." He didn't flex, the way Michael did, being more the long and limber type — moving, he was graceful, balanced, light — but yet he still had muscles, definition. He must have done some exercises out at those campsites, Riley thought. She wondered if Karen Archibald had watched while that was going on. Jordan looked as if he'd be extremely nice to touch, to her. *Fun* to touch, the same as she would be, as a matter of fact.

Jordan made the call to Gilson's Funeral Home the first morning he was at the Rouxs'. Michael and Riley stood right there beside him, just in case he needed any help. He didn't.

"My name is Rodney Archibald," he said, and he gave out some address on Ridge Street, Pocatello, Idaho. He got the Gilson guy to total up the bill while he held on, and said he'd work out something with a friend in Northfield who'd mail the cash to them from there. They'd have it the next day, he said.

When he hung up, he turned to Riley and he said, "I'd never used a telephone before."

Michael wanted to do some phoning, too. The idea was his own, but seeing as he wanted to use her father's phone, he'd checked it out with Riley first. He wanted to call the FBI, in Washington, D.C.

"The thing Jordan said about Karen telling him not to be fingerprinted?" he said to Riley, by way of explanation. "What did you make of that?"

"I don't know," she said. "I thought it might have been a little joke, to tell you the truth."

"I don't think so," Michael said. "To me, it means she knew the federal government — specifically — had an interest in the guy. And in her, as well. You know what *I* believe is possible: I believe she may have kidnapped him. And what I want to do is call the FBI and ask. Maybe help the guy get back with his parents."

Riley moved her chin and made a little face.

"No, wait," said Michael. "It all fits. Let's say Karen Archibald was one of those women who finds out she can never have a baby of her own. It gets to her; she broods and broods about it, and then one day she just flips. It happens; I've read about cases like that. So what she does is grab the first kid she sees — from a carriage outside a store, or playing in the yard while its mom's on the phone. She had no idea whether a baby's fingerprints are a matter of record or what. The story — all that mystery bullshit she told Jordan — is totally contrived, made up; to keep the kid in line, attached to her, and so on."

"But why wouldn't she just settle down some-where?" said Riley. "And bring the kid up normally? That's what I'd do: settle down and have a normal life."

"Yeah, but you're not nuts," said Michael. "This woman's off the wall; she's paranoid. She's scared to death they'll catch her, take the kid away. And remember, she may have felt that given the . . . well, the difference in their looks, they'd, like, stand out too much. Face it, Jordan *could* be black, just like he said. And from what you told me, she definitely wasn't."

"Maybe," Riley said. "And I guess she could have gotten most — or all — of that money in ransom from the family." She nibbled on a thumbnail. "They must have spent a *ton* of money. In fourteen years?"

"You bet," said Michael, making what she always thought of as his big-deal face: lips together, corners down, eyes a little narrowed, whole head nodding. "Of course she could also be some sort of an eccentric millionairess, could have *been*, I *should* say. I mean — face it, Riles — your mother could probably put her hands on that kind of dough without too much trou-ble."

Riley looked away. She didn't like to hear refer-ences to her parents' affluence. She liked *being* rich, but she didn't like it coming up in conversation.

"But you don't know their real names," she said. "So suppose you call up the FBI. What do you say?"

"I don't have to say much," he said. "Just ask if

they've got any unsolved kidnapings going back . . .
oh, ten or fifteen years, let's say. And if so, who and
where. There can't be *that* many — do you think?"

Riley wasn't sure. About that, or about the idea
in general. But she agreed it wouldn't hurt to try.

And of course, she couldn't wait to hear what
happened.

"Well, it was a bit of a fiasco," Michael admitted.
"In the first place, after I told them what I wanted,
they shuffled me around to three different offices —
'Would you mind holding, puh-leez?' — before I got
to the right one. The one where they supposedly
kept the records on that sort of thing. And then, get
this, the guy said he had to have my name and
address, first. Before he'd tell me anything. Well, I
said, 'Whoa. I'm just asking for, like, *public information*, aren't I?' And he goes, 'Yes *but* . . . blah-
blah-blah.' I hung up on the guy. I mean, what
business is it of theirs who I am? I probably should
have just told him I was Rodney Archibald from
Pocatello, Idaho, but I didn't think of it. Maybe I'll
call them back."

Riley told him no, forget it — unless he wanted
to use his own phone. He just shrugged and said,
"It's up to you," making that sound a lot like, "It's
your funeral."

Riley didn't see where it'd make any difference to
them whether Jordan had been kidnapped or not.
In her book, Michael just wanted to be difficult.

But on the second day, surprisingly and suddenly,
Michael was won over. Though after Riley thought

about it, she realized she shouldn't have been surprised at all. Once Michael had had a demonstration, after all, how could he *not* embrace — or anyway, solicit further information on — "a science of the future." Or at least a part of such a science. The part that had to do with pendulums.

Here's the way it happened. That second day, while the four of them were sitting by the pool, Jordan happened to ask how long it took to fill a pool that size. And Riley explained how they'd had to drill a second well for just that reason: filling the pool.

"They ended up having to drill down something like five hundred feet," she said. "Daddy said it would have been cheaper to fill the pool with Perrier. And even with *that* well, it still takes days."

Jordan said he bet her father hadn't hired a dowser. "I can't believe you had to go that deep," he said.

Allison naturally asked what on earth a dowser was ("anyway"), and Jordan explained that he or she was a diviner, a person with a kind of ESP, who could tell you where there was a vein of water, underground. "And other things," he said.

"But how? What happens?" Allie asked.

"They use a forked stick, sometimes," Jordan said. "Or a pendulum, though that's a little less likely, for water. But you can use either one."

Michael picked up on the "you," of course.

"What do you mean?" he said. It was a tone of voice he used a lot in class, and teachers didn't like. "Have you actually seen it done? I mean, you haven't learned how to do it, have you?"

Jordan smiled his vague and dreamy smile and

63

said, "Well, yes, I have. Karen showed me, actually. You don't exactly teach or learn it, though. It's something you just come to, more or less. Almost an attitude, you *could* say."

As Riley could have predicted, Michael went a little crazy. He wanted more, much more; he had to learn what dowsing's "future" was. He insisted that Jordan show him how to "do it." He didn't remind Jordan about all the help he'd given him with the funeral home stuff, but if he'd had to . . . Riley thought. It's fair to say that she and Allison were also . . . interested.

Jordan hadn't jumped at the idea. He said it wasn't a parlor trick, an entertainment, but Michael kept pushing. He was serious, responsible, he said; they all were. Riley giggled at that, put both her palms on Allison's smooth cheeks, and looked into her eyes. "Is this the face of a thrill-seeker?" she asked the pool deck.

"Oh, cut it out," said Michael, crossly.

Riley sobered up, and Jordan Paradise agreed to show them just one thing. "I'll show you how it's used to tell a person's sex," he said. Allison goggled her eyes, but he ignored her. "In this case what I do will just be . . ." Riley thought he almost smiled, "*confirmation*. Of the obvious. But country people use it with a pregnant woman, to tell the baby's sex before it's born. If the pendulum goes round and round, it's female; back and forth is male."

So they all walked back to the house, and Jordan went up to his room and brought back a piece of black thread and what looked to Riley like an antique wedding ring, but a tiny one. "Karen gave me this," he said. "It was her granny's once; I love it." He tied the thread around the ring and that was it: the pendulum.

First, he held it over Riley's hand, and steadied it till it was still. When he let it go, it hung there motionless a moment; but then it slowly, slowly stirred, and started going round and round in tiny circles.

"You're *doing* that," said Allison.

Jordan smiled and shook his head. Again, he steadied the ring, then moved it over Michael's hand. Again, the pause, and then a different sort of motion: straight lines, back and forth.

"You *must* be doing that," said Allison.

So of course Jordan Paradise pulled out a clean, red country handkerchief and handed it to Riley to blindfold him with. And of course, he did — it did — the same thing six more times. If the hand was Allison's or Riley's, the thing would move in circles; when Michael's hand was there, it just went back and forth.

"Amazing," Michael said, and Riley bet herself she knew what he'd say next. "Would you . . . help me to do it?"

"I don't know," said Jordan. "As I said, you kind of have to teach yourself. Karen only told me certain things. First, you must believe it's going to happen — work. Then, your purposes — the reason that you do it — must be good. Or anyway, not *bad*, self-serving. And finally, you must try to clear your mind of other things, and only think about . . . whatever." He smiled and raised his eyebrows, looked at Michael.

Michael scowled, but said, "I really want to try." And Jordan handed him the thing.

It didn't work. The ring just hung there. "Come on, dammit," Michael said. He was staring fixedly at the ring; Riley thought he was holding his breath. Different people put their hands under it, but nothing happened. In the end, Michael started to force it. You could see him swinging the thread.

"Ach, yes. A-may-sing!" he exclaimed. He had controlled his anger, and was goofing now.

"Sometimes it takes a while. You have to practice," Jordan said. He took the little apparatus back, slipped it in the pocket of his shirt.

"No, seriously," said Michael. And he was. "I really want to learn to work it. Maybe . . . I don't know — but maybe if we go with you, you'll help me get my mind organized, or whatever it takes. All right?" Jordan nodded, and Riley felt an invisible smile just spread across her head, from one ear to the other.

"And you use it for other things, too?" she asked. "For this, and finding water, and for other things?"

"Yes." He looked at her. "I ask it questions, too. Yes is going in a circle; back and forth means no." And then he said something pretty odd, as he was standing up. "It can be like talking to your heart, sometimes."

Then he'd gone upstairs and put the thing away, and that was that, for the time being.

"Well," said Riley to Michael later on that afternoon, Jordan and Allison being in the basement, playing Ping-Pong, "it sure would make things a hell

66

of a lot easier if we *did*. Just in not always having to move on the bus company's schedule, for instance. And — like getting around in a strange town. It'd be so darn much more *convenient*."

It was simple for her to stress the totally impersonal advantages of traveling with Jordan, Riley realized, which also kept Michael from giving her any of his all-knowing, I-can-see-right-through-you looks.

"That's true," said Michael. "*But*, let's just suppose the story Karen Archibald was telling *was* true, and they — some sort of 'they' — were still after him, or them. I guess they'd still be looking for a kid and a woman, probably, but suppose they'd gotten ahold of their license plate number, somehow. Well, no matter who this 'they' is, it'd still be a hassle to get caught. Even if it was government people of some sort, I wouldn't want *my* name to be mixed up in it, be in their files, and all that garbage. Would you? You know what I mean? It's something to think about."

"For sure," said Riley, and she chewed a lip this time. "But wait, I've got an idea. About the license plates and that? Suppose we leave his car *here* and take my parents' Fiesta? Their snow car. It's a bit of a rust bucket, but it's got good tires and it runs great. And they never use it, really, except in winter, around town. I bet they wouldn't mind, if I tell them he's got a license and everything. I could call them down at the sweat center. I bet they *wouldn't* mind, or at least Daddy wouldn't. You know how *he* is."

Michael had to agree. He'd made his last objection, and when they went and asked Jordan Paradise, he said it'd be all right with him, if it was all right with her parents. So Riley called them right away, hoping to catch her father after one of his massages. When he was in a certain kind of mood, at home, after a particular number of drinks, he sometimes mentioned Suki, his masseuse, to the women of his household, wearing an expression on his face that even Allison objected to. "Don't be disgusting, Daddy," she had told him primly, once.

Riley's luck was good. He said that if there was a licensed driver going, who'd leave his car behind, and she was prepared to take responsibility, and Michael was going to be along. . . . Then, changing tone, "But you damn well better bring it back in one piece, pal."

Mr. Roux enjoyed telling the men in his regular foursome that he didn't go for any double standard, that he'd taught both Riley and Allison to swim by throwing them into the pool and that, in general, he'd raised the two of them "like boys with tits."

"You can't wrap up a girl in cotton wool," was one of his pronouncements. "Not in this day and age. The best protection you can give 'em is a little common sense and a whole lot of insurance. Plus a credit card from the phone company and a prescription from the family physician." And he'd wink and chuckle.

Mrs. Roux often wondered where he got to be this big authority on females, and once (she felt like wrangling) she even asked him that, out loud. To which he answered, "The same place that Gebel-Williams or whatever the hell his name is learned about tigers." Which got a big guffaw from all the men around.

So, by the third day it was set, agreed upon. Fiesta-time would be after breakfast the following morning. Allison said she was so jealous she felt like puking in the gas tank.

10

CLOSING IN

"From what you said," said Eric, "she isn't even marked, to speak of."

Not that there was going to be any problem identifying Karen Archibald, anyway. The fingerprints were the first thing, and they were carrying a photograph of Dorothy Simon — over fourteen years old, but probably still useful — and they'd brought along her dental records, just in case.

Having the body comparatively unmarked, though, also meant they wouldn't have to stand around making small talk with something gross on a table in front of them. Morgue guys seemed to do that: They'd get going on and on about the A.L. East, or whether

Wendy's fries are crispier, and all the time you're standing belly-up against the lifeless last remains of John or Janey Doe, often with some holes or dents in it, or pieces missing. Eric knew that Sweets accepted this — call it by its right name — *squeamishness* of his, but *he* never would. It reminded him too much of a rather plausible question he'd heard a vegetarian ask once: "How can you eat the stuff, if you wouldn't be willing to kill it?" Though in his case it was closer to the other way around, of course.

"Broken neck," said Sweets. "A nice, quick, tidy way to go. Quicker than the Goodspeeds' method, even. And if it *is* ol' Dorothy, sure enough, then all *we* got to do is figure what the boy'll do, and it's all over." His fingers riffled all the papers in the big thick folder in his lap.

In the very back of that folder was the start of it, the clipping from the paper, the one about the Goodspeeds' death. RESEARCH TEAM FOUND DEAD IN RICHFORD PLANT, the headline said. And below it was the text, which started: "A custodian at the Norris E. Richford Research Center discovered the bodies of Dr. Amos Goodspeed, 43, and his wife Susan, 36, also a physician, shortly after 8 P.M. this evening. The Goodspeeds, both research associates, had been employed at the facility for the past nine years, and worked together in viral research. The bodies were found in their laboratory, during regular cleaning rounds. A police spokesman said the cause of the deaths was still under investigation, and refused to comment on reports that there was evidence of suicide. Calls to the home of the custodian, believed to be Edmund Wilson, 58, of North St., were un-answered."

The article went on to speak — a bit confusingly, it seemed to Sweets — about what made a "super" virus, and why anyone would want to. It also detailed both the Goodspeeds' academic histories and honors, his having served in Vietnam, and mentioned, as the sole survivor, Amos Goodspeed, Jr., two.

Very slightly closer to the front of the folder was another newspaper article, dated two days later, which told about the "mysterious" disappearance of that same Amos Goodspeed, Jr., two, only child of Drs. Amos and Susan Goodspeed, whose deaths "by suicide" occurred two days before. The article mentioned that police believed this disappearance was related to another one, that of Dorothy Simon, 25, a free-lance dress designer, who was described by colleagues at the Richford plant as "a close friend of the Goodspeeds." Police would neither confirm nor deny a report that the child's disappearance was listed as a kidnapping, and that a warrant had been issued for Miss Simon's arrest.

"The boy will run," said Eric, flatly. He smoothed the front of his vest. "Run and keep on running for a while. The boy will panic." Eric had an undergraduate degree in psychology. If you knew him for an hour, you probably knew that.

Sweets slid the picture out of the folder, as Eric talked. It was one of those artist's renderings, a pencil sketch by someone from the agency's art department, done on the basis of the last two eye-

72

witness descriptions they'd gotten. He was a handsome young dude, Sweets thought, curly-haired and bright-eyed, dark-complected, "maybe twelve years old," the last witness had said. She'd also said he could be "white, or Spanish, or a Negro," but that he'd talked like a regular person. "Just the same as you or me," she'd said to Sweets, and smiled. Sweets had smiled back; he figured Amos talked like him, not her.

In Sweets's mind, the picture in his hand *was* Amos; he'd decided that. Amos Goodspeed, age of twelve. But he also realized Amos must have changed some in the past four years. Maybe lots. He was sixteen now. He'd be different, grown. Sweets remembered when he was sixteen; he remembered how he felt, back then.

"The boy may very well have loved her," Eric was saying. "She was mother-father-sibling substitute, you read me? Without her he'll be rootless, rudderless. So he'll just run, run fast — out of his mind — away from where it happened."

It didn't seem to Sweets the boy had panicked. If anything, the opposite. He'd kept his head and taken care of business, taken care of Karen Archibald, seen that she was rightly taken care of. Whatever anybody thought, the kid had shown some class. Sweets didn't speak. He just sucked air around the mentholyptus in his mouth; that made his tongue feel cold and clean. Sweets had a bushy, thick mustache, but was otherwise clean-shaven.

"And he'll be thoughtless, careless, too," said Eric. "He'll make mistakes. We'll hear about them. This could be it: the beginning of the end, my man."

Eric used expressions like "my man," sometimes. Black expressions he'd picked up. Language could bridge the gap between people, he believed; if you were going to work in Spain, learn Spanish. Hey, that's common sense.

"The situation is analogous to marriages between old people in isolated regions of rural America, where you have the two of them living almost exclusively with each other. Proximity studies have shown, consistently, that close confinement of a nonpenal, nonpunitive nature produces a. . . ."

Eric talked on, supplying Sweets with a mix of information, lies, conjecture, theory, smoke. From time to time, he snuck a peek at Sweets, who only sat there, pulling on the Kool he'd lighted, with his eyes half closed. Sweets was the only person in the world who had the capacity to lull Eric into a state — not sleep, not even boredom exactly — where he'd talk without thinking first. And an annoying corollary to this ability was that he, Eric, never really knew what Sweets made of the little things he said, but maybe shouldn't have, in some instances. With white guys he could tell how smart someone was — pretty quickly and accurately, he thought. But with a black guy he was never really sure. You had to use some — what? — some different *criteria* with blacks, and Eric didn't have a glimmer what these were. Which also meant he was never sure if he was smarter than Sweets or not, and who would have been driving the car if both of them were white.

He liked Sweets. He *thought* he liked Sweets. He thought he liked everyone he worked with. He wondered all the time if Sweets liked him. He wondered if Sweets had worries like his own. Or if he was just kind of happy-go-lucky, like they said.

PART TWO

11

FIRST FORTNIGHT

"Let's get our you-know-whatses *out of* here," had been the words that Riley said (followed by a joyful chuckle) on the morning that she and Michael and Jordan Paradise piled into her parents' old Fiesta and pointed it away from Northfield.

And for the next couple of weeks they certainly did more driving — three hundred miles or so a day — than any other single thing. But still, that left a lot of time for other things to happen in.

One pretty regular occurrence was a meeting, held almost every day, between Michael, Jordan, and the pendulum. Riley would have liked to be a part of these sessions — see if she could get the thing to work for her — but Michael vetoed that idea. It'd just be too "distracting," he had maintained, to have another person "in the picture."

"This could be very important for me," he said to Riley.

So the two of them would go off by themselves, usually after supper, and "try our luck," as Michael said at first. If Riley wanted to stay in their motel room, they'd go outside (or sit in the car, if it was raining); if she wanted to walk around wherever they were, the two of them would set up shop in the room. She peeked at them once, through the window, and saw them sitting tailor-fashion on one of the double beds with their heads bent slightly forward. She thought they looked pretty intense.

"But what do you *do* all that time?" she asked Michael once. "Are you actually doing it, yet?"

Michael looked a little annoyed. "It isn't a question of *doing* something," he said. "Like *doing* a dance, or doing — I don't know — your homework. It's more like letting something happen. The function of the person is to receive, rather than cause. In a way, what you try to do is the exact opposite of what you've been trained to do for your entire life. *You* know: Be aggressive, be in charge, make it happen, think it through. That makes it very difficult for me — someone like me."

"Hmm," said Riley. "I guess *so*."

"It sounds a little bit nutty, but Jordy says when he does bird calls — like that mourning dove, remember? — it's the same sort of thing. Instead of it being *you*, making a bird call, you just let the call come through you. You sort of are the *instrument*."

80

Michael looked embarrassed. "I told you it sounded nutty. But I like it. It's relaxing."

"I can see that," Riley said. She also saw — guessed — that the pendulum wasn't working for him, yet. She thought it was interesting that he was staying with the process, trying to take in this strange new way of learning something. That wasn't typical Michael at all.

Riley probably enjoyed the driving most of all of them. They didn't go in a straight line toward Jettison City, their first destination, but zigged and zagged all over the place, going out of their way to hit a lot of spots with weirdo names, like Big Man's Bottom, Hog Shooter Creek, and Dead Horse Canyon. Riley wished she lived in one of them, instead of Northfield. She thought she'd be another kind of person altogether, if she lived in Dead Horse Canyon, say.

It would have taken another kind of person, Riley thought later on, not to be a bit nonplussed — and then impressed — by Jordan Paradise, their very first night on the road. That was a happening, all right.

Because it was the first day, they'd made it a long one, and it was almost eight o'clock when they checked into unit five at the semi-sleaze-bag Valley Rest Motel. Michael had said, as they approached the place, that he "assumed" they'd all bunk in together, in one room; and with economy as one consideration and sophistication as another Riley wasn't about to (immaturely) holler, "Wrong," and grab herself a single. Besides, she was still naive enough to believe that there was safety in numbers — as her mother always said.

They dropped their stuff in the room and went out again and ate. When they came back, Michael flipped on the tube, and he and Riley flopped on the matching double beds. Jordan asked if anyone else wanted the shower. The two of them said no and help yourself, respectively; so Jordan Paradise rapidly undressed down to his briefs (stacking his clothes neatly on the floor beside his suitcase) and then, instead of stopping and going on into the bathroom (as Riley expected he'd do), he took off one more item, first. Then stretched, *then* went.

Riley was pretty sure Michael noticed. He'd flopped face forward on the bed and was staring fixedly at the TV screen. His pose was pretty relaxed, but his unblinking stare betrayed him. Riley didn't twitch, herself, and during the first commercial they began a discussion that soon turned into an argument: Who was going to get which bed, with whom? No one mentioned you-know-what.

Riley said she'd "just assumed" the boys would share one double bed, and she would have the other. Michael said it seemed to him that *they* should "sleep together," on the grounds of familiarity breeding propriety, or some such nonsense. Riley was not about to spend the first night she'd ever spent in bed with a man in a bed with old Michael — no matter who was breeding what. But of course, she didn't want to say that. So the issue was still unresolved when Jordan came out of the bathroom.

His head was partly covered by the towel he

was using to dry his hair, but the rest of him was still — and this word popped up, classically, in Riley's mind — *undraped*.

Jordan got clean underwear out of his suitcase and unhurriedly slipped it on, while asking them what they were watching. They told him *Cheers* (not guess, don't ask, or *Solid Gold*, which Riley thought of later), and he, without another word, picked up the foam pad and the sleeping bag he'd brought in from the car, unrolled them on the rug between the beds, and slid right into down-filled comfort. And that was the way they did it from then on. No discussion, no problem, no sweat. One night out of three, you "got" the floor. Instant solution, courtesy of Jordan Paradise.

The other issue, though, the one touched off by Jordan's casual nakedness, sort of hung in the air for more than a week before Riley finally made a speech about it. She realized later she should have said something the first night, because when she didn't, and then kept putting it off, the situation just got more and more . . . dramatic.

It was pretty obvious to her that Jordan and the late Karen Archibald had had — *must* have had — a very open and relaxed relationship, when it came to bodies. That was why *he* was that way. Not that they were nudists, or anything, but just that they didn't care who saw whom, how. For example, Jordan was perfectly capable of coming into the bathroom to brush his teeth when he *knew* Riley was in the shower. And even if she turned off the shower, he didn't necessarily head right out of there. The way he acted, though, seemed entirely natural to

83

her — not the least bit planned, or sneaky.

With Michael, however, she got no sense of some-one doing what came naturally. No way. It seemed to Riley that he was both competing with Jordan Paradise *and* taking advantage of her. Examples: The second day, that night, he started sleeping in the nude, and on the morning of the fourth day he ac-tually suggested that they help conserve water by him joining her in the shower. Riley turned thumbs down on that one. This trip was meant to be a time for them to see a lot of places that they hadn't seen before, but . . . what the hell (thought Riley).

So she finally made a speech, on the eighth day, asking them both to cut it out: the various skin shows *and* invasions of her privacy. Jordan didn't react one way or the other to her request, at the time; he just said, "Sure. Okay," and changed his habits. Michael sighed, and Riley heard it as a "what a baby" sound. She wasn't sure, but he might even have winked at Jordan Paradise — although, in fairness, that was not like Michael. Riley was glad she'd said what she did. But she also looked forward, she realized, to the day she'd be able to act like . . . Jordan Paradise. With a man, of course. That'd be pretty neat, she thought.

The day after she'd given her famous modesty speech (or the "Modroux Doctrine," as Michael al-ways referred to it), Jordan came and stood beside her as she was leaning up against the hood of the Fiesta, stretching her hamstrings. They'd pulled over to the side of the road while Michael walked back to take a picture of a defunct rural gas station they'd just passed. It appeared that someone was now living in the single-bay clapboard garage, because there was a stovepipe that angled out one boarded window, with smoke coming out of it. And leaning against one of the gutted gas pumps was a hand-lettered sign: WOOD 4 SALE.

"Well," said Jordan Paradise, when she kept on stretching one leg, then the other. "You figure anything out yet?"

Riley pushed away from the front of the car and turned around.

"What do you mean?" she said. She was slightly on her guard, still. "About what?"

Jordan smiled. "About *everything*," he said. "About what you want to *do*, this fall. *You* know. All the stuff you wanted to get clear about, this trip."

Riley laughed. She felt relieved. "Not *yet*," she said. "My gosh, we've barely started. Gimme a break." She saw Michael walking back toward them. Jordan was nodding, but she thought he looked a little disappointed. "I haven't even gotten clear about *you* yet."

That just popped out. She certainly hadn't planned to say anything that . . . *personal* to him, at that point. Much less lie.

Or not exactly *lie*. She wasn't totally clear, but she did keep on finding out things about the guy she *thought* she liked. The way he lived in the present, for instance, and didn't seem to lay a lot of expectations on . . . people. She mentioned that to Michael once, when Jordan was in a food store buying peanuts. Michael immediately equated "expectation" with "caring." And got himself into it, of course.

"You've got a perfect right to expect me to do certain things," he said, "just because I'm your friend." He sounded very proper, saying that.

"Like what?" she said (with an "Oh, yeah?' in her heart).

"Well," he said, and stuck a special grin on his face, "to give you a recent example: like coming right over to your house when you've picked up some kid downtown you're not sure you want to be alone with."

"And then you expect me to be grateful, right?" said Riley.

"Well . . . ," Michael shrugged. "Probably. I mean, you would be, wouldn't you?"

"Of course I would be," Riley said. "But I wouldn't feel I owed you anything. Like a little token of my gratitude, that you decide on. That's the trouble with expectations — you can get jerked around by them, real easily." She made her voice a whine. "After all I've done for you, you'd think you'd let me — "

"But suppose I'm always doing stuff for you, and you never do anything back?" Michael interrupted. "I mean, that's where you get a lot of divorces, right? Love's got to be a two-way street." He gave her a look that *she* thought *he* thought was positively dripping with meaning.

"Of course it does," said Riley. "But just naturally, of its own accord. If people only do stuff for each other because they think they *should*, or to get something back in return, then they don't love each other anyway. Love is" — she waved an airy hand "giving for the fun of it." She wished she had a chiffon scarf to toss over one shoulder as she turned away.

"Hey, listen to the big love expert," Michael said. "That *sounds* great, Riley, but it isn't realistic. No shit. Everybody's got their expectations and they should. Jordy may look like he doesn't expect anything of us, or anybody, but just wait awhile. Life is just a lot of deals — and love's a part of life. Believe it. You scratch my back; I'll scratch yours."

That sounded more like Michael than when he was talking about the pendulum. It was interesting, Riley thought. They'd been gone for less than two weeks on their big search for clarity and self-discovery, and Michael seemed to have already trotted out a bunch of different selves.

As a matter of fact, a new one began to surface during that expectations talk, she felt, and it remained in place for the three or four days before they got to Jettison City. In this edition, he seemed to become the big brother that she'd never had, and sure as hell had never really wanted. A guy who, on the one hand, would pass along advice like: "Maybe we'd be smart to take things a little slowly with the guy" — his eyes darting toward the gas station's men's room — "until we know there isn't any *mob* connection with his parents' death, and all the money that he's got." And who, on the other, if she happened to sit down in a booth at HoJo's, or on a seat in a movie theater, would come and plunk himself down beside her, as if that was *his* spot, by some sort of kinship right or other. And he took to touching her, too, much more often than he'd ever done before. They were just little pats on the shoulder or swats on the ass, or an arm thrown around her neck, but they seemed to her like signals. Maybe to her, but possibly to someone else, too, she thought.

"Someone else" seemed completely oblivious, of course. Jordan. She didn't even know if he noticed her punching Michael back, pushing him away, and saying stuff like, "Get outa here, you dip! Go find yourself another squeeze!"

He might have. He smiled at most things she said. But she thought he smiled a little differently when he'd look over to his right, after a rest stop somewhere, and see her riding shotgun, once again.

12

MEANWHILE . . .

Eric was excited. It had definitely been Dorothy. Dorothy Simon. Karen Archibald and Dorothy Simon were one, one and the same, and that was good. Now, he and Sweets were sitting in the doctor's waiting room, Dr. Illuzzi's waiting room, and doing what the room was built and furnished for. Eric was excited, but relaxed. This was a classy doctor's office; the guy must know his stuff.

Sweets was looking at a magazine. He'd picked it up before he'd even sat down — just one quick look around and grab the fattest magazine they had. He slowy turned its pages, one by one, looking slowly, carefully at all the pictures. The magazine was *Vogue*.

It was pretty clear to Eric that Sweets didn't feel like talking, which was unusual. He was a little afraid that this meant Sweets had seen, or thought of, something that he'd missed and was trying to decide how to use it — maybe blow the case wide open, somehow. That didn't seem possible to him. But Sweets was so damned . . . *enigmatic*, you might say. Almost like a Chinese or a Japanese or one of them, thought Eric.

At the funeral home, Sweets had stood staring at her body for the longest time — at *the* body, at her face, that is — and he hadn't said a single thing about it, after. Eric hadn't needed more than a glance to *know* that it was Dorothy; she still looked mucho like the picture that they had, except she'd cut her hair and curled it some. The picture was a snapshot of her and the boy's mother, taken on top of a hill or a small mountain somewhere, in the summertime. Dorothy'd had on shorts and a T-shirt, and her long wavy hair was pulled back and tied behind her head. She looked trim and vigorous in the picture, a nice-looking chick, Eric thought, if you happened to go for healthy outdoor women — "the old chum-buddy type," as they used to say in college. Hell, she'd only been twenty-four when the picture was taken, and the truth of the matter was she didn't look any thirty-nine or whatever she was, lying there dead on that table.

But she did look dead, all right, not sleeping — "damn healthy-looking corpse," as the Gilson guy had said — and Eric had laughed along, but moved off with him to go and stand by the window and compare the chart the local dentist had made with

the one he'd brought with him. It was just a for-
mality; there wasn't any question, really. Turned
out she'd only had one other cavity in fourteen years.

Sweets had just stayed by the table, staring at the
woman's face. He'd pulled the sheet up over the rest
of her, as soon as Eric and the Gilson guy had moved
away, and just kept staring at her face. He also took
the photograph, of course.

"Gentlemen." They both looked up. The receptionist was looking at Eric. "This way, please. The
doctor will see you now."

Sweets closed the magazine and put it down, and
both of them got up and followed the young woman
in the striped blouse and the bulky, shiny dark blue
skirt that made a silken rustle when she walked. She
opened a door near the end of the corridor and stepped
back to let them enter; Eric smiled at her and led
the way.

Dr. Illuzzi had already come around to the front
of his desk, which was large, brown wood, and very
highly polished. The doctor also shone in places:
hair and nails, the buttons on his blazer, the bracelet
and the watchband on his wrists, his teeth. He shook
hands with Eric and with Sweets, but then he just
leaned back against his desk, half turned, and put a
slender haunch on it. He didn't ask the two of them
to have a seat.

"Of course I'm anxious to cooperate in any way
I can," he said. He spoke each word both carefully
and clearly, as if he were a robot — or addressing
someone slightly slow, or deaf, or foreign. "But yet.
. . ." He smiled and raised and spread his very clean,
soft hands. "As I told the officer at the time, and

then Chief Hansen only yesterday, I didn't see her struck, nor did I see the car that struck her. Sometimes, when I'm thinking of a case, I walk along just staring at the sidewalk. I imagine I was doing that. I also told the chief I have no recollection of the other people at the scene, other than the officer and rescue personnel, of course. The people from the ambulance," he said to Sweets. "Believe me, there is nothing I'd like more than seeing this man caught. Or woman, as the case may be. But. . . ." This time he just shrugged and made a face that Eric read as signifying sorrow, or at least regret. And as the doctor shrugged, he also checked his wristwatch.

"We understand," said Eric. "But if you would. . . ." He held out Amos Goodspeed's picture to the doctor, who slanted it to catch the light and stared at it.

"I ask you, first of all, to imagine how this boy would look if he was four years older than in that picture," Eric said. "Make him six feet tall, or so, and sweet sixteen, which is, in fact, his age." And Eric chuckled.

"Now, if you please," said Eric, "I'd like to try a small experiment." Eric's voice took on a more familiar tone. "You're probably familiar with Gestalt psychology. I'd like to ask you, Doctor, if you'd close your eyes, and piece by piece attempt to reassemble what you saw — the exact same scene that was in front of you when you looked up and saw that woman lying there."

Doctor Illuzzi made a little mouth sound, and he took a breath. His lips tightened, and he looked at

Sweets for an instant. Nothing happened, so he closed his eyes.

"Put it all in," Eric urged him. "The street, the sidewalks, City Hall. Now there's the woman, lying in the intersection. And right in back of her, behind the body, Doctor? Who was there, how many people are you getting? And was one of them this boy?"

The doctor kept his eyes closed for a count of ten, perhaps, and then he opened them again and shook his head.

"I'm sorry," he said. "But I really *do* remember nothing. Believe me. I am a trained and practicing observer — but trained to see the things that I'm concerned with. What isn't relevant is to be ignored, looked past, in medicine as in life. I'm sure you understand."

Suddenly he smiled again, and took another gander at the time. "Forgive my curiosity," he said. He took a full step toward the door. "But would you tell me why . . . *you're* interested? You folks, specifically? I realize it isn't only medicine that's specialized these days, and so I can't help wondering. . . . That picture makes me think there might have been a — what? — *abduction* of some sort? Something of a political nature, perhaps? Say, four years ago?" He smiled once more.

"Hey, better watch it, Doctor," Eric said, now smiling, too, and holding out his hand to have it shaken. "Or I might have to do some diagnosing in your waiting room out there. Just to make things even." He threw in a little comradely laughter, even swung his left hand in a wide, fraternal arc and squeezed the doctor's forearm while he pumped his hand.

"Thanks a whole lot for your time, sir," was his exit line.

Sweets went out the door ahead of him, nodding at the doctor as he went. There were some fresh new patients in the waiting room, and one of them — a woman in a brown linen skirt and penny loafers — smiled at Sweets as he went through it. And they still didn't know what Amos Goodspeed looked like, now.

As soon as they'd arrived in Northfield, Eric had checked himself and Sweets into the Northfield Arms, which was an older, vaguely Tudor-style hotel, not big. The day after, they'd gone to Gilson's and the doctor's office, and that evening Eric had prepared a memo to go out to all the sheriff's offices and all the local police departments within five hundred miles. With it was to go a copy of the photo Sweets had taken of the late Dorothy Simon and (unfortunately) that *old* artist's rendering of Amos Goodspeed as he'd looked (perhaps) at twelve. For the next week, Sweets and Eric walked and drove around the town, sometimes together, sometimes not, talking to the citizens, and waiting.

Nothing happened. There weren't any calls, and no one that they asked — which included a pretty fair percentage of the population, after a week's time — could remember having seen a boy, a *strange* boy to the town, who could have been *that* boy, except grown-up some. Some people asked Eric if the boy in the picture was "colored" or not, but nobody asked Sweets that.

Eric, who liked both Northfield and the Arms, decided that they'd stay in town another week. It made as much sense to stay there (in his opinion) as it did to go. Or, as a matter of fact, a good deal more. Talking psychological sense, that is.

"A lot of people believe it's just something out of Agatha Christie or one of them, 'the murderer returns to the scene of the crime,' but it isn't," he said to Sweets. "We're talking casebook facts, there. And in *this* case there's another likelihood — what one might call a corollary — that the boy, the one who's closest to the victim, will come back, too."

They were sitting at an outdoor table on the property of Burger King, finishing a cup of coffee and watching kids walk in and out the door. And also some adults, of course. Sweets could have called a few of them by name, a few of both varieties, and some of them gave him a wave, a smile. Eric waved right back at them, each time.

"Thought you said he'd panic," Sweets replied. "Run and keep on running. Didn't you say that? But now you say he's going to go in circles, is that it?"

Eric chewed on that, wondering exactly how Sweets meant it. Sweets's babbling was bad enough, but he'd got used to it; this new Sweets being (mostly) quiet, looking thoughtful, took some further getting used to. Eric didn't know exactly what was going on, but he was pretty sure by then that Sweets wasn't going to start pulling any rabbits out of any hats. Eric hoped devoutly they were almost done. That the kid would do exactly as he said he would, and he could take him out within the week: case closed and Amos . . . who? Eric figured Sweets might be a little . . . bummed, if he saw Eric do it. But what the hell, they both were on the same side, right? Perhaps he'd tell the guy what had to happen a little bit ahead of time, to spare him, like, the shock.

"Not exactly," Eric said. "I'm looking at a two-stage possibility. Stage one's the panic: running wild, chicken with its head cut off — quite literally, in this case. But after he's been running for a bit, and four-five-six days pass, let's say, and nothing happens, *then* he'd probably come back to earth again and stop, collect himself. And then you'd get stage two, a deep depression. It hits him: Karen Archibald is dead and going to stay that way. Up until that point, he's only known it intellectually, but then it hits him where he lives, gut-level. He has a need to mourn, go through some rituals. Someone else could spend time at the grave; he can't do that. But what he *can* do, more or less instead of that, is drift back here — the place it happened, the place he never will forget, where he saw Karen last."

"I *see*," said Sweets. He had a twinkle in his eye. "And so he goes and stands there on the corner, and . . . and you'n me are sitting by a window on the second floor of City Hall, I'll bet. Hey — maybe we should get right over there, you think?" He snapped his fingers. "And then — hey, there he *is*! And look, that Datsun with the dented fender, waiting at the light? So first I get that rascal's license number down, and then — hey! — quick as salt and pepper, we run out and pick *him* up, the boy, and then. . . ." Sweets grinned and fished for cigarettes.

Eric knew that Sweets was only . . . *jiving*, as they say. But still, he wasn't wild about that kind of joke, where somebody seems to be more or less making fun of somebody else's education. The stupid-people-they-know-best approach. The psychology-is-egghead-horseshit syndrome.

"Can't say I'm counting on *that*," he said, with a foolish grin of his own, a good-ol'-boy-type grin, he thought. "But stranger things have happened."

"Mmmm," said Sweets. "And speaking of that: Strange thing happened more'n a week ago down in D.C. Boys got a call from right here in Northfield. F.B.I. boys. Person asked if they got any unsolved cases — like, say, kidnappings, for instance, ten to fifteen years ago, specifically."

"What?" said Eric, hitching forward on the bench, no longer smiling. "A call from here, from Northfield? How do you know that?"

"How else?" said Sweets. He sucked his cigarette and blew a long light stream of smoke through lips he'd pursed as if to whistle. He made a little smile and dropped his eyes and batted them a time or two. "Came in through the office."

Eric started to speak, but Sweets just kept on going. "Happened — hell — about two weeks ago, almost. Of course they stalled the caller some and traced the number just in case — the way they always try to do. I guess it figures no one thought of this case right away. Anyway, the guy hung up on them. He wouldn't give a name." Sweets opened up the hand that didn't hold the cigarette and offered Eric what he had in it: a slip of paper. "Number's listed to a family named Roux. That's R-O-U-X." Eric was already standing up. "Live just outside of town, on Dixon Hollow Road."

Thalia met them at the door and told them that the Rouxs were not at home and not expected for another ten-twelve days.

The younger fellow asked her who *was* living there, besides herself, and she said she was just the cook and not about to answer any questions such as that, or any other such-as, come to think of it.

As he requested, she then listened-up some more, but after that she said she didn't care one damn bit *who* they were; they'd have to talk to Mr. Roux, who paid her salary, and see if *he* said she should tell them anything, or not.

Then she said, yes, she guessed they might as well come in and use the telephone to try to get in touch with Mr. Roux.

The younger fellow also did the talking on the telephone, and Thalia guessed real easily that Mr. Roux was not exactly thrilled with what he said. There wasn't *no*body that she met yet was going to tell old Mr. Roux what *he* was going to do.

And pretty soon the younger fellow started saying, "Yes, but, sir . . ." a lot and, "All we're asking is . . ." a few times, too. And at the end he said, "All right, yes, sir, we'll do that. We'll be there in the morning."

When he hung up the phone, he said to Thalia, "We'll be going down to see the Rouxs; we'll probably be back on Thursday. I imagine Mr. Roux will call you on the telephone tomorrow, and we'll also bring a letter signed by him."

Thalia saw the younger fellow wasn't happy, not at all. He looked like he was smelling something awful bad. Something that "wants flushing," as the saying went.

The other fellow, Mr. Reid, did not look *exactly* happy, either, but Thalia knew that he was just as pleased as punch inside, the same as her. You could always tell with a black person, Thalia thought, and even more so if you'd met the man before.

13

COMPLICATION

Two days later, Sweets and Eric came back to the house. This time they were not invited in. Thalia came outside to read the letter that they bore, and saw that it contained, in writing, the things that she'd been told already, on the telephone. She took the two men straight to the garage and left them there with Jordan Paradise's wagon, and their powders and their fancy cameras, and all that nasty stuff.

The next day another young man came and sat with her and Allison, and tried to put a face together out of all the drawn-up parts he'd brought with him — which he could also change, and did, at their suggestion. He went away with a face that she and

Allison agreed was "pretty close" to Jordan Paradise's. (Thalia'd given up his name, before, to Sweets and Eric.) This "artist's rendering" looked a little like Michael Jackson, and a little like Ron Darling, the pitcher for the Mets; and a little like Rachel Ward, the actress; and a little like a real young Groucho Marx; and probably a few others. It even looked a little bit like Jordan Paradise.

Sweets and Eric had also received, from Mr. Roux, all the facts concerning the Fiesta: color, license number, model, and condition. And, of course, one other fact as well: that the Fiesta (chances were) would have his daughter, Riley, in it. Whatever business they might have with Amos Goodspeed — that was no concern of Mr. Roux's, he said. But (the two of them were told), they'd better step real light around Miss Riley Roux.

This was an attitude, indeed a *complication*, Eric could have done without, real easily. There were some guys — apparently this Mr. Roux was one of them — who thought that their own personal affairs came first, even before the interests and the strength of Uncle Sam.

All he had to say to them (though not out loud, of course) were two real little words: "We'll see." There were lots of different kinds of power in this world, and the Mister Clean-Hands Rouxs, they had to *buy* — and even to beware — the kind that Eric wore clipped to his belt in back, well-hidden by his nicely tailored jacket, every working moment of the day.

14

JETTISON CITY

Jettison City, where the state university is, is named for Jeremiah Jettison, the famous Indian scout who led no fewer than thirty-eight wagon trains across some of the most trackless wilderness on this continent, in spite of having lost the power of speech (after winning one too many kinds of "cutthroat" poker).

A number of people thought "Dumb" Jettison was luckier than he was smart, but there's never been any question about his son Donald's business sense. He, of course, was the founder of what is now the Dee-Jay discount chain, which began with the one department store, right at the start of the trail. It was originally stocked — or so the story goes — with the various and sundry items different people would leave behind when they lightened their wagons before the final dash across the wilderness. This lightening was old "Dumb" Jettison's idea — or, I should say, *insistence*. Before each train got underway, he'd pass through every wagon, pointing at stuff (treadle organ, side of bacon, chamber pot), and the people'd take whatever it was out and leave it by the side of the trail. It was either that or pull their wagons out of line. Then Donald, he'd come by and pick those items up, as soon as they were out of sight, just minutes later on.

D.J., Jr., was governor when Jettison City got that name (changed from Lushwell), and it was he who spearheaded the drive to move the University from right behind the state capitol to there. The members of the Legislature did a lot of talking about the superior climate in Jettison City, and the availability of room to grow in, but basically what they wanted was to be able to get a better deal on apartment rentals and be rid of all those know-it-all professors.

D.J., he just chanced to own the land — though under many other names, of course — on which they up and built this brand new U.

By the time Jordan Paradise steered the Rouxs' family Fiesta into Jettison City, the University had been there over fifty years, had grown to an enrollment of over twenty thousand, and looked, to Riley and Michael, like a pretty nice-looking place ("if one were going to do this kind of thing," as Riley said).

Most of it was brick and classical, trimmed in white, of course; the trees were large and shady, and the frequent lawns seemed extra lush and green.

"Everybody looks so happy," Michael said, suspiciously. "Kind of makes you wonder."

They were driving west on Prospect Street (it's hard to find a college town that doesn't have one) as he spoke those words, and the sidewalk next to them was thick with summer session students on their way to classes, or coming back from classes, or taking breaks from classes. Most of them wore shorts, and tans, and carried either book bags, beach bags, or — can you believe it? — shopping bags.

At her present age (of innocence) Riley didn't know that sixty-eight percent of them were there to make up incompletes and outright flunks, or to keep from being made to take a summer job, but even if she had, she would have seen what Michael meant. The kids on the sidewalk mostly looked as if they belonged in a soft-drink commercial. They looked *prosperous*, for sure, and (somehow) very much as if they planned — perhaps *expected*, even — to have as good a time, oh, ten years up the pike, as they were having then, that very day, while walking in the sunshine in "J-City."

"I could imagine coming here. I really think I could," said Riley.

They'd talked about colleges, she and Michael, off and on while they were driving. They'd mentioned big and little ones; public ones and private; what they'd heard from different people's sisters, brothers, parents — not to mention Barron's and the guidance staff at school. Jordan Paradise had just listened, taking it all in. Sometimes he shook his head, as if he didn't really understand.

"What do you think, J.P.? Could you see coming here?" Riley was riding where she liked to now, scrunched up, with her bare feet up on the padded dashboard, just above the glove compartment.

"Sure," he said. "Of course. It's hard to drive when you can't, you know." He smiled and wrinkled up his nose, and looked at Riley out of the corner of his eye. He'd started to joke around more as the days had gone by, though he still had times he seemed a million miles away.

"You know if you could pass the G.E.D.," said Michael, jumping in, "and have a high school equivalency diploma, you could probably get into a big state school more easily than a lot of other places."

Riley listened to that, and wondered what she heard. Was that the way a back scratch sounded? Michael hadn't yet gotten up the nerve to ask Jordan how much money was in the suitcase, so his financial aid rap was still pending.

"What you'd have to do," he went on, "is set up residency here in state, and explain to the admissions office that you hadn't actually come from anywhere, before that. I'm sure we could think up some plausible story. They might get really turned on. My guidance counselor told me that admissions people are always on the lookout for unusual and interesting cases."

"Well, he's a case, all right," said Riley. "And *unusual* is putting it mildly, I'd say." She took one foot off the dashboard and — mildly — tickled Jordan Paradise's ribs with one big toe. She'd only started touching him in the past week (Michael would touch *her*, and she'd sort of pass it along), and it was going very well, she thought. Putting hands — and feet — on him was surprisingly easy (as opposed to awkward) and nonstressful. And once she started touching him, he touched her, too, again so easily and naturally (that word, again) that she wasn't even getting looks from Michael — ones she noticed, anyway. She didn't check too often, truthfully. And she wondered if Michael wondered why she wasn't telling *Jordan* to stop.

"*Interesting*," she added now, "is a whole other question, of course."

"It's too bad they don't have colleges out in the middle of nowhere," Jordan said. "Like deep in the woods some place, away from everywhere. Maybe the middle of Alaska."

"Or how about a college in a car?" Riley said. "That's what you're really used to, right? Maybe a Winnebago, or something." She noticed this, and felt a little weird about it: She never used to kid around so much, except with Allie, maybe. She used to be a pretty serious person.

"Well, actually, the thing that I'd be best at," Jordan said, "is that other idea you talked about. You know, back at your house, the first day. The one where you just go off" — he motioned with his hand — "and meditate some place. Were you serious about that? Being Siddhartha or someone, right?" Riley thought she saw his eyes flash upward, to the rearview mirror.

"*Exactly*," Michael said quickly, maybe even *approvingly*, it sounded to Riley. "Sure we were serious. You see, Riley's family just happens to own" — she made a face, but no one saw it — "this enormous tract of pure wilderness that her father's father bought during the Depression for seven cents an acre, or two, or something — some totally ridiculous sum of money, like that — just as a speculation, and that her old man's held onto all this time. This is like a hundred square *miles* I'm talking about, mind you, not acres. Maybe some day we could all hike in there — if you're such an Eagle Scout and all — and then split up. I guess it isn't *that* far from here, right Riles?"

She nodded — but also waved a hand at him. "Yeah, but now we're *here*," she said, "and I'm excited." She bounced a little in her seat. "It seems so different than back in . . ." She slacked her jaw and drooped her eyelids. ". . . *Nawthfeel*, man." She shook her head. "Yes, *I* feel different. And I'm hungry. Oh, look there." It was another large expanse of green, green grass, with walks and trees and kids on it, a glass-faced modern building just behind. "Doesn't that look like the place for a picnic? We can get some stuff. . . . Fantastic!" Jordan had nosed the Fiesta into a parking space. "Aren't we having fun?" She reached and rumpled Jordan's curls; his hair was soft but springy, nice to touch, and it couldn't get messed up, no matter what you did to it.

"She says she's hungry," Jordan said to Michael, turning, peering through the headrests. "And she *also* says she's feeling different."

"Right," said Michael, and he switched to his all-purpose Viennese accent. "Ve can't accept dot, can ve? Vun uff dose stadements hass to be a liddle fibbyvibby, no?" But he, too, thought that eating on that wide expanse of college lawn would be a very cool, collegiate thing to do.

A half an hour later, all three of their mouths were snatching bites of bagel mixed with other things like swiss and sprouts and turkey slices, dripping Russian dressing. Around them, scattered on the lawn, were students reading, eating, talking, tossing things for dogs or one another, smoking, listening to music. From time to time, people would get up and go into the library — the modern building right behind the lawn — to use the washrooms there. Or possibly to meet a friend, or try to make a new one. Every so often, some summer session student would actually pick up a book out of that library, but it was much more apt to be a blonde, brunette, or redhead, either sex.

Riley really did feel great, and also didn't think she looked too bad, for her, sitting barefoot on the grass with just a tank top on above the briefest pair of running shorts she owned: the silky, sexy striped ones, green and white, stripes up and down, of course. Now that she was halfway tan, her legs were pretty close to excellent, and she didn't (ever) mind not having the kind of breasts that got asked out on dates regardless of what sort of kid came after them. Here, on this genuine college campus, she felt she was tasting what her life might well be like, quite soon, she thought; when she — an older, freer she — could have a life-style of her own, when everything she did would not "get back" to Dixon Hollow Road, for judgment and analysis. It was a dizzying, and terrifying, and very much delightful thought, she thought.

"So, anyway," said Jordan, taking a piece of twig and running it along the bottom of Riley's foot, "Michael told me this college here would be in one of the safer areas, if there ever was a nuclear war, right? Do you suppose these kids all know that?" He rolled his head to mean the entire group there on the lawn. "I mean, they don't *look* as if they — "

"No, of course not," Michael interrupted. "Hardly anybody thinks about it. I told you that already. Not because it's so remote or impossible, but because it's too obnoxious. They'd rather build and deploy a few hundred more missiles and think about Star Wars. Hey, that'll solve everything." He seemed to be talking a little louder than he had to. "And besides, with the kind of debts that a lot of them have, they've got" — he changed his voice to dopey — "real problems, buddy. Plus" — himself again — "maybe trying to get into grad school so they'll be qualified to make some big bucks later on. But the trouble with *that* is, they depend on the wrong sources for their information, so by the time they hear some field is hot, it's cooling off already, and by the time they're trained for it, there's a glut. They'd be better off consulting the pendulum, I swear, than a lot of career counselors. Even at a place like this. The system's completely screwed up; I'm not kidding you."

Riley'd heard that speech before — futurists believed that only *they* — et cetera — and for a second there she wondered why, exactly, she was hearing it again, at just that moment, and so loud.

And *then* she saw the girl, sitting by herself a little ways away, apparently absorbed in her thin paperback. She had a short, punky haircut, blonder at the ends than at the roots, considerable eye makeup, but carefully and neatly applied, and (ditto) lip gloss. Her toenails were also freshly painted — a rather pretty coral, Riley thought — and she was wearing faded cutoffs and one of those white cotton peasant blouses that you can almost but not quite see through, unless they get wet, of course. The girl was as braless as Riley, but much more of a . . . chunkette.

Riley was pretty sure she was about fourteen, and just as certain Michael would believe she was in college.

It wasn't the first time Riley'd observed the Michael-method for trying to hit on a strange girl. Such as it was. She guessed that different guys were just like different species of birds or wild animals, and that each of them had his own little mating ritual (or *display*, better) that he couldn't anymore change than he could change his fur or feathers. She supposed (well, *hoped*) there were some Michael-hens (Micheles?) somewhere who'd go for his routine. The ones he tried it on were apt to look like real fast poultry, Riley'd noticed in the past. But she was delighted — for her own sake far more than his — that he was taking a shot at this girl. Actually, she looked like a pretty alert and healthy kid — though you never knew, these days.

"You can say that again," the girl said, looking up from her book and speaking directly to Michael. The book, Riley saw, was Rilke's *Letters to a Young Poet*, and the girl had a clear and pleasant speaking voice. No evidence of disease, so far.

In the little pause between Michael's speech and the girl's reply, Riley had forgotten what he'd ended on — what he could say again — but apparently *he* hadn't.

"It's really true," said Michael, back to her. "What happens is, these guys — a lot of the counselors — just talk to corporate headhunters, the ones who — "

"Yup," the girl said. "But one good thing about this place is that you can crash in some of the dorms for a while, if you know which ones, even without ID from anywhere." She laughed. "Or any future plans at all." She closed her book; then keeping it in one hand, she crawled on all fours over to where the three of them were sitting.

"Hi. Where are you all from?" she said. She stuck out a hand at Riley, who smiled and shook it. Another Jordan Paradise, she thought: a mover and a shaker. The girl had a good firm grip, and her hand seemed completely slime-free.

"I'm Lisa," she said. "When I saw you guys coming, I said to myself, 'Aha, more tourists.' I didn't blow it, did I?" She looked around at all of them. "You don't go here, do you? You're still in high school, right?" She aimed the last of that at Michael.

"Well, yeah," he said, reluctantly. "We're kind of on a scouting expedition, though, looking for a halfway decent place to go — that's *if* we go to college. I'm Michael, this is Riley, he's Jordan. Riley and I are both from Northfield, back in — ." He named the state. "Jordan, he's from almost every-where."

"Like me," the girl said, giving Jordan just a glance and turning back to Michael. Riley had a funny sense that she'd been sent a message.

"Though I haven't been thinking too much about college, myself," the girl went on.

I bet not, Riley thought, being maybe three years' worth of credits short of getting into one.

"I never officially dropped out of high school," Lisa said, "but I didn't drop in much, either, after March or so. Don't ask me why." She laughed. "My parents own the concession for that one: Why? Why? Why? Why? Why? How the hell do I know?" She laughed again. "That's what I used to tell them, too. I was doing great — all A's and B's, that kind of shit. It's weird, the stuff you do." She shook her head.

Michael was looking a little stunned, processing this flood of unexpected information. Riley figured he'd be taken aback, at first, to learn the girl was not in college; but once he'd chewed on that awhile, he'd probably be pleased. Of course he'd think she'd been a senior or a junior, in her high school.

Riley also thought she understood what the girl was talking about. It was amazing. She'd hardly ever missed a day of school in her life, but she could imagine doing exactly what Lisa had apparently done — just suddenly stopping going. On the one hand, it didn't make any sense at all, but it also made all the sense in the world.

"When did you leave home?" she said to Lisa, and she held out an open bag of corn chips, feeling like some Pocahontas offering a string of friendship beads. "Are you from far away?"

"About two months ago," the girl said. She smiled and took a corn chip. Got the message, Riley thought. "My parents live outside of Preston, way down there. I've been all over, and I'm nowhere near done. I'd kind of like to see the ocean, maybe, next. And to tell you the truth, I don't really plan on going home. For now, I'm just here — and this resident faculty adviser or whatever he's called told me I was welcome to stay in his dorm for a little while; so long as I help clean up a little and don't fuck with the students. He knows I'm jailbait, but he's cool." She laughed. "So, of course I promised. I don't know if he meant the last part or not, but *I* did. You ought to come on over, if you need a place. They've got lots of empty rooms."

"Do you suppose there're people looking for you still?" asked Jordan Paradise. "The police and all? I saw this show on TV once, called *Runners*? All about . . . well, kids like you, I guess. Or some of them might have been, a little bit. And they said on there — "

"Yeah, I saw it," Lisa said. "It was pretty good, didn't you think? I guess I'm one of what they called the 'mutual consent' variety, where . . . *you* know. My parents gave up. I don't blame them. How could I expect them to understand me, when I don't even understand myself?" She made her voice real deep and sorrowful. " 'I don't know what's going to become of you' — that's what my mother kept saying. And I couldn't give her any sort of an answer, except, 'I'll probably just get cindered-out, or vapor-

113

ized, like you and Dad and everybody else.' Somehow," she put a finger up to one pink cheek and made a mock of looking thoughtful, "that didn't seem to be *exactly* what she'd hoped to hear."

"You know," Jordan Paradise blurted out, "I've been thinking about that. About the same sort of thing you said to your mother." This was classic *type-JP* behavior, Riley was starting to realize: When a connection got made in his mind, he'd let you know about it, fast. "And you know something?" Of course the girl, Lisa, shook her head. "I think it's pretty absurd for you to believe something like that might happen — you getting cindered-out, or whatever you said — and for Riley and Michael to believe more or less the same thing. And then for them to be actually looking at colleges, in the safer parts of the country, of course. And you to just head off and see the ocean."

"Oh, really?" Riley jumped right in, this time. She had no idea if he was serious, or not.

"So what were *you* planning to do, big stuff? Hold your breath till all the countries cross their hearts and promise to disarm themselves?" Riley asked. She pushed his shoulder. "Stop eating apple pie, maybe?" She shoved him harder. "Write a letter to the editor of *Ranger Rick*?" The other girl was grinning, by then.

"No," he said. He raised his chin in comic dignity. "But I'm going to do *something*. Something positive and active." He nodded forcefully, then sniffed and held his hand up. "No, no, don't ask me yet. I'm not quite ready to . . . reveal myself." Riley started giggling; she couldn't help it. "But I'm thinking. You see" — he turned to Lisa, pointedly — "up to now, I've been preoccupied, and on the road a lot. But at last my schedule is lightening, *and* I've just recently met these . . . *freaked* young people, here. They've impressed me by the things they've said, I must admit, so I intend — Hey! Watch it, you, just watch it!"

This, when Riley dove on him and started digging at his ribs.

Jordan Paradise, she'd learned, was very, *very* ticklish.

Michael had sat and watched all that, moving his head back and forth between Lisa and the other two. He'd plastered an expression on his face, in case he caught her eye. It was (he hoped) a tolerant but also lofty little smirk. The kind that goes with saying, "Children, children, *children*."

15

DORM LIFE

"Hey, be my guests," grinned Dr. Larry Benjamin, Ph.D., Department of Sociology. "Any friends of Lisa's are a friends of mine. I'm Larry."

The guy was balding, long-haired, bearded, curly-chested, with wire glasses, sandals, drawstring shorts, a walnut tan, and muscles made by Nautilus (thought Riley). Standing in the doorway of the resident faculty advisor's apartment — the inner doorway, that is, the one that opened onto the first floor corridor of Chisholm Hall — he was shaking a container of Dannon cherry yogurt with one hand and holding a fat paperback in the other, a finger jammed into its middle, more or less. Riley would have guessed his age as thirty-five, which meant she would have had to give the guy a kewpie doll if she'd been guessing ages in a boardwalk booth; Dr. Lar was twenty-eight years old.

"Though the sad fact of the matter is," he continued, "that after you three the NO VACANCY sign lights up, I'm afraid. LANE CLOSED, NEXT AISLE OVER, all that shit. Nothing personal, you understand. Just part of the continuing power struggle between *El Magnífico*, otherwise known as the Dean of Residential Life, and this untenured *peon*. He wants anyone who shelters in the U to be an enrolled, dues-paying laborer in the academic vineyard; *I* see no point in having good beds empty while homeless, cootie-free kids sleep out on the streets. He wins, I lose. What else is new? But I'm calling you four and David, the other one who's here already" — he looked at Lisa — "you met him, right? — my personal guests, who I just happen to be putting up in the dorm for a few days. What you'd probably better do is go in and out through my place, here, and not only not fuck the students" — he winked at Lisa, this time — "but also pretty much avoid them, if you can; even if you *are* cootie-free, which I'm assuming for the moment. Aside from that. . . ."

Riley snuck a look at Jordan Paradise, to see if she could tell what he was thinking. His face wore its usual pleasant, neutral expression as he listened to Larry explain "the one or two common sense requests I'll have to make of you," and that "check-out day, regretfully, had better be next Tuesday," four days hence.

At the end, he said, "Any questions?"

And Jordan said, "Yes, I have one. You're a professor here, right?"

"No," he shook his head, "I'm an instructor. That's the lowest form of academic life. An amoeba in the ocean of the intellect."

"But you do *work* at this university," Jordan persisted. "You teach students."

"Well, I conduct classes," Dr. Larry said. "I don't know how much *teaching* I do." He stepped back and started to turn away from them. "Did I answer your question all right?"

"Not really," said Jordan. "I haven't asked it yet. This is my question: Do you, a teacher here at this university, believe there's going to be a nuclear weapon used in the next ten years?"

The man stared at Jordan, and then switched his eyes to each of the other kids. None of them was giggling, though Lisa was looking at the other girl, Riley, with a sort of half smile on her face.

"Well," he said, "if you're serious, my answer is that, yes, I think it's plenty goddam possible." Nobody moved or said anything, so he added, "I might drop one on the Dean of Residential Life." He waved the hand that held the book at them and strolled back into his apartment, still shaking up that little thing of yogurt.

Because "no cooking" was one of Larry's "common sense requests," they brought in a minimum of stuff from the Fiesta, figuring that for those few days they could do just fine on things like bread and milk and cheese and canned tuna, along with fruit and vegetables, the kinds you didn't have to cook,

118

and — oh, yes — maybe ice cream, chocolate fruit-and-nut bars, a cookie here and there. They felt like savvy travelers, already. Lisa asked Riley if she'd like to share her room, and Riley said she would. After two weeks with "the guys," that would be kind of nice, she thought, a break, a change of . . . something. Tension? Pace? She didn't know — just nice. Jordan and Michael took the room across the hall, next to the one the other kid, this "David," had his stuff in.

"You've met him," Riley said to Lisa. They'd knocked, to say hello, be friendly, and there was no one in his room. "What's he like?"

"*Very* quiet," Lisa said. "Kind of cute, except he looks so solemn all the time — like, edgy, almost pissed, you know what I mean? Tall and skinny, light brown hair that he's usually got pulled back in a ponytail, sort of sharp features. He has this beat-up old Yamaha, but he isn't what you'd call a great musician, by a long shot. I asked him once if he wanted to walk on downtown with me — he was just sitting there kind of strumming on the thing — and he goes, 'Hell, no,' just like that, real snappy, like I was interrupting some major rehearsal. Then the next time I saw him, he was outside on the steps, smoking, and he smiled and asked me if I'd like a hit, and I said sure, and we actually had a little conversation. He said he'd been traveling for just a couple of months, and did I know whether the troopers around here hassled hitchhikers much, so I asked him where he was from and how old he was, and he kind of laughed and said what did it matter. I think he's about your age — *our* age. His last name is Gracey; David Gracey. I think that's a nice name, don't you? It sounds like a movie star, or something."

And with that the four of them had gone out and gotten into the car and cruised around downtown a bit before heading out to find a shopping center on the edge of town, where they could buy some food. Then they came back to the dorm and ate — still no sign of David Gracey — before going out again for a stroll around the campus, and down to the lake that bordered it in places. From time to time, they'd stop and sit and talk and listen to the sound of . . . *college*, you could say: all those kids, almost entirely on their own, just doing what they felt like, more or less.

"It seems so free and easy," Riley ventured, at one point. They were walking toward the dorm again.

"Hardly free," said Michael. "Even for the in-state kids, it's something like a hundred dollars a credit hour, I think, plus — "

She turned around and batted him. "Come *on*, you know what I mean. Like, *peaceful*." And Jordan Paradise had looked at her and nodded, licked his lips as if to speak, and then just put a hand on hers — gripping the back of her hand. She managed to turn it around, so they were actually holding hands as they walked along, and Michael began to whistle. She wasn't sure, but it could have been "Subterranean Homesick Blues," the Dylan song that has the line: "You don't need a weatherman to know which way the wind blows." That one.

By the time that they got back and she and Lisa used the bathroom, went into their room, and started to undress, Riley felt she'd known the other girl much longer than a half a day. Lisa was *accessible*, there wasn't any better word for it; she was a person you could come up close to, easily, the kind of person that you'd like to get to know. Her last name turned out to be Shay.

"How old are you, really?" Riley asked her, switching from her tank top to a T-shirt for the night. "Fourteen? Fifteen?" With most of the makeup washed off, Lisa could have passed for twelve, Riley thought, at least from the neck up, anyway.

Lisa grinned at her. "*Just* fifteen," she said. "My birthday was two days ago. Guys can never tell, it seems like; but girls can, can't they? Another woman's age, I mean. I've been around older kids a lot. Mostly, really. I was the youngest kid in my class. People my age always seemed like such *babies*. So boring. And they think they're so cool, I swear. Anyway, when I had my birthday, like that, and nobody else knew it, nobody around me; that's what made me feel older and more different than anything that's ever happened to me. A lot more, even, than the first time I ever did it, did." She paused. "You still a virgin?"

Riley nodded. Didn't hesitate or speak, just nodded.

"I thought so," Lisa said. "That's another thing I think you can tell a lot. I kind of wish I was, still. *Kinda* wish. But I'm glad I'm not, too, because now I've got it over with. I'll tell you this much, though: I've already changed my attitude — you know, about doing it, the whole bit. I was really pretty crazy for a while. Like a kid with a new toy, almost. Some toy, right?" She laughed, reached into her pack, and brought out a little metal contraption, which she proceeded to attach between the door and the door frame. It was a separate, second lock, one that made it completely impossible for anyone to open the door from the outside.

"You can see how much I've changed," she said to Riley, and she laughed again. "I even carry my own locks around now. Like a modern chastity belt, right? But what's happened is, ever since I've been away, I've felt I . . . I don't know, I *matter* more. To me and — *you* know — just in general." She paused. "Do *I* sound like the baby now?" She batted her eyes. "Like, wow, kids — look at me! Can you believe it?" She shook her head. "I never said this stuff out loud before. Maybe it's one of those things a person ought to just shut up about."

"No," said Riley. She'd spread her sleeping bag on the other built-in bunk, and now she pulled the zipper down a foot or so and wiggled into it. "I think I know exactly what you mean. At home, sometimes, going to school and all that stuff, you sort of feel you're not anything, just by yourself. That you don't have a separate identity, and it's almost like nobody wants you to. You're a Roux, or a Shay; or a member of the junior class or the Spanish Club or the swim team, or whatever it is. You're just a good little, special little *girl*, who's meant to more or less blend in — like disappear. Outstandingly, but quietly. And as far as . . . *you* know, *doing* it goes, I'm sure I would have, too — *if* I could have done it quietly enough, and *if* I'd had the opportunity. You know what I mean: an opportunity with someone halfway decent. Part of my problem was: No such person asked."

"Gee, that's hard to believe," said Lisa. She was lying on her stomach with her head down flat and turned to look at Riley. "I think you're really cute. And someone else thinks you're *outstanding* by the way. That Jordan. I can't tell you what his *plans* are, but he's sure doing some serious looking."

Riley stared straight back at her. "You think so?" she said. "You're not just saying that, are you?"

"Hell, no," Lisa said. "I'm sure of it. And he is gorgeous, isn't he?"

"Well," Riley said, "he *is* a little bit gorgeous, all right." She laughed and knew she sounded nervous, but still, she felt relieved for having said a thing like that out loud, admitted it. "Not that I'm planning to rape him, or anything. But I really think I like him, and I wish I did know what his plans are — except I'm not so sure he works that way, like, *planning* things." She reached for the light switch by the head of the bed. "Shall I turn this out now?" Lisa nodded.

"Do you three know where you're going after this?" Lisa's voice was softer in the dark. "I mean, don't think I'm trying to mooch a ride or anything — I'm not. I'm just curious. Really. I've gotten used to traveling alone. I think I actually prefer it."

"I don't know," Riley said, almost whispering herself. We haven't totally decided yet. We're talking about doing some camping sometime soon." She smiled in the dark and Lisa could hear the smile in her whisper. "No one's brought up the ocean yet, but it's a possibility, for sure."

In the little silence after that, the sound of a key going into their door's main lock was clear and unmistakable. It turned; the door handle turned; there was the very slightest grunting sound.

And then a whisper — a whisper of the "stage" variety. "Hey, Lisa. Whattaya done to the door? It's Larry."

"Gee, it must be jammed, or something," Lisa said. "And I'm in bed already, Larry. What do you want?"

He sort of chuckled. "Oh, I don't know," he said. "I thought I maybe ought to run a little cootie check, you know? Just so's I don't have any trouble with the Dean. I've got this real neat stuff you just rub in. . . ."

"Gee," said Lisa, one more time, "that's really thoughtful of you, Larry. But Riley's sleeping in here, too, and she was telling me just now how strict her father is about the people that she sees. I guess he's county prosecutor down in Jackson Falls and so he's extra sensitive and cautious, seeing all the weirdo perverts that he does, like in his *job*, and everything. . . ."

Larry made his chuckle sound again, this time followed by a sigh. "Oh, well," he spoke a little louder. "Who can blame a guy for trying?"

Lisa whispered softly, quickly, in the dark: "One-two-three — we can. Real loud, okay? Ready? One. Two. Three. . . ."

"WE CAN!" they chorused.

And cracked up, when his door slammed.

A little later, Riley whispered, "Suppose you'd

been alone? Suppose we hadn't come to town?" She giggled.

Lisa whooped, rolled over on her back, and said, "Why, Riley Roux! I really am ashamed of you. Asking such a question! You think I'd ever do it with a guy with yogurt on his breath?"

"Of course not," Riley said. "I lost my head."

Maybe twenty heartbeats later, Lisa added, "I'm really glad you *did* come, though."

And Riley said, "Same here."

Riley came awake in stages. She'd been dreaming, flowingly, of horses in a field: running, wheeling left and right together, such a gorgeous group of horses. And then the noise, the hollering, got through and pushed the dream away, and opened up her eyes to absolute pitch darkness, and that sound of someone hollering not words but more like, "Hey. . . . Hey. . . . Hey!"

Let's see, where was she? (Riley's foggy mind insisted on an answer to that question.) No, not a motel . . . that's right! . . . a college dorm, and Larry, *not* Larry, so a college student on the next floor, up above. Then — no, again (she thought), it came from closer, like across the hall . . . Jordan, Michael. She had her feet down on the floor when Lisa said, "Hey, what the hell . . .," and hit a light.

By the time they got their locks unlocked, the noise had stopped, and when they came out into the corridor, they saw that both the doors across the way were open, and that David Gracey's light was also on.

They crossed the hall and looked inside; Riley felt a little . . . vulnerable, in only underpants and T-shirt, not a lot of underpants.

A person she assumed was David Gracey was lying on the bed, propped up on his right elbow and part way out of an old blue nylon sleeping bag. He had tousled light brown hair, real long, and deep-set, dark-rimmed, staring eyes; and he wore a gray T-shirt black with sweat under both arms, and even down the front. Jordan Paradise was sitting on the bed in red briefs and a green T-shirt with the words WHY IS A CROW? on it, in gold, and he had his left hand on top of this guy's right hand, and (she could see) the boy was gripping on to it so hard his knuckles whitened. With his right hand, Jordan was sort of patting the other guy's left shoulder, and between pats giving it a little bit of a shake, and saying, "Hey, it's okay. Everything's okay now, see?"

It didn't seem to be working, Riley thought. David Gracey just reclined there, looking like a vegetable, a stone (yeah, super-stoned). But then, the next moment, something happened to his eyes and she could see that he was there, behind them, understanding, seeing things: the room, and Jordan Paradise, then Michael, crouching right beside him by the bed, and finally Lisa and herself, standing just inside the door — two maiden forms. Later on, she thought, until he noticed Lisa's face, he must have wondered if he'd waked up in the middle of an ad for underwear, or what.

"David, it's okay," said Lisa, forcing him to look at her. "They're cool. I know them. They're all right;

they're staying here. Just wait, I'll get a towel." She went back out into the hall.

"*Shit*," the boy said, struggling to sit up straight. "I'm sorry. Jesus, look at me." His voice was a little gravelly. He touched his forehead, looked down at his shirt.

Lisa came back. She'd wet one end of a yellow bath towel, and she handed it to the boy, who buried his face in it, then ran it up his forehead, pushing back his hair.

"Thanks," he said to Lisa, and he gave her just a flash of smile.

"This is Riley, and Jordan, and Michael," she said, speaking slowly and pointing at each of them in turn, as if it was a foreign language class and they were different kinds of fruit. "They're staying here, too. I've been with them all day." She paused.

"That was a really, really awful dream," said Jordan Paradise. He'd put a hand back on the guy, just resting easy on his forearm.

David Gracey closed his eyes a second, then opened them and blinked a few times, hard. "The worst," he said. "The worst because . . . because it was about some stuff that really happened." He shook his head. "Do you suppose I'm going to dream that son-of-a-bitch for the rest of my life?"

"I had a friend who told me dreams are smoky picture-shapes, inside your head," said Jordan. "But once you *say* them, put them into words, they're *stories*; true or otherwise. Not dreams. And once they lose their *dreaminess*, they can't be dreamed again." He looked around at Riley. "Karen used to tell me

127

that, when I had nightmares. And you know something? That's the way it works."

Riley didn't know if it was Jordan's matter-of-fact
voice, or two-thirty in the morning, or the boy's
spacey-ness, or what. But anyway, he started talking, telling them about himself and then about his
dream, which was, of course, this stuff that really
happened, as he'd said.

First, he told them that he'd been — just as Lisa'd
said — out on the road for just two months, having
left his home in Clayton for quite a standard reason:
He simply couldn't hack it anymore. Of course there
were some special circumstances, out of his control.
His father'd been laid off the year before and, as
David put it, he "hadn't made a good adjustment,"
not at all.

"It was more or less as if he took it personally,"
he said. "And so, to punish them, the bosses at the
plant, he started drinking. I know that sounds ridiculous, but I swear that's why he did it. He really
thought that maybe they'd find out, and be real
sorry."

The situation at his house had deteriorated pretty
quickly, after that.

"Even when it was happening," David told them,
"it seemed like I was living in a big cliché. You know
what I mean? There we were: the drunken father;
and the weepy, ineffective mom; and the resentful,
wise-ass kid who makes things worse, not better —
it was perfect. When I finally decided to leave, I
almost left the note on the kitchen table — wouldn't
that have been just classical? Luckily, though, I came
to my senses in time and Scotch-taped it under the

toilet seat. I wasn't a *total* disgrace," he said.

For the first month, and more, things didn't go too badly for him. He had a couple of hundred dollars saved, which helped, and he also lucked out a lot, in terms of meeting decent people.

"You won't believe this one," he said. "It's just like *Little House*, or something." And he told them about the week he stayed with the lady minister and her family ("I think her husband was Mr. Goodwrench, or somebody."), helping paint the church in exchange for room and board. And playing the guitar and singing with the oldest daughter. "All part of the deal," he said.

"Actually, she was a *really* nice kid," David said. "As a matter of fact, she was *exactly* the sort of girl I've always thought I'd end up getting married to. Real quiet — sweet — you know?" He laughed, a mocking sound. "I told you you wouldn't believe it."

Anyway, when the painting was done, he'd moved along ("Come back, Shane . . ."), promising to write as soon as he was anywhere for any space of time. That hadn't happened yet, he said — the writing or the roosting.

He sure didn't write to anyone from the next place he stayed. That was the old county jail in the city of Darwell, where he was picked up in the bus station and held while they were checking out his story, slowly, making sure he wasn't wanted anywhere. Even by his family. He'd never dreamed that such a thing could happen: that a person could be put in jail for no better reasons than his age, and hair, and luggage — that guitar case, plus an old brown backpack. But he sure had dreamed about what happened there.

They'd put David Gracey in a cell in the old section of the prison, the part that really wasn't used for people anymore now that the modern jail had been added on to the other side of the courthouse. Generally, the old cells were used for storage, and the only time a prisoner got put in them was if the prisoner was a juvenile who they wanted to keep separate from the other inmates — for his or her own good, as the saying went.

Well, after David had been there most of a day, they brought in another kid, a fifteen-year-old local boy named Remmy Torrant, David said. One of the jailers told him that this was Remmy's "second coming," that the judge had put him in for truancy that winter, a weekend's worth of time, "to teach the little so-and-so *one* lesson, anyway." This time, he was in because his old lady swore he wouldn't mind her, sassed her back, and the judge had given him exactly twice as long a term to think it over, four whole days; and promised he would double it again next time, and so on, on and on, as long as it took.

"He wouldn't talk to me," said David. "His cell was right across the way from mine, but up one; and he just sat on the edge of his bunk and looked at the floor. He didn't touch his supper when they brought it, even. And he was still sitting there when the lights in our cells went out, and there was just the one in the corridor.

"I kept on talking to the kid for a pretty long time after that," said David. "Partly, I was lonely, I guess, and it was something to do, almost a kind of a challenge to get him to say something. Plus I thought I could identify with what he might have been feeling, having taken all the crap I had from my old man. So I told him all about *that*, and how I'd realized since I'd been on the road that not everything and everywhere was quite as rotten as it seemed to be at home. He just kept on sitting there, not moving. He wouldn't even *look* at me, even when I begged him to. I'd go: 'Remmy, Remmy, please. Just look at me,' like that. I don't know what I expected him to see, if he did. Just a different human being, I suppose, a person who was *with* him, not against him. But he wouldn't even look. So finally I got tired and gave up and went to bed. For all I know, he might never have heard a word I said."

Sometime later on that night, David Gracey'd heard some sounds from Remmy Torrant's cell; and he had gotten up and watched while Remmy Torrant, moving thoughtfully and slowly, taking care, had hung himself with pieces of his shirt, torn up in strips, and wound, and knotted.

"First I yelled at *him*, of course, to try to make him stop." David Gracey told them that while looking at his sleeping bag and playing with the zipper. "And then . . . once he'd *done* it, and was hanging there, I yelled for *anyone*, to come and get him down, to come and *save* him, for gosh sakes. Nobody came. I'm pretty sure that nobody could hear me, but I couldn't swear to it. Possibly they figured *he* was yelling, and they just said, 'That'll teach the little bastard,' I don't know. Anyway, they finally came to bring us breakfast. He was long since dead and I'd completely lost my voice, which was probably all for the best, at that point. There's a period in there I can't remember much about; I must have been a little crazy for a while. So later on that day, around noon or so, they put me in a squad car and drove about five hours and let me out on the edge of Robinsville and told me never to show my face in town again. Like it was all my fault, or something."

David Gracey blinked his eyes a few times. "As if I'd ever want to," he said. "Anyway. This is about the fourth time I've dreamed of being right back there in jail and . . . and watching Remmy. And each time it's so real I guess I start in going just the way I did when it first happened."

"Who wouldn't?" murmured Jordan Paradise. "That's just so terrible."

"It really *stinks*," said Riley. "It's about the worst thing I've ever heard in my life."

"I've heard that some of those small towns are pretty awful," Lisa said, "but to think a thing like that could — "

Michael cleared his throat. "Like Jordan said," he said, "it very well could be you had to verbalize it once — to tell somebody else, so your brain won't have to keep on thinking that it has to take total responsibility for remembering something as terrible as that. Something that somebody ought to get in real big trouble for, sometime." He looked around at the other listeners, everyone other than David; they nodded encouragingly.

"Do you see what we mean?" he said to David. "How you could have been holding onto this so hard because you were the only one that knew it? Like the only unprejudiced witness, you might say?"

David nodded. "I guess that *could* be right," he said. "*I* don't know. I sure as hell hope it is. And no matter what, I sure want to thank you guys for coming in like that, and — ."

"Look," said Riley, interrupting. "I'm wide awake, and guess what? I'm — "

"*Hungry*," Jordan and Michael finished for her.

And that's how come the five of them happened to spend from three to five that morning, roughly, eating chocolate, peaches, cole slaw, apple-raisin cookies, milk, and cheddar cheese. They also talked: about jails, and justice, and kids killing themselves, and how terrible it is to feel so powerless. After which, amazingly, they all slept dreamlessly (they thought) for four more hours.

16

AFTER-DINNER DRINKS

Eric was sitting on the bed in his room at the Northfield Arms. He had his shoes off and his legs stretched out in front of him. It was nine-thirty at night, and there was a half-full vodka Collins, Eric's usual nightcap, on the bedside table. What was very *un*usual — make that *unprecedented* — was that next to *it* there was an empty glass that had also held a vodka Collins that same evening.

From time to time, Eric picked up this second drink of his and sipped; the level of the liquid in the glass did not go down an awful lot when that happened. Nothing like when Sweets, across the room, bit into his second Seven and Seven. Eric had noticed that Sweets seemed to take bigger mouthfuls of liquor than anyone else that Eric had ever known, in or out of the agency. It irritated Eric that he, Eric, had a very low tolerance of alcohol, while Sweets, apparently, was almost unaffected by the stuff. He'd often wondered if it was a racial thing or just a question of practice, so that night when Sweets got up and said good-night and started down to have his second drink — which he usually drank in the tap room by himself — Eric'd said, "Hey, why don't you bring me up another one, myself?"

As soon as he'd said that slightly garbled sentence, he'd regretted opening his mouth, but he wasn't about to change the wording or his mind. Chances were, Sweets hadn't even noticed; he was no big Strunk and White himself. Mind over matter, that was all it took; Eric didn't feel the least bit drunk from that first drink, he told himself.

When Eric had taken off his wing-tipped oxfords, he'd placed them side by side beside the bed. He had shaken foot powder into his clean socks that morning — as he always did, each day — so he was confident his feet were inoffensive, odor-free. Eric liked to get out of his shoes in the evening and sit around in his socks, even though he realized that doing so was slightly unprofessional. A man in his socks was patently less ready than a man in shoes. But on the other hand he felt that he, by sitting shoeless in his room during their last official meeting of the day, very unmistakably (but softly) underlined the fact that he, not Sweets, was running things, in charge. *His* room, and *he* the one with his shoes off (Sweets still kept his jacket on), stretched out on *his* bed. A subtle series of points, thought Eric, but definitely *there*. He'd also put his pistol on the bedside table.

The decision to stay on in Northfield had once again been Eric's, naturally. They'd gotten the Fiesta on the teletype, so all they had to do was sit and wait, and Northfield made more sense than other places. In Northfield, they could check the mail for Roux and Gordon every morning; a letter or a postcard signed by Riley or Michael and they'd know which way the kids had headed, maybe even where they were, right then. Eric hoped they'd find the three of them before some local cop, cruising up and down some local street on overtime, checking plates, lucked out and made the Fiesta, picked the trio up.

Ordinarily, waiting didn't get to Eric, but in this case . . . well, it slightly did. Maybe it was because Amos Goodspeed was a kid. He'd never done a kid before.

"There's something I been meaning to ask you," Sweets said now. The second drinks were halfway down and the business of the day long done with. "It's about Dorothy. From a psychological point of view, what would you say the likelihood would be that she told Amos much about his parents. I mean, wouldn't the decision to tell him or not tell him depend a lot on her psychological makeup?" Sweets was lounging in his armchair, with his hand cupped 'round his drink and holding steady on his belly, for the moment.

"Interesting question," Eric said. And indeed, he thought it was. Maybe, after all this time, Sweets was getting interested in broadening himself a little. "And I'd have to say it would."

Sweets didn't speak but raised his eyebrows, looking interested.

"For instance," Eric said, "her insecurities would work in favor of her telling him . . . lots of things about them. That way, she could identify herself with them. By telling him a lot about their work, their attitudes, their natures, their intelligence and education, she could show the boy that she was close to them and therefore *like* them. 'Your parents were smart good people and I was their best friend. Draw your own conclusions — about me.' You see the way it works? By extracting positive vibes from the boy, she gets to feel better about herself."

This was going to be an interesting conversation, Eric thought. He was glad he'd gotten Sweets to stay, to have another drink with him.

"I *see*," said Sweets. "That's interesting." He nodded. "But I was wondering. . . . Wouldn't some of that — the stuff about his parents — be pretty heavy going for a little kid? Like, hard to comprehend? Sure, you can tell him his mommy and daddy were *doctors*, all right, and you could even tell him they were trying to learn about diseases — right? — that they were doing research, in a lab. But at what age you gonna tell him that what they were studying, developing, were superviruses? That they were *making* diseases, as well as cures for them — brand-new diseases that could wipe out an entire country. Or damn close to it, right? I mean, that's heavy, man."

"Oh, I don't know," said Eric, cheerfully. He took

a sip of his drink and thought it was even more refreshing, in a way, than his first one had been. And, if anything, not as strong. "*I* learned about the great plague in Athens when I was in the sixth grade, I think. Pericles's funeral oration and all that?" It'd be flattering to Sweets if he acted as if he assumed Sweets'd know all about the plague in Athens back in the fifth century B.C., or whenever the hell it was, Eric thought. "I could handle it all right."

"*Right*," said Sweets, and he smiled, "but like they say, man, that was ancient history." He set his glass down on the table, plucked a Kool out of the pack in his jacket pocket, and lighted it. "You didn't have to learn your parents were the ones that started it — or could have, anyway."

Sweets put up a palm as Eric shifted weight up on the bed. "I know, I know. Not that the Goodspeeds' discoveries were going to cause anything. *We* know that. But did the Goodspeeds, did Dorothy? We're pretty sure the Goodspeeds thought their company had tipped off the government about what they were getting close to. Now, would Dorothy *want* to tell the kid that she believed his parents killed themselves so they wouldn't have to tell his government — her government, our government — what they'd found out?" Sweets laughed and waved a hand, dismissing the stupidity of all that.

Eric narrowed his eyes. The utter contempt he felt for people like the Goodspeeds attacked his gut sometimes, and changed his breathing slightly, and his heartbeat. They weren't just wimps and assholes; they were blind and weak and self-deluding — very near to being traitors.

"Well," he said, keeping his voice both calm and reasonable — instructive. "That would depend in part on another . . . aspect of her personality: how radical she was — how *sick*, in that sense. If she was fanatical enough, she'd want the kid to know that kind of thing, at a really early age. She'd want to hammer in her set of twisted facts. Bend his mind against his country at as young an age as possible. That's what they do, Sweets; you know that. Why, you hear about kids ten or twelve years old fighting in some of those guerilla armies, right? You probably fought against some little gooks that age in 'Nam."

"Yeah," said Sweets. "Could be." He hated it when Eric brought up the Vietnam war. *He* could bring it up, and talk about it, and it'd just come back to him as fucking miserable, the way it was. But when Eric started in, he always made it sound like the U.S. cavalry against them dirty, thieving aborigines, or something. Eric was big on the word *gooks*. Our gooks and their gooks. Eric gave the word the same inflection, either way. And if you asked him, he'd probably tell you that some of his best friends were Vietnamese.

"But what I wonder is," Sweets said, "could you call the Goodspeeds radicals, exactly? Or Dorothy Simon, either? They all seemed to have been pretty much into money, cars, good old free enterprise. They all had dough, real bucks — like all the Goodspeeds' assets in the suitcase Dorothy took with her. And she, herself, that job she had. I don't think of dress designers as the revolutionary type, exactly."

"I know, I know," said Eric. "But what you have to do, you see, is look below the surface, beyond the surferficials." Eric didn't even notice how he'd said the word. "You can't ignore the implications of the Goodspeeds' actions, understand? No, they weren't agents of a foreign government, not anything like that, but there are radicals and radicals. Like different breeds of cat, you follow me?" Eric winked and nodded, and Sweets nodded back at him, his brow furrowed — in concentration, Eric thought — trying to keep up. ("Like different kinds of gooks," was what his partner was thinking.)

"The Goodspeeds," Eric said, "were two private citizens attempting to interfere with the conduct of their country's foreign policy, that's about the best way to look at it."

Eric picked up his glass and took quite a sizable mouthful of vodka Collins. He felt good laying this stuff on Sweets, who really *was* an okay guy. The drink was mostly ice water by then; that's the way it tasted, anyway. Sweets seemed to be waiting for him to go on, so he did.

"These self-righteous bastards like the Goodspeeds and that Dorothy Simon just never will face the facts," he said. "You know what I mean? They refuse to see that making any sort of lasting peace is not an easy thing to do. At all. I mean, all they think we have to do is be good guys, and they'll be good guys, too — everybody's buddy-buddy-buddy. Shit. What a good government uses is whatever it takes, right? If someone has to die to save a bunch of others later on — well, then, so be it. And you sure as hell have to have access to the work of everybody in your whole goddamn country. The fact is — and you know this just as well as me, my man —

that the people, meaning all of us, have a certain set of *rights*. And one of them happens to be called 'eminent domain,' which means what the government needs, the government has a right to take — for a fair price, sure — and use for the good of all the people. The Goodspeeds' discovery belonged to science — *our* science and that means our people — and only the government, not any individual and not any corporation, is in a position to know how to use it best, for all of us. I feel sorry for the Goodspeeds, in a way, because they weren't able to see that, but I'd never feel so sorry for them that I'd let them fuck things up for the rest of us, the way they wanted to." Eric nodded strongly, once, and left his chin down on his chest. He knew his Constitution; you can bet your life he did. Words like *fuck* were strong language for him, but guys like Sweets — and Eddie Murphy, and that Richard Pryor — they were used to talk like that. Like all their lives. Eric's hands were fists, now, resting on his thighs.

"Right," said Sweets, looking down at the ice cubes in his glass. He thought the "government" that Eric was talking so confusedly about sounded a lot like the government that had decided (so confus*ing*ly) to put a lot of young men in Southeast Asia for reasons (and also with results) that most of them would never understand (or quite get over). The "government" that hung out in that five-sided building down there.

"And that's why we're in business, right?" he said. "Guys like you and me. To keep things from getting fucked-up, any old way at all. *Any* way. For instance: What are the chances Amos Goodspeed's got a single secret in his head? I've been wondering.

That's part of why I asked you how you analyzed that Dorothy."

Eric had knitted his brows, trying to really *penetrate* what Sweets was saying.

"Look," said Sweets, "try this scenario. Let's just suppose: Dorothy Simon gets a phone call from the lab, from Amos Goodspeed's mom, let's say. She's told that they — the Goodspeeds — gonna take some poison, kill themselves; they can't go on like this no longer. Would she take care of Amos, bring him up? Old Dorothy, she just goes hysterical; she tries to talk her best friend out of this, but can't. They hang up. She's totally flipped-out, she don' know what she oughta do. She panics, scoops up little Amos and the suitcase full of dough, and just takes off. Only later — two or three days later, say — she thinks how that must look. How guys like us would think that she had something that we wanted, maybe. But by then, she figures, it's too late. We'd *never* believe her. Being spooky, like the Goodspeeds themselves, she gets to thinking what we'd 'do' to her to make her talk, or possibly to little Amos. And so, she just decides to 'disappear' — forever."

Sweets made a gesture with both hands, as if he'd magically made something disappear. "You see what I'm saying?" he asked. "I got a sneaky suspicion that Amos Goodspeed, sixteen-year-old person, isn't any threat to anyone. That, number one, it's perfectly possible his parents never did *finish* making their discovery at all. And number two, that if they did, they never gave — and never would have *thought* of giving — anything at all to Dorothy. Anything but money for their kid. It just wasn't *like* them. And

142

now that Dorothy's dead, anything they might have said to her is not just old, but secondhand — unusable, unprovable. The ravings of a coupla loony suicides. The way I see it, with Dorothy dead, young Amos doesn't matter anymore. Could be we ought to tell our uncle down in Washington that we believe this mission can be scrubbed, abandoned, let alone, forgotten."

Sweets took one last suck and rubbed his Kool out in the ashtray. Then he blew a long light line of smoke and settled back, relaxing in his chair, big fingers clasped across his stomach.

Eric didn't raise his head, but he looked at Sweets out of the tops of his eyes.

"The trouble isn't Amos Goodspeed as a *person*," he began. "Or Michael Gordon as a *person*, or Mr. David Roux's young daughter *Riley*. This matter isn't personal at all. Never has been. Never-ever-ever." He shook his head. "I'm going to tell you something Sweets. This may surprise you, and it sure as hell should please you. But the fact is" — he paused, portentously — "some people of our own have come up with something every bit as good as whatever supervirus the Goodspeeds might have made. Or better. Or maybe it's the same one, who knows? But the point is: We don't *need* whatever it is the Goodspeeds might have gotten and might have given a copy of to Dorothy Simon. Not anymore. So it doesn't make any difference if she had it on paper, or in her mind, or if she put it in Amos's mind, or what. The only important thing now is that the Russians don't get it. Period. Exclamation point."

143

He took a deep breath. "Which brings us to Rule One, of course; you know this just as well as I do, Sweets. Probably you learned this baby in Vietnam. The first rule of security is . . . " He held up his hands the way an orchestra conductor might. "*When in doubt, shoot.*"

Sweets had not joined in, but Eric smiled regardless, smiled because he felt like smiling, smiled because it all was very simple, very clear. "There's no way we can *know* that Amos Goodspeed doesn't have the knowledge — and that he hasn't shown it, taught it even, to those other two. But there is a very simple way of ending all the doubts and questions, and seeing to it that the people of this country are a little better off — like, safer — than they were the night before." He held his hands up, both palms down and level with his chest, then moved them side to side a little, like the "safe" sign in a baseball game.

"All three of them?" said Sweets, picking up his glass and draining it. It was time for him to ask the question, to be absolutely sure. "You're saying that we've gotta . . . snip all three of them?" He stood up — hoping he looked real cool and casual, totally relaxed about it. *Snip?* He buttoned up his jacket.

Good man, thought Eric, surprisingly good. Not totally educated, maybe, or used to doing all the things the job required, sometimes. But, thank God, no faggy bleeding heart.

"All three of them," said Eric. He'd just decided it, that very minute, and he felt good about the decision, and having the power and the right to make it. "One plus the other two. So sorry, Mister David Big-Shot Roux."

And Eric smiled his charming, chilling, clean-cut smile.

Sweets went on out the door, carrying his dirty ashtray.

17

FUTURE COMPLICATIONS

Riley and Lisa were a little bit amazed when they realized they were both not just awake but *wide* awake before nine o'clock the next morning.

"Maybe our bodies counted that as breakfast — the stuff we ate at three and four A.M.," said Lisa, "so now it's time for lunch."

"Well, I *am* hungry," Riley said.

They got dressed and went across the hall to wake the guys, so that Jordan could drive them some place for breakfast. To their surprise, that room was empty.

"Those so-and-so's. If they've gone out without us. . . ," Riley said. They headed for the outside door to check the car.

On the lawn in front of Chisholm Hall, they found a celebration of a sort in progress. Jordan was sitting on the grass, grinning, and Michael was standing facing him, with one hand on his forehead and the other hand held out, waist high, in front of him.

And what he was saying, over and over, was: "Holy shit! It works! It really works!!"

That gave them their first clue, and when they'd gotten another ten steps closer, they could see the "it" quite clearly. Michael had the pendulum held out in front of him, and the little ring was swinging back and forth.

When he looked up and saw them, he started shouting their names and babbling some more. They got the message: This was the most amazing thing that had ever happened to him in his entire life. Within a couple of minutes, of course, they'd heard the whole (amazing) story.

Michael and Jordan, it seemed, had also waked up surprisingly early, considering their bedtime, and had decided to let the girls sleep on a little longer while they did their pendulum practice. After they were done, *then* they'd wake the girls and go to breakfast.

Well, Jordan had suggested that they try a different sort of thing that day. He reminded Michael that the first and best use of the pendulum — and the divining rod — was as a water finder. It was, he said, "infallible" as that. The other things — the sex test and the questions — were most definitely "extras." Even when the forked stick or the pendulum was in the hands of the most experienced diviners, it wasn't always accurate, or even active, on these other missions. A search for water — underground — might really be the best, if not the only, way for Michael to get started. Michael had, of course, agreed to try.

So, first of all, Jordan went out and located a vein — somewhere in front of the building — while Michael stayed inside and didn't peek. It was important, Jordan said, that there be something *there*, to look for. And also, this way, if it seemed that Michael might be getting something, Jordan'd already know if it was real, or Michael forcing it, or what. When he came back in, he explained to Michael what he had to do, the method. The dowser, he said, points with his free hand in different directions until the pendulum he's holding in the other hand goes back and forth. Then, by moving around the area, and pointing, the dowser can triangulate the vein of water and eventually stand right on top of it, with the swinging pendulum marking the direction of its flow.

Michael said he understood. They went outside. He pointed here and there, and then — *amazingly*, to Michael — the pendulum began to swing. Entirely on its own. Within ten minutes' time, he'd found the same vein Jordan had. And gone bananas.

Naturally, he had to show the girls *exactly* what he'd done, and both of them had to admit it was pretty amazing to see that little ring begin to move.

"I'm not *doing* that," Michael kept saying. "I swear to God I'm not. Isn't that the most amazing thing you've ever seen?" He seemed to have forgotten that Riley'd watched Jordan Paradise work the pendulum more than two weeks before. But she said yes anyway, and Lisa was the perfect first-time witness — just incredulous.

"My God," she said. "That's *spooky*. Do you, like, *feel* it happening at all?"

"I get a sort of tingle," Michael said, and Jordan nodded in the background. "Not *exactly* like a small electric shock, but something on that order. It's peculiar. Maybe my imagination, I don't know."

Lisa wanted to try it herself, right away, but no one seemed too anxious to indulge her. Riley realized *she* thought of the pendulum as Jordan's thing; she didn't even much like Michael knowing how to do it.

"Well, look," she said to everyone, once the ring and thread were back in Jordan's pocket. "We've got to decide what we're going to do about David."

"In what sense?" said Michael, cautiously.

"In the sense of including him, or not," said Riley. "What did you think? I mean, are we at least going to ask him if he'd like to do stuff with us around here, or are we just going to more or less ignore him?"

"That sounds awful," Michael said. "Especially since" — he stopped and grinned and jerked a thumb toward Lisa — "since we seem to have adopted little waiflet here, without so much as a saliva — "

"Hey, wait," said Lisa. She hadn't put much makeup on, and maybe did look younger. "If you think I'm leeching on to you guys, let's get crystal-clear on that. Riley *asked* me if I'd like to hang out with her — with all of you — for the next few days, and see if maybe *I* — "

"No, no, no, no, *no*," said Michael in tones of

149

outraged protest — fake-o soothingly. "Don't mis-understand, I beg of you. I think that's *won*derful. Superb. Hey," he said, lowering his voice, "why do you think I picked you up there, yesterday?" He wiggled his eyebrows, pounded his chest with one fist, and gave his version of a Tarzan yell, while Lisa muttered, "*You* picked *me* up, sure." And Riley smiled and put an exaggeratedly protective arm around her shoulders, saying, "Don't you pay him no attention, hon."

"Anyway," said Jordan, "I vote we wake up David. I liked talking to him last night, and he'd probably *love* to be around the kind of excitement we just take for granted — doing stuff like eating, and looking at stuff, and having a nice day. Our usual amazements, *you* know." He smiled blandly.

"That's right," said Riley. "And *today* he'll even have a choice of entertainments, won't he? Once we've hearty-breakfasted, of course."

"Of *course*," responded Jordan and Michael, in chorus. And they all tromped off in the direction of D. Gracey's room.

It turned out David *was* delighted. Delighted to be waked up, and to see the four of them again, and to *not* be coming off the back side of a nightmare. He even had a piece of priceless information he could share with them: He'd found this place, he said, where for ninety-nine cents you could get two eggs, with home fries and. . . . Lisa stared. She'd really fallen in with some *eaters*, all right.

So they all went and ate their ninety-nine cents worth, and then split a few extra orders of this and that while running through the morning's plans again. David opted to join Michael and Lisa on their visit to the state headquarters of the Society for Futurism.

"Sounds interesting," he said. "Maybe I'll get in on the ground floor of something, for once. Be the first one on my block and all that jive."

"Hey," said Michael, still sky-high, "in futurism, you *start* on the fifth floor, baby, and all the elevators just go up." He laughed, delighted with himself and pleased at the prospect of having two witnesses to the sort of respect he expected to get on this visit. As the founder of the Junior Futurists of America, he was generally looked at by older future-freaks with both esteem (for what he'd done), and also jealousy. Being sixteen, he had lots more years ahead of him than they did.

The three of them set off from the café on foot, heading for the center of the city.

Jordan and Riley went the other way; their destination was the Office of University Admissions. But when they got there, they were told that they could not be seen by anyone, just then, but that *maybe* Ms. Medina might just "slip them in" a little later, if they'd come back, "Oh, say, two-ish?" They smiled and said "Just wonderful. . . ," showing how untroublesome and downright *nice* they'd be, to have around full-time.

Once outside the admissions building, they looked at one another and they smiled again, but differently. This was — actually — the very first time since they'd met that they were going to be alone together for more than a few minutes. They probably had a couple of hours, maybe even more. Not to kill, to

151

cuddle, Riley thought. She stopped smiling when she felt her mouth go dry, and then she said the first thing that popped into her mind.

"Let's go back to the dorm," she said.

Jordan Paradise's eyebrows jumped, but then he smacked his lips, and grinned, and said, "Well, sure. Okay." And, just a moment later, "Great idea." After they'd taken a few steps in the right general direction, he also sort of seized her hand and held it. But as they walked along, he didn't speak; instead, his hand perspired.

Riley's mind was tripping all over itself, trying to figure out exactly what she felt — it *was* — in addition to excited. Judging from his immediate reaction to her suggestion, she had to think that maybe — probably — her earliest guesses about Jordan's level of experience with girls were pretty much correct. He was a Level A Beginner. On balance, she realized, that pleased her. There was a part of her that would have liked Jordan Paradise to have been the most godlike lover since . . . Zeus, or Dionysus, one of those. Not *promiscuously* experienced like them, of course, but more of a sexual prodigy, schooled by the late Karen Archibald (perhaps) in every nuance of the art of giving pleasure to a woman (including blushing virgins, natch). But at the same time another section of her being — a much, much larger one, she thought — was delighted that he *wasn't* such a person. That they'd be starting out on this trip to Elysium, or Eden, or even Carnal City, taking off — that's both of them — on People Express, from the same Newark Airport of experience. From Level A, that is.

It crossed Riley's mind, at that point, that it might not be terribly unwise to say something like "a penny for your thoughts" to the guy, to Jordan, before she started tearing at his clothes, or hers (not that she really *planned* to do that), just on the off-chance she'd been totally misreading the "signals" she'd been getting, him touching her and holding her hand, and all that. Lisa'd thought she'd seen the same things, and Lisa was sharp; but Lisa was also just fifteen and newly on the scene. She was not the Pope, or Elizabeth Taylor, face it.

But at the same time she felt that "a penny for your thoughts" was just about the most immature and antifeminist cop-out line in the entire English language, given the present circumstances. Look, she told herself, what Lola wants, Lola goes after. Damn the torpedoes, here comes Miss Liberty, right? Full speed ahead now, baby!

"A penny for your thoughts," said Riley.

"Oh," said Jordan. "Actually, I was just thinking about what I ought to say to this Mrs. . . . *Medina*, was it? About whether I ought to tell her that I probably didn't want to go to college next year, even if I can. I mean, the year after."

"What?" said Riley, feeling that a rude, cold hand had suddenly come down on the sexual thermostat of Jettison City, and then had twisted, cruelly, counterclockwise. "Are you serious?"

"Sure," said Jordan cheerfully, and he let go her hand as he said it. Then, to her amazement, he put his arm around her shoulders, gave a squeeze. Stunned, she seized his waist, and they were snugged together, hip to hip, still walking toward the dorm.

"I wasn't kidding, yesterday," he said. "I *have* been thinking a lot about what you said — about what you and Michael said — about you two being so freaked by this whole nuclear war deal."

"You know something?" Riley said. "After you said that, I started to think about it myself. And I realized I used to feel just the way you were saying you did, but that what happens after a while, when you don't *do* anything, is you just get . . . *I* don't know." She shrugged.

"Well," he said, and he gave her shoulder another squeeze, "here's what I thought, before I fell asleep last night. If there's a good chance of some sort of nuclear thing happening — like a lot of people seem to say — and then it *did* happen, and I hadn't done thing one about trying to *stop* it from happening, it'd be almost like I was one of the *causes* of it. You know what I mean? It's like what Karen told me once: If you can't be part of the solution, then you're part of the problem. That made sense to me when she said it, and it does now."

Riley nodded. "Did you and Karen ever — *you* know — talk about this sort of stuff? Like war and all that?"

"Not really a lot," Jordan said. "Or she did, some, but I didn't react much, I guess. Maybe sometimes I was thinking about other things. Like myself, mostly. Trying to figure out how everything would ever work out for me. *You* know, later on, and everything. But a lot of the time I'd just say: Bag it, that's up to someone else. I just wanted to have fun. She told me what she thought, but she didn't really push it."

"And it was just meeting us that changed you?"

Riley said. "That, and having Karen be killed and all," she added and felt like an insensitive clod for having it come out like that. They were getting close to Chisholm by then, and she wished she could slow their progress down a little, so they wouldn't *necessarily* be talking about nuclear war as they walked in the door of her bedroom. Or whatever room they ended up in. Hoping for the best, she gave his ribs a little extra pressure.

"Well, actually," Jordan said, "it *is* both of those . . . events. Meeting you, and having Karen die. What that made me realize is, it's up to me to look after . . . well, whatever matters to me." He'd been staring at the walk, but now his head came up. "*Who*ever matters to me, too. And in this case, what that means is I've got to do whatever I can to keep you from ever getting hurt — much less *killed* — in such a stupid, awful way."

His head went down again. "You'll probably think this is the craziest thing you've ever heard in your whole life, but I'm going to say it anyway. *You* matter to me more than anyone I've ever known. In a whole, completely different way. I really think I . . . *love* you, Riley."

They stopped, and then, still joined together like a hinge, they swung around and faced each other.

For a moment, they just stood there, looking into each other's faces, and holding one another lightly, just above the elbows. His look was wide-eyed, timid, questioning — no more than *hopeful*, at the most.

Until she smiled into his eyes and said, "Oh, Jordy."

Then, almost in slo-mo, their hands slid out, around each other's backs. They pressed and pulled their fronts together, chests and bellies, all the way to kneecaps (thighs-to-thighs — that just felt unbelievable). And, while that was going on, the kiss that both of them had thought about for days (quite possibly) began quite . . . cautiously, as if they were afraid they'd mess it up, or that her parents might come driving by, or something. Both of them had gone this route before (Jordan many fewer times than Riley), she mostly in the context of a party, perhaps a little high, for courage, always with some thoughts or reservations: *What on earth will I do next? I hope this person isn't getting any wrong ideas.* This time, though, there wasn't anything to think about, except . . . *fantastic, goody.* Their mouths got nicely matched and comfortable; they pressed and opened wider; explorations, wet and cavernous, took place. And no spelunkers ever came up happier, or breathing more . . . enthusiastically.

"Hey, watch it, kids. You'll give the students here ideas," said Dr. Larry, passing — and he chuckled off to class.

The office of the state headquarters of the Society for Futurism was probably not a disappointment to Michael. Michel*angelo* might have been put off, tending as he did toward the use of natural materials (like marble for the "Pietà"), and anatomically recognizable human shapes (for instance, Adam, on the Sistine ceiling). But not Michael *Gordon*. For him, the fluorescent bulbs did just as well as what came in the windows other places, and the shapes of some of the molded plastic furniture and standing conversation pieces (one called "Jealous Jezebel," par-

156

ticularly), not to mention their colors and materials (its: green acrylic, streaked with fire-orange flashes) were way beyond what anyone could ever do with wood, or stone, or metal, he believed. Michael didn't know art — for sure — but he knew what he liked.

Lisa slowed, then stopped inside the office doorway — and maybe even tottered back a little (maybe dazzled, Michael thought), while David Gracey pursed his lips (as if to whistle, possibly).

Michael had called ahead, and at a buzz from the receptionist, Mr. Mason came bouncing out of an inner office. He was a round and balding little futurist who wore the first pair of rose-colored glasses Lisa'd ever seen on a guy. But she *was* impressed by his outspoken glee at seeing Michael. He ushered all of them into his large, light corner office and announced this was "a treat."

From almost that point on, things slid downhill, at first so slowly that the tilt was imperceptible. Mr. Mason ("Alan, Alan, Alan — *please!*") babbled happily about the need to have, "our point of view" established in the high schools of America, and said that now it had been, "thanks to you, friend Michael."

"In my view" — he aimed this at Lisa and David — "the whole futurist concept equates superbly with the vision of America the founding fathers had." David Gracey nodded, stroked his chin.

"Which, by the way. . . ," continued Alan. And he told them how the founding fathers' ideas were certainly under attack here and there around the country, nowadays. As for instance when state legislatures — "even ours, right here," he said — had wasted valuable public time discussing, and even voting on, a nuclear freeze resolution. This, to him, was an example of despecialization at its very worst.

"What kind of a foreign policy could we expect to have — and link our future to — if it's the product of the thinking, or *emotions*, better, of a bunch of rural farts from Nowheresville?" he asked them, chummily.

"Like Thomas Jefferson and them?" piped Lisa, wide-eyed, innocent. Her best just-asking-sir expression. She knew she should probably keep her yap shut, but she didn't really care that much.

Alan Mason laughed and waved a "cut-your-kidding" palm at her.

Michael would have answered Mason anyway — who already reminded him, unpleasantly, of his social studies teacher in the ninth grade — but with Lisa having stuck her neck out, he felt a little extra motivation.

"We-elll," he drawled, and stretched out in his chrome and imitation leather chair, matching Alan Mason's laid-back posture, "it isn't *just* the rustics and the birders, is it — really? That're alarmed by recent trends in U.S. foreign policy. I mean I'm sure you're *au courant*," smiling, just to punctuate, to *underline*, the French expression, "with what's been happening at the major foundations: the sums of money *they're* putting into the search for new and different ways to slow down the arms race and reduce the threat of nuclear war. I hardly think one could call the Carnegie Corporation, or the Ford Foundation, or the Rockefeller Brothers Fund hayseed operations, exactly. Or mired in the past, either."

Michael liked saying "one could call." He snuck a quick peek at Lisa, and liked what he saw.

"Maybe not," said Alan Mason, looking suddenly surprised — and sounding, for the first time, slightly patronizing. "But still, it goes without saying that the problem is largely one of *access*, isn't it? Access to information, as much as information itself, is the key that unlocks the future. The national security people have the best insights into Ivan's plans, I'd say. *They're* the government's designated futurists, if you will, and in this case I agree with them absolutely: that massive threats of force are the prescription. To train a bear and keep him docile, you have to show him the stick," said Alan Mason, folding hands across his Orlon middle, delighted with *his* access to such vivid, forceful language.

"So, when William Dietel over at the Rockefeller Brothers" — Michael tossed the name at Mason as easily as if it were a card at a hat, a mouse to a cat, a pearl before a swine — "says that the prevention of nuclear war is going to be to the eighties what civil rights was to the sixties — *the* major issue, in other words — *you* say, 'Calm down, Bill. We already know how'?"

"More or less," said Alan, his fat face wreathed in smiles. "There's a fine old saying, Mike — perhaps you've even heard of it: 'Let the cobbler stick to his last.' Huh? Not his last pair of shoes — that's what I first thought it meant, when *I* was a kid." He chuckled, man-to-kid — no question. "No, a 'last' is also that metal foot-shaped gizmo you see in shoe shops, if you're lucky enough to find one, nowadays. Well, anyway, that's in a nutshell what I was saying

159

to you before. The Rockefeller Brothers and the other funds should stick to what they know: sending some of that old money of theirs up to Harvard, or to Harlem, reconstructing Williamsburg, that kind of thing. And the government should stick to what *it* knows, dealing with the Russkies, for example, and stay the hell out of business. And *we* . . . here, just to give you one example. . . . " He paused. He had a zinger ready, clearly.

"*Truffles!*" he exclaimed. "Fifty dollars apiece, and lucky if you find them. In the wild, of course, and *only* in the wild — up till now. But now this little Frenchman, in his lab, has found a way to cultivate. . . ."

When they finally left the offices, almost an hour later, Michael felt obliged to say that Alan Mason was in no way a typical futurist, that he seemed more like a . . . well, a greedy, pig-shaped moron, a dangerous, power freak.

"Not that there's anything wrong with being on the cutting edge of any new . . . er, *enterprises*," he went on. "But that crap about leaving the whole matter of nuclear disarmament and all that to just the people down in Washington. That is such bullshit. If people don't really say what they feel about weapons and stuff, and what sort of ethical standard they expect from government, how the hell can you expect the Third World countries to ever — "

"Oh, well," said David, interrupting. "I can see where he's coming from, in a way. I mean, if everyone in the world could be guaranteed a decent medium-priced truffle sometime in the not too distant future, why, then. . . ."

He said this deadpan, his long face looking thoughtful, solemn — and Michael stopped and stared at him, and even caught his breath to answer. Then behind him, Lisa whooped with laughter, and that made David grin, so Michael blew the breath back out and pushed him on the shoulder.

"Get outa here," he said. "Go snuffle up your own damn truffles." And he shook his head and started laughing, too, trying to make what sounded like a "good sport's" kind of sound.

When Riley first started to think about such things, in fourth or fifth grade, she imagined that one day she'd meet a man, some perfect man (like Mr. Shackleford, who taught both English 9 and skiing) and he'd sweep her off her feet with presents, kisses, and those special looks of his, and they'd marry and do that stuff (a little bit unthinkable, but so they said) she'd lately learned that married people did.

After a while, however, she thought differently. She believed that sometime — fairly soon, in fact — she just might meet someone (probably *not* a film or rock star, but you never knew) and they'd just fall for one another like a ton of bricks. And show it, by kissing up a storm and then gradually getting into all manner of neat touchy-feely stuff (that, by then, she knew would feel just *great*) before they eventually decided to live together — probably married, but maybe not — at which time they'd go for the Big One.

And then, after that, there was the stage where she really thought she'd like to "get it over with." At that time, however, she hadn't even gotten totally relaxed with the kissing routines, which was her first problem. Her second was that she'd already come to hate — resent — having her chest pawed at, and her rear end grasped by awkward boys who smelled of beer and told her that she "owed" them "satisfaction." Her resentment, and her way of putting it in words, won her a bit of a reputation in junior high ("stuck-up," "ice-cold," "a baby," or "that dyke," depending on the zitty-slicker speaking), and that led to the situation she'd described to Lisa: a lack of opportunities to do . . . well, much of anything with anyone halfway decent.

Now, though, magically, the world was different. This new, exciting, early-summer model Riley *had* a (much, much) more than "halfway decent" someone, whom she loved (she thought, was pretty sure). And furthermore, she'd also given up — as she had said to Michael — *expectations*. She had no plans and no scenarios for Jordan and herself; what's more, she didn't feel they needed any. What she knew, that day, in Chisholm Hall in Jettison City, was that she felt like taking off her clothes with Jordan Paradise. Not in order to do anything that could *conceivably* make her pregnant, but just to do that, to make that sort of statement with and to the guy — show him who she was, and really take a full-fledged, unsnuck look at him, of course. It didn't hurt that Jordan was already on record (you might say) with a willingness both to look at her and take off everything of his with her around. In any case, the act, their doing that, would be a sort of proof (thought Riley) of both that kiss and what they'd said to one another. Of their love, you could say.

So that's what they did. There was a moment there, as she pushed down her underpants, that Riley felt as if she'd skipped from . . . oh, sixth grade, let's say, to twelfth, in fifteen seconds flat, and now was faced with — possibly — an hour test in calculus. But then she looked at Jordan, and she knew that he had not misunderstood, that everything was A-OK.

And so it was. They hugged and kissed and touched and talked — and found that both of them, while acting so grown-up, felt very much like children. Man- and womanchildren, to be sure, but children just the same: full of wonder and delight with this new, silky, sudden world that they'd discovered. Riley'd never felt more beautiful . . . or *natural*. She *was* fun, just the way she'd always known she'd be.

And she'd never felt more surprised — such is the way time flies, when you are having you-know-what — than when someone tried the door (she'd single-locked it from inside, of course), and Lisa's voice said, "Riley?"

She thought a second, answered, "Yes?"

There was a sound of muffled conversation from the hall, and then who else but Michael, saying, "Jordan?"

Riley put a hand over Jordan's mouth, and said, "None of your business, Michael."

And he said, "What the fuck . . ." and David Gracey laughed.

18

ACTIONS AND REACTIONS — 1

Here are three statements Riley Roux believed were true, and lucky for her they were (she also thought).

One: When a person is fully dressed, it's impossible for another person to tell, just from looking, how long ago she put her clothes on. Or *back* on. Or *his* clothes. Whatever.

Two: Human skin doesn't show fingerprints.

Three: What she did, or didn't do, or planned to do with Jordan Paradise — person to person — was, is now, and always will be absolutely none of Michael Gordon's business.

* * *

It was in full knowledge of these three great truths (giggled over in the midst of whispered, earnest conversation) that she and Jordan put their clothes on, noticing that it was close to one o'clock already, and walked — or make that *wandered casually* — into David Gracey's room, there to meet, if not the probing questions of the press, at least some normal curiosity, let's say.

"Hi. What's happening?" " said Riley (feeling unexpectedly . . . *self-confident*, she realized). "Did you all eat already?"

Lisa was sitting on one end of the bed, with her legs curled under her. She looked straight at Riley, smiling in a happy, friendly way, very much as usual — oh, perhaps an extra twinkle in her eye. David was at the other end of the bed, leaning on a pillow propped against the wall, his long legs stretched toward Lisa. He dropped his eyes when Riley and Jordan came in, and then seemed to take a lot of interest in smoothing his jeans along his thighs. Whether this was normal behavior for him, or not, Riley couldn't be sure. Michael was sitting in an armchair, a sturdy piece of institutional furniture, with wooden arms and green naugahyde upholstery. He had both feet on the ground, his legs apart, and his hands on his knees. He looked right up at them, smiling in much the way vice-principals of many high schools seem to learn to smile somewhere, somehow.

"Well, well, well," he said. "Here they are, fresh from their college interview. You can't tell me admissions isn't staying abreast of the times, the way they handle those interviews. But they still want to know how the applicants are scoring, don't they? Or *if* they are. I imagine you got in all right," he said to Jordan Paradise.

David looked at Lisa, then at Jordan, then at the door, then at the window. This wasn't his beef, was how he felt.

"Michael," Riley said, "try not to be an asshole, will you? Try growing up a little? You're not my father, or my keeper, or the God of the Israelites, so do me a favor and stop acting like you were, okay?"

"Hey, who's acting like anything?" Michael protested. "I'm just kidding around. How'd it go, no fooling? I've had a couple of interviews myself, so I know that they're exhausting, man. You just feel like going straight to bed when you get back from one, am I right?" He rocked back in his chair and brayed a laugh at them.

"We didn't have the interview yet," Jordan Paradise said to him, before Riley could speak. "We're going back at two o'clock. And Michael, I want to ask you a favor. Please don't make jokes about Riley and me, if that's what you're doing." There was nothing threatening, or scornful, or angry in the way he said that. And nothing worried, or apologetic, or uncertain, either. "What's going on is important to us, and it's serious. How you take it may not be the way it is; I hope you realize that." He cleared his throat. "Here's something I'm sure of, Michael: Nothing major is easy. Not to do, not even to have to look at, sometimes. We think we love each other — a lot — and we're asking you to believe we know what we're doing. Do you understand?" He looked at Lisa and David. "And of course we ask the same of both of you."

When he stopped talking, nobody said anything. It was definitely one of those silences. David Gracey kept looking at the backs of his hands and Lisa, though still smiling, was fiddling with the old faded cleaning tag, on the end of the old blue sleeping bag. Michael was wrinkling his nose and staring at the carpet between his feet. Riley looked at Jordan, smiled, and shook her head — not "no." She was (she felt) entirely "yes," more so, in more different ways, than ever before in her life. Affirmative. A little while ago, they'd felt like children: innocents, unformed. But now she felt responsible, grown-up. It crossed her mind that "act your age" was one of the most absurd things that anyone could say to someone else.

"There's something more I'd like to say," said Jordan Paradise. "It's about next year — this fall, I guess. I've decided I want to do something, besides maybe go to school, or study for some test. I've gotten an idea." He looked around at all of them. "It's from my heart, I think — or somewhere way inside myself. I don't know. Maybe this isn't a good time to bring it up — it probably isn't — but I really wanted to tell you all, and see what everybody thinks." He cleared his throat.

"I feel a little foolish," he said. "Please don't laugh." *He* laughed. "I seem to be saying that a lot, all of a sudden."

He stopped laughing and looked down at the floor.

"First I'd like to tell you *why* this idea happened, maybe. It's what I think, anyway. It has to do with Riley." He cleared his throat again.

167

"When I was little, Karen used to tell me stories all the time — she was this sort of guardian of mine," he said to Lisa and David. "Hundreds of different ones, it seems like; neat stuff: about foxy animals and fairies, and vegetarian sharks, and talking furniture, and how the burp began — all kinds of stories. And some of the ones I liked best were about the olden days, when knighthood was in bloom, or in clover, or whatever it was. Well, it seemed that whenever you had knights, you also got dragons," he said. "At least in those stories, if you were a knight and you loved someone, you'd go out and try to kill the fire-breathing monster, right? And it seemed the only reason you thought of doing that, and maybe the only reason you could do it, was that you really loved someone. Either that, or you did it for a whole bunch of people, like the poor but honest woodcutters on the edge of town. It wasn't that you were such a . . . I don't know, such a *chicken salad sandwich*, all of a sudden, such a real perfecto of a person. It was more like something that you *had* to do. And you wanted to.

"Well, this is just like that — not that I'm comparing myself to a knight or anything. But I think I got this idea because of feeling the way I do about Riley." He paused and rubbed the side of his face. "And wanting to do something that'd be good. Like she is. Sort of as a celebration, you might say." Riley couldn't help but smile at him again. And she also felt, ecstatically, like crying.

"The problem is," he said, "that the idea I got isn't something I can just do by myself. The dragon's much too big. And besides, it's everybody's dragon, not just mine. But I actually think that maybe there's something we can do about nuclear weapons, getting rid of them. Kids like us, I mean — millions and millions of us, all over the world."

David looked at Lisa again, and Jordan caught the look and laughed again.

"See? I ask you not to laugh and keep on laughing. This is crazy. Maybe I'm crazy. Talk about unrealistic, right? Talk about — what's the word? — presumptuous? Starry-eyed? But listen. Suppose we could get kids — people who are too young now to go into the Army, even, but who would eventually be the ones who'd have to fire the missiles or drop the bombs — suppose we could get them, by the hundreds and hundreds of thousands, in all the different countries to agree on one thing: that they'd *never* do that. Never do anything that would ever, conceivably, set one of those things off. Maybe that they'd never even help to *make* one. Do you see what I'm getting at?

"It wouldn't be like someone refusing to register for the draft, or having to quit a good job making nuclear subs, or something. The kids wouldn't be breaking any laws; they'd just be sending a message: Here's what we're *not* going to do. Believe it. I think it first hit me when I was talking to Allison — that's Riley's little sister," he said to Lisa and David, "that even a younger kid — she's twelve, I guess — can see this whole thing, this nuclear deal, a lot clearer — more *personally* — than . . . oh, say some senator can, or some guy in the Politburo, or whatever it is.

"So if millions of kids could only find a way to

169

tell these leaders . . . well, not only what they thought, but what they were going to do or not do. . . . You see? At first it sounds far-out — but then you think about it. Kids *know*. Maybe *because* they get right down to basics, the important part. Don't you agree? And if they spoke together, saying something simple and direct. . . . Do you see what I mean?"

Everybody except Michael was looking at Jordan by then. Michael still looked at the carpet. Riley was pretty sure he was dealing with a lot of different things, inside his mind: their ten-year friendship; the way he liked to see himself (liberal, fair-minded, on the cutting edge); anger; jealousy; whatever. And not enjoying himself at all.

David Gracey smiled that oddly shadowed smile of his. "Well, I'll tell you what *I* think. I think it *sounds* like a good idea," he said, "but I don't think it'd work. A lot of kids probably don't give a shit, or feel it isn't any of their business, or think that they don't count, so what's the use? Besides, nobody *does* take kids seriously, you know that. Plus what you're talking about would take a hell of a lot of time to organize and probably a ton of money, one of which — for sure — most kids don't have."

"Wait, wait, wait," Lisa said, reflexively holding up her hand as she spoke. "What you said about kids not giving a shit, or feeling it's not their business? I think you're wrong. I think that's much more adults than it is kids. Older people with all their other worries. Kids are still hopeful. Even me, after all the shit I've seen go down."

She laughed; David shrugged: maybe.

"And as far as money goes," she went on, "how

about those big foundations Michael was talking about over at the futurist place? Who's to say they wouldn't be interested? Don't you think they might be, Michael?"

Lisa got one leg out from under her and waved that foot at Michael. She was actually bouncing up and down on the bed a little.

"I doubt it," Michael said, still not looking at anyone. "I can't see their boards of directors handing over any money to a bunch of fruity kids, I really can't. And anyway, the idea's pretty simplistic and vague. Arms control's a complicated issue. Countries can't just give up nuclear weapons cold turkey, like a person gives up cigarettes, or something. I mean" — he actually raised his head and turned toward Jordan Paradise — "it's one of those ideas that sounds pretty good — like David said — but sort of as a *concept*. Practically speaking, I doubt it'd get off the ground. I just can't see it." He shook his head and went back to looking at the floor.

"Oh, Michael," Lisa said, "you sound like . . . what's his name? . . . Alan *Mason*. Leave it up to the experts, right? The government's 'designated futurists,' did he say? Bull*shit*. We've seen how far that's gotten us."

Michael looked at her, this time.

"Anyway, it sounds too much like the Children's Crusade," he said. "That's another thing about it. Back in the Middle Ages. When that whole bunch of kids were going to take over the Holy Land, or find the Holy Grail, or whatever it was."

"Really?" David Gracey said. "Wow! How did that turn out?"

Michael looked at him. "It was a disaster," he said. "I think most of the kids died of exposure, or got sold into slavery and shit. It was an utter and complete disaster."

"*But*," said Riley, "look at all the differences between that crusade and what Jordy's talking about. In the first place, those kids wanted to take something that somebody else had. We wouldn't. Plus, nowadays an idea can spread about a million times faster and better than back then, with TV and everything. And if there are foundations we could ask. . . . Who knows? They might think Lisa's cute and write her a blank check."

"Including where they sign their names," said Michael. His eyes had gone back to the carpet and stayed there. "They're *real* interested in cuteness. Just like all the dukes and counts and earls that didn't do diddly for those other kids."

"But the biggest handicap they had, compared to now," said Jordan, smiling, "is they didn't have. . . ."

He pointed at Michael and everybody else laughed, which made Michael look up quickly.

"They didn't have guys like you — which I realize this idea really needs — to organize the thing," said Jordan Paradise to him.

Michael smiled, but wryly. "I'll give you that," he said. "But neither do you, *amigo*."

"Yipes," said Riley. She'd just looked at her watch. "If we're going to keep that appointment at the admissions place," she said to Jordan, "just to keep all our options open, and all that. . . . And we haven't even eaten yet." Even to her, that sounded like forced cheerfulness, like pushing it.

"I think you'd better do that," Michael said, still speaking to the floor. "Have something else besides this . . . other plan."

"Well," said David Gracey, getting up almost as if his bed had caught on fire, "me, I'm going swimming." And to Lisa, "Want to come?"

"Gee," she said, "what a choice. A cool swim on a hot day, or a chance to sit around a crowded waiting room and maybe get off on a college syllabus. . . . Bye, Riley. Jordan. Michael. I'll just run and grab a towel."

"Maybe I'll go with you," Michael said. "You mind?" he said to David, who just shrugged and said, "It's not my water, man."

Michael waved a hand. "Well, fuck it," he said. "I changed my mind. I swim enough in the winter, and I just thought of something else I'd rather do."

"Why don't you come with us?" said Jordan Paradise. "You were planning to check out the college, anyway."

"Yes, Michael, come on," said Riley. "We'd really like you to. That'd be good. We'd have a chance to talk, and. . . ."

"Oh, we would, would we?" Michael said, finally looking straight at Riley Roux. "But are you sure we'll feel like *talking*, for all afternoon? You know what they say *three* is, don't you, Riley? And, personally, I hate crowds."

He said that as he left the room, not bothering to close the door behind him.

The other four looked at each other.

"Ouch," said Jordan Paradise. And — just the way he said it — everybody nodded, no one smiled.

When Riley and Jordan finished with their interview, and with their little campus tour, they came straight back to Chisholm. There wasn't any sign of Michael in any of the rooms (other than his stuff, which was still there), so they went outside and sat on the grass to wait. Riley borrowed David's guitar, and Jordan watched and listened; she seemed pretty great, to him.

The interview with Ms. Medina had not been terribly enlightening. Jordan's total lack of scores and schooling ("I don't suppose you have a guidance counselor, either?") was something . . . well, unique in her experience; she didn't have a set response to offer, and she was much too junior to invent one. So, she just hedged, and made the standard, safe, suggestions. ("Give the SAT's a try, why don't you? Meanwhile, I'll present this to the Dean, and we can see. . . .")

Riley was a different story; Ms. Medina recognized a catch. She suggested *she* should take a little campus tour (" . . . you and your friend, of course."). She bet that she could find a student who. . . .

Her name was Amy something; and she was very nice, an officer in her sorority, good clothes. Some bits of what she said got stuck in Riley's mind awhile.

" . . . quite a lot of drinking, actually . . . the dorms are zooey, some of them . . . lots more pressure . . . *great* parties, and they just brought back the *prom* . . . parents spend a fortune on . . . job security, for one . . . I wouldn't call it *apathy*, exactly . . . get ahead . . . if *you* don't, no one else is going to. . . . Good Lord, I *hope* not, but if it comes, it comes, I guess." That last was aimed at Jordan, and an answer to the question he'd been asking lately.

Around five o'clock, Lisa and David came back from their swim; their heads were damp, their eyes a little red, and they were very hungry. A picnic was suggested and approved, again. Jordan and David went to find some food, while Riley and Lisa waited on the lawn for Michael.

On the drive to the store, David said to Jordan: "That idea of yours?" He was speaking fast, intensely. "The one about getting kids all over the world to get their shit together against nuclear weapons? Well, I'm completely convinced; I think we ought to do it. I mean, Lisa 'n' me were talking about it, a *lot*. It'd be something to do, you know? She even brought it up, kind of, with these other kids we met down by the lake. This one guy, he kept going, 'Far- *out*, that really is far-out' — over and over, like that. He'd go, 'That's far-out, man — you know?' and just keep shaking his head. You know what I mean? He wanted to tell everybody down there, but Lisa told him to be cool. He made us promise we'd tell him, when we had it organized and all." David laughed. "The 'far-out' kid," he said.

Jordan, driving, nodded. "We talked about it some ourselves," he said. "We were thinking maybe we should go somewhere else to discuss it. Try to be a little more specific, you know? We thought it might be good to get away from — I don't know — all the distractions, and just be by ourselves. . . . We were going to ask you and Lisa if you'd like to come with us, and camp, and we could see what we come up with. I've been thinking of some more stuff, and Riley's sure that Michael will want to *talk* about it, anyway, once he gets over . . . whatever it is he's feeling."

"Hey, man, that'd be *great*," said David. "Like I said, I really want. . . ."

Jordan listened, drove the car.

Michael still wasn't there when they got back, and the four of them sat on the lawn and had their picnic. The swimmers ate like sharks; David said a few times that it was the best potato salad he'd ever tasted. He also said he couldn't *believe* how it had just happened that they'd all come to this particular place at that particular time. At one point, when he'd gone inside to the bathroom, Lisa said to Riley, "He said that all afternoon, too. Before we got the dope, even," and Riley nodded, thinking that she maybe understood. As Jordan said, nothing major is easy. Not loving, seeing someone die, or starting over.

Before ten o'clock, they were ready for bed. Michael wasn't back. They wanted to leave the next day and head for Riley's father's land. But not without Michael, obviously. They didn't even consider any other possibility, not out loud, anyway. A little after ten, they went to bed — everyone to the bed where he or she had been the night before.

Michael was completely shit-faced; that was the way that David Gracey put it, later. Jordan had been unfamiliar with that way of saying "drunk," but he got the point. He didn't think it was all that great a way of saying it. Michael hadn't *looked* that bad. It was his *attitude* that stunk.

Jordan heard him coming just before the door banged open; he flipped the bedside lamp on.

"Oh, there you are, you bastard," Michael said. He stood just inside the door, feet spread, but still rocking a little and blinking in the sudden light. Then, typically, he added, "That's a stupid thing to say. Of course you're there. Where the hell else would you be at two A.M.?" But then he held a finger up. "Well — maybe in *Riley's* bed. That's if you could weasel your way in there, again." He shook his head. "But the point is, you're a bastard."

"Yes. Well, I'm glad you're back," said Jordan Paradise. "I hope you had a good time." He'd never chatted with a drunk before. "Maybe in the morning we can talk. There's something — "

"What do you think you're doing to Riley, anyway?" said Michael. "Just answer me that. And *then* maybe we can talk. Trying to get her all messed up, you bastard. What do you think you're doing? She's m' *friend*."

"I'm not doing anything to Riley," Jordan said. "Nothing bad. Michael, *you* know that. I *told* you. I *love* her. You do, too, I guess. I wouldn't ever hurt her any more than you would."

"Oh, yeah?" said Michael. "That's what you think. I asked the fuckin' pendulum — I can do that, too, you know — whether you might . . . fuck her up. And you know what? It didn't move. An' you know what that means? Means *yes*. Like, you know, 'silence means consent,' or whatever it is."

177

Jordan Paradise actually laughed. "I never heard that," he said. "Not with the pendulum."

"Well, anyway — now I'm asking *you*," said Michael.

"And I'm not going to answer you, either — any more than I have already," Jordan said. "If you don't know the answer yourself, hearing it from me again isn't going to do you any good. What do *you* think, Michael?"

The natural and normal thing for Michael Gordon to do, faced with such a question, was to pull up a chair, sit down, furrow his brow a little, and begin to answer. For almost all his life, people, starting with his parents, had asked him what he thought, and for almost all his life he'd tried to give them a truthful and convincing answer. Often, at the end of it, he'd ask the exact same question of his questioner: "What do *you* think, so-and-so?" What people thought was important to this kid; Descartes would have loved him.

But now, instead of answering, he took a clumsy run across the room and leaped on Jordan Paradise, flailing at him with his fists and screaming, "Answer me, you bastard, answer me." And if he'd had a piece of pipe, or a tire iron, he'd have used that, too.

Jordan struggled, trying first to get his arms out of his sleeping bag. His muscles were uncharged, relaxed; his adrenal glands still very much off-duty. He took a shot to the cheekbone that made him see a flash, and stunned him; his head rang from another punch on the side of it, just above the ear; he could taste blood in his mouth. The thought, *This guy could really hurt me*, crossed his mind. He tried to roll and wriggle, shake the body off him; it was almost like a straitjacket, that down bag of his.

It was a lucky thing for Jordan Paradise — one of his pieces of luck — that Michael *was* drunk. Although Michael wasn't trained at punching people, he was strong, and motivated. But he couldn't aim his punches right, and a lot of them went wild and wide, landed on a pillow, shoulder, mattress.

"Answer me, you bastard," he kept screaming; soon, he started crying, too. To the extent that he was thinking at all, he thought that he would have to keep on punching Jordan until he got an answer from the bastard. Of course there was no way in the world he could have told you what the *question* was, by then.

Jordan's other piece of luck was that first David Gracey and then Lisa and Riley were wakened by the noise. ("What *is* it, with this place?" said Lisa.) And that David, as the first arrival on the scene, didn't need a diagram to figure out what he was looking at, and what he had to do. His dive took Michael off the top of Jordan Paradise, and off the bed as well; his long arms wrapped him up — he also got his legs around him — and just for emphasis he swung the side of Michael's head against the indoor-outdoor carpeting. By then, the girls were also on the scene.

There continued to be a lot of sound, and a certain amount of fury, for a few more moments, though, and by *that* time, Dr. Larry Benjamin had joined them, shirtless once again and wearing judo training pants, and barefoot. But he didn't chuckle this time, not at all.

"All right, you little assholes," Dr. Larry said. "You've got five minutes to be out of here, the bunch of you. Bag and baggage, out, out, out. Otherwise, I call security and throw you in the can for trespass, got it? And don't you think I wouldn't. Five minutes, fuckin' moron ingrates," and he left.

It took them less than four. The Fiesta squatted down a little with the load. At a diner on the edge of town they stopped for coffee-and, and Riley bought the postcard there and sent it to her parents:

Dear 'rents,

Leaving Jettison for Shangri-La today, to get a little p and q, and sort out what's been happening. Very interesting trip, so far, a lot of possibilities emerging. We'll keep our fires small and won't feed the bears (Daddy); the Fiesta says to say it's "<u>muy bien, gracias.</u>" Much love to Allie-doodle, too.

yr. deautiful dotter,
R.

PART THREE

19

TWO-LEGGED BEASTS

" 'Oh, give me a home, where the buffaloes roam,' "
sang Sweets, in a tuneful, bluesy, whiskey-baritone.
He had the road map open, spread across his lap.
"It's a *big* country, man, and no mistake," he said.

Eric had actually been thinking the exact same
thing, as he drove. The words "wide open spaces"
had kept cycling into his mind every half minute or
so, over and over, along with "for spacious skies,"
and "it's a *big* country," too. Probably Sweets had
gotten those words from *him*, telepathically. Eric
didn't swallow ESP — you could color him *extremely*
skeptical — but at the same time he had a healthy
respect for his own powers of concentration, and

transmission, even. Possibly. After all, it went with the territory, in a way: He *did* have a powerful mind, a magnetic personality.

"I'm not seeing lots of deer and antelope," he said, "but I guess this is what they call 'the range,' all right. Personally, I like a few more trees around my home. This is a little too empty for me." Sometimes they wouldn't even see another *car* for ten minutes or more, let alone a person or a house. Scrubby growth, some unimpressive-looking cattle, an occasional group of horses — that was it. Some range.

"We'll soon be seeing trees enough for anyone," said Sweets. "Tomorrow, anyway." He ran his big, square-ended finger three, four inches on the map, going right to left. "Where we are headed to, there's trees enough for anyone. For *everyone*, more like it. Trees and wildlife, both. Wildlife in a lot of shapes and sizes, and by no means all of it four-legged. No-sir-ree." He peered down at the map some more, but also snuck a rapid sideways look at Eric.

They'd been out on the road for two days already, making decent mileage every hour, steadily, but still not going *fast*. Sweets had gotten fanatical about obeying what he called a sensible law — the fifty-five miles per hour speed limit — and Eric, given his role, and in light of who they worked for, couldn't very well defy him, or the law, actually. It graveled Eric to be controlled by Sweets (or really by the *law*) this way, but he kept a careful eye on the speedometer. He *really* hated it when Sweets would clear his throat and make a little hand signal toward the dashboard, and *he* would have to look, and then slow down.

They knew where they were going. Where and also why, of course. Three days before, they'd picked up Riley's postcard to her parents at the main Northfield post office — picked it up and Xeroxed it, both sides, two copies. Then, naturally, they'd put it back where it belonged, some twenty minutes later. The carrier who took it to the Rouxs would never know that they had huddled over it, excitedly, like schoolboys with the latest *Penthouse*, earlier that morning.

"I'd never rob the U.S. mails. Why, that's a federal offense," said Eric, primly. "Interrupt, interpret in the nation's interest, sure. That's different. But never rob the sucker."

Sweets chuckled, shook his head, staying in his character.

There wasn't much interpretation necessary. Riley's message was straightforward, completely clear to anyone who knew, as Sweets and Eric did, that Shangri-La was Mr. Roux's not terribly imaginative name for that huge, hidden, undeveloped valley (with surrounding wilderness) his father'd bought as an investment over fifty years before. They'd had, for sure, more than enough time to find out almost everything about this Mr. Roux, his habits and his holdings, that anyone might ever want to know, including an item or two that Mr. R. would be *most* unlikely to confide to . . . anyone. Like what he'd always shout (to Suki? to the stars?) at the moment her massage became unbearably, delightfully . . . well, *therapeutic*, you might say.

Of course, finding three kids in a territory that big might pose a bit of a problem, but locating their *car*, somewhere on the edge of it, should not. And (as Eric had mentioned to Sweets) once they had the car staked out, they were in charge. They'd have them — in the sense they'd *know* that they were there: in there somewhere, and that if they tried to come out, it'd be at the place where their car was. Of course, Eric didn't plan to wait for them. That wasn't his way. Somehow or other, they'd find the kids, and tie the loose ends up (and bury them), and after that there'd still be all the time in the world to clean out the Fiesta and get it to a crusher, lacking plates and serial and motor numbers. Other than having them accidentally join the dinosaurs in the LaBrea tar pits, Eric couldn't think of a better thing for the kids to have done than go camping in a wit- nessless and isolated wilderness. The job would be as easy as one-two-three. Jordan, Riley, Michael — in this case. All disappeared, all "missing." Hap- pens with a lot of kids, these days — almost an epidemic, nationwide. Some of them turn up and others don't. This'd be a type-B situation: Chalk up three more "don'ts."

"Say — *what?*" said Eric, being (so he thought) extremely pal-sy, even funny. He tried to copy Sweets's voice. " '. . . *by no means all of it four-legged.*' What's that supposed to mean? You telling me there's *people* living in these woods we're going to? Like, native aboriginals, perhaps?" He'd made his voice a parody of professorial as he said that, so Sweets wouldn't think he was trying to flash his (big) vocabulary. "Or do you possibly, perchance, refer to local legend? Some Big Foot sort of creature?" He switched his sound again, to fake-dramatic, like Dick Butkus on the tube. "A creature who comes out when the moon is full, and howls? With great big staring eyes, like Rodney?"

Eric laughed, then snorted. "That stuff is strictly tourist feed," he said. "Baloney. Sasquatch and the Abominable Snowman — hogwash, both of them! They *do* keep the Winnebagoes rolling, though."

"Winnebagoes!" Sweets let out a snort of his own. "They's the abominable *slow*-men, what *I* think." He chuckled, paused, then snuck a glance at Eric, before he spoke again.

"No," he said. "What I meant is simpler than that. They got some *people* in those woods, from what I understand. Just guys, no women, living by themselves — sort of like rogue elephants, you know?, but different. They had this big piece in the *Times* about them, not that long ago. I'm surprised you didn't see it. What they are is guys from 'Nam who couldn't, like, adjust when they came back. It said they've gone into the woods in lots of places, places where there's really wild and empty wilderness. Like where we're going, where the Rouxs' land is, near Drumbee. What they call them — the psychiatrists and social worker guys — is 'trip-wire' veterans."

" 'Trip-wire' veterans?" Eric shot his eyebrows up. "Sounds more as if they've got their wires *crossed*. What's it supposed to mean? Like, booby traps or something?"

"Exactly," Sweets replied. "Over there, the VC used to plant 'em by the thousands, right in the different jungle trails. Patrol'd come by and one guy hooks a toe on just this little strand of filament, okay? — can't hardly see the wire — and ka-boom, wham-bam, and oh-no-thank-you-ma'am. Like, jagged bits of metal blow right up between his legs, and one or two guys after him, sometimes. Wouldn't kill so much as maim a guy, you know? Guys used to walk along bent over, knock-kneed, anything to try and cover up a little."

Eric shook his head, his mouth all twisted in disgust. He didn't like to think about the Vietnam war, and especially he didn't like to hear Sweets tell about it. It never sounded to Eric as if Sweets had been a real gung-ho campaigner in the military. His stories always had a lot to do with getting back in one piece, avoiding casualties, and understanding local points of view. It also seemed as if he didn't always follow orders to the letter (as he should have), and that he got real buddy-buddy with enlisted men on his patrols, instead of with his fellow officers.

"So, who exactly *are* these men up there?" asked Eric. "Guys who got . . . *wounded* like that?" He imagined, to his horror, a strange fraternity of ex-servicemen who had this mutilating wound in common. Like Jake Barnes in *The Sun Also Rises*, though he, of course, had stayed in Europe.

"No, not really," Sweets replied. Quite cheerfully, thought Eric. "A lot of what *we* called trip-wire men over in 'Nam were sort of the opposite — the guys who *didn't* get wounded, who had, like, this amazing sensitivity to where the damn things were — a sixth sense, almost, you could say. Another set of *instincts*. They couldn't tell you themselves where they got the talent from; it was just the way they were, or learned to be, I guess. Some of the guys thought they were pretty weird. They didn't hang out much, or do drugs. They weren't all that friendly to a lot of people, but with the ones they liked, they were the sweetest guys imaginable. What the doctors seem to say is, well, they learned to be like animals in 'Nam, and now they can't go back to living regular."

"Great," said Eric. "I can see us having to shoot our way through a few platoons of psychopaths before we even *see* a kid."

"Hey, no — I doubt it," Sweets said soothingly. "They be more like bears or wolves — *wild* animals, but not that dangerous, necessarily. They don't want thing one to do with *you*. What they are is *solitary*, man. They *could* be diagnosed as paranoid, I guess, or suffering from post-traumatic stress disorder, but I wouldn't call them *dangerous*. Unless you tried to mess with them somehow — which'd remind them of the war, and all — or you forced them into social situations." And he smiled.

Eric didn't answer. He wondered what the hell was going on. What did *Sweets* know about paranoia and "post-traumatic stress disorders"? How come *he's* Mister Psychological Terminology, all of a sudden? Was this some little smart-ass takeoff on his present boss, perhaps? That certainly was not out of the realm of possibility. Earlier, Sweets had told Eric some Army stories where he'd done the clever slave routine with his superiors, the staff officers, getting them to think he was a lazy, shiftless sort of combat second looey and then suddenly suggesting some pure stroke of military genius, adapted out of Hannibal's campaigns. Was he up to something now? He certainly didn't *look* it, sitting with that stupid road map open on his lap, his finger pointing, head bent over it.

"The life they lead, from what I understand," said Sweets, his voice all innocence, his finger on the tiny town of Drumbee, "is lots like what the early trappers went for, back a hundred fifty years ago, or so. Mountain men, they called 'em then, and I guess they were another bunch of misfits. Guys that couldn't cut it in the towns or cities, not for long, no way. But like I said, I don't think we'll *see* one, where we're going. Not if he sees us first, for sure." And Sweets reached into his jacket pocket, took a mentholyptus out, peeled off the crinkly cellophane it came in.

"Just out of curiosity," said Eric, in a very offhand way. He'd decided you catch more flies with honey than with vinegar. "Are these guys mostly black, from what you've heard? Something *I* never knew, until pretty recently" — he kept his voice real chatty and informal — "was that a whole lot of the *cowboys* in the Old West were black men. So I was just thinking: I bet a bunch of the old-time trappers — these mountain men you were talking about — were, too. Black, I mean. And that got me to wondering about these guys."

Sweets looked over at him. The smile he felt inside was nowhere on his face.

"Sure," he said, "just like you'd expect. Put a brother in a crazy jungle war that don't make sense, and he'll bend out of shape just like the next guy.

190

When he gets home, back to the *local* jungle, he finds the neighborhood's too stressful, man. Yeah, what I read was: A lot of them *are* black. About the same proportion as you had in combat units over there."

He took a Kool and lit it up. Everything he'd said to Eric was the truth, and though he didn't think it'd make Eric change his plans, it might . . . well, change his *attitude* a little. Let Eric have a taste of walking through an unfamiliar wilderness with cotton in his mouth and tom-toms in his chest, one time. It might not do him any harm at all. But then again, it might (Sweets thought); hell, why not look at the bright side?

Eric, glancing over once again, now saw Sweets smiling, as he smoked. That was a pretty ignorant thing to do, Eric thought: to smile while you were getting cancer of the lung.

20

PINDY

When the five of them came out of the Jettison City Diner, Michael made straight for the car and got in first, without speaking, sitting once again in the backseat on the right-hand side. He had just had black coffee, and he hadn't looked as if he'd enjoyed it. It, or anything else about his life. The melee back in the dorm was like a lot of border clashes: It hadn't really settled anything.

While they were in the diner, the other four had talked around Michael, pretty much. They all had different reasons, different attitudes. Jordan wondered whether Michael still wanted to kill him; he'd never even *seen* anything like that before, not in real life. Riley was working on a fury she couldn't quite believe. She wanted nothing more to do with Michael Gordon for the entire rest of her life; yet she couldn't bring herself to tell him to take his stuff and get the hell out of her parents' car. So she was simply pretending he didn't exist. That was her position. He'd forfeited his place in civilization.

David Gracey was plain uncomfortable. Just when it had looked like he had something really good going. . . . And Lisa, when she saw Michael sitting in the backseat like that, she didn't hesitate, or mill around, or talk about who got which seat; she just climbed in and took back-center, next to him — simply the worst place to ride in the whole car. Riley got in beside *her*, letting David have the leg room in front. The guitar case had to go along their laps, in back.

Riley and Jordan had talked about the route they'd take, before they left the diner. The trip was not that long, perhaps four hundred miles, and considering the hour — not yet four A.M. — they knew they ought to be there by midafternoon, or earlier. Exactly where they'd park was still a bit uncertain — Riley's memory was not too strong on the alternatives — and of course they had supplies to pick up, still.

"Well, uh, how long do you see us staying out there?" David asked. He'd turned halfway around, and so he threw the question into empty air, in back of Jordan's head, but still not straight at Riley. Jordan was driving, but it was her car and her land. He just wanted to see what someone would say.

She didn't mind answering.

"Who knows?" she said. "That's up to us. It seems

to me it sort of will depend. On lots of different stuff." She didn't look at Michael, or even turn in his direction.

"I vote at least a week," said Lisa. "I'm really up for peace and quiet, just being a hundred percent by ourselves, with absolutely no one around to hassle us. No creeps like Dr. Larry. We can make our *own* common sense rules this time. I'd like to sleep and eat and talk and lie in the sun, and swim — you said it's great swimming, right? — and maybe fish. There must be fish, wouldn't there be? I plan to just vedge-out. Become a real tomato. Finally." Her tone of voice reminded Riley of her mother at the dinner table, when Allie, age of six, was sulking in her seat, not eating.

"At *least* a week," said Lisa. "Maybe two."

About halfway through her speech, she moved her left hand across the front of her body, hidden by the guitar case, and found Michael's arm and took a hold of it, just in the crook of his elbow, not squeezing hard but holding him, like that. He didn't look at her, but neither did he move, or try to get away.

"Sounds good to me," said Jordan Paradise. "In fact, that sounds about like heaven. We camped quite a ways north of here one time, Karen and me" — his eyes found Riley's in the rearview mirror the — "trout we caught were unbelievable."

"That's right," said Riley. "I keep forgetting. We've got Kit Carson in this car. Jim Bridger. Shmokey da Bear. Why, this boy's got more merit badges" — she reached and, very much on purpose, patted Jordan's head, or stroked it, really — "than . . . than

Brigham Young got things of after-shave on Father's Day."

In one particular respect the idea of this trip was getting her excited, too. She hadn't really had time to focus yet on all the lovely implications of having a boyfriend. And not just any boyfriend, no, but this one: Jordan Paradise, who in addition to being the sweetest, neatest, maybe also smartest human being she'd met in her entire life, also didn't even have a home he'd ever have to better-hurry-back to. A boyfriend she was *with*, both on this camping trip, right now, and for all the rest of summer. And who knows how long after that?

Of course she immediately thought of Michael again, and got that heavy feeling in her chest, again. The bad, unfinished-business feeling. Final exams, a dentist appointment, going out to eat with her uncle who drank too much.

"Pindy," Riley said, not even realizing she was saying it out loud.

"What?" said David, turning.

"Pindy," she said again. "It just happened to pop into my head. Actually, it's what my uncle says, whenever something rotten happens in his life. He's an alcoholic; but when he isn't drinking, he's a pretty good guy. 'PINDY,' that's an acronym. Proves, I'm, Not, Dead, Yet. P-I-N-D-Y. He says when he finally dies and goes to heaven, everything'll be good, great — like, *perfect* — so whenever something lousy happens to him, or he reads about some terrible disaster happening, he just shakes his head and says, 'Pindy.' Proves I'm not dead yet."

"I like that," Lisa said. "Pindy. That's cute."

"Well, it's one way of looking at it, I guess," David said, nodding his long head and pursing his lips. "And I guess as long as you *are* alive, there's always going to be *something* shitty happening, or just about to happen. Or just getting over with," he added hopefully.

"But maybe, just to avoid having to say it every hour when we're camping," Jordan said, "maybe we could make a list of stuff we've got to get, if anybody's got a pencil and — "

"Fish hooks, fishing line," said Riley, who'd already dug a pen and pad out of her bag. "Do we really *need* to get a pole? What else . . . ?"

The list, when they had finished it, was just enormous, much too long, so then they had to go back over it and cut down.

Michael actually suggested a couple of things, when they were getting started.

"Rice?" was his first word, and then, "Spaghetti?" and Jordan and Lisa both said those were great ideas, being good filling foods that weren't really heavy to carry. But later, when the goofing began, and people were insisting that they doubted they could do without chilled canteloupe, a blow-dry job, their morning soaps, real store-bought, greasy fries . . . Michael didn't enter in at all. Lisa kept stealing little glances at him, as the miles went by, and she thought he was either thinking hard about something or was so hungover he didn't dare to blink, or move his eyeballs.

They stopped for lunch about eleven, at one of those little places with a homemade name, where you stand outside and order through a window with a sliding screen. Inside, there's always a girl in just regular clothes, who looks as if she's never taken an order in her life, and when you get your food, you go and sit at a picnic table, or in your car if you prefer. This one was called The Farmer's Ice-Cold Daughter's and featured foot-long hot dogs and soft ice cream, which is exactly what everyone had, with potato chips and Cokes, except Michael, who chose a large tomato juice and two pieces of cellophane-wrapped raisin pound cake, followed by another cup of coffee.

When they got back in the car and started up again, he cleared his throat and made a speech.

"After what happened last night," he said, "some of you — or maybe all of you — are probably wishing I wasn't in this car, or maybe even in this *country*. I can't say I blame you. Riley's right: I *am* an asshole, and I owe all of you an apology, especially Jordy, of course. I'm sure he hasn't done anything *wrong*, or anything I wouldn't have done, if I'd had the chance. If I were him — or Riley either, for that matter — I don't know how I'd feel right now, about hanging out with a maniac like me, I mean. But I can at least guarantee them both that nothing like that'll ever happen again. I don't *think*." He swallowed. "I hope the two of them have a . . . really good relationship. I really do."

He cleared his throat again, and Lisa thought both Jordan and Riley said, "Thank you, Michael," softly, pretty much at once. She was sure Jordan did. Riley said *something*.

"But what I mainly want to say," Michael went

on, still in a very formal tone of voice, "is that I do want to stay with you all, at least while you're camping, and talk about Jordy's idea. What I did last night was like a revelation; it really jarred me. It showed me anything can happen — anything. The most unexpected and unlikely thing in the world can happen. Just think: A week, a month, a year ago, I would have said that the chances of my attacking someone and trying to hurt him as badly as I could were absolutely zip. No way. Self-defense, *maybe*. But I would have bet anything I'd never start it. That isn't me, being violent. I think even Riley would tell you that much."

She nodded.

"But then, last night, I did it. Never mind the reason or the explanation, the act itself is the only thing that matters, in this case. Same as with a nuclear device: The act is everything." His voice rose. "*There isn't an acceptable excuse. I* did something I know better than to do — that I really don't believe in. The sort of thing I'd always believed that only someone *else* would do.

"So what I realize now, and what I've got to face, is this: If I can be that way, so can anyone else be. A nuclear war could be started by me, by the President of the United States, by *anyone*. By the best person in the whole world." He laughed, but weirdly. "By Magic Johnson, or the Pope, or my *mother*." He hitched his body forward in the seat a little.

"Sure, one of the religious fanatics, or the Russians *may* be more likely than any of *them*, but the point is, everyone's got the temptation. You know what this is like? I was just thinking. It's like in the

Odyssey, when they were going by the island where the Sirens were. You remember how Odysseus made his sailors put wax in their ears so they couldn't hear the song, and tie him to the mast so he wouldn't get sucked in by it?

"Well, this is *like* that, with this nuclear shit — except wax in the ears isn't good enough. You've got to take away the rudder. Or better yet, turn off the song. Otherwise, it's just a matter of time, I'm sure of it. *Some*body'll do it, somebody'll fuck up. And Riley's uncle will say Pindy, except after he says it that time, he *will* be dead."

"You know," said David, earnestly, "this isn't exactly what you're talking about, but did you ever hear about how many of the military guys that have something to do with nuclear weapons have actually had to be replaced because they're heavy into drugs or alcohol? I was listening to the radio, and — "

"That's right," said Michael, interrupting. "I did know that, but let me finish." David nodded, gestured with his hand: Go right ahead.

"What I'm saying is," said Michael, "that we've got to get everybody in the world to really see the danger — how it's a *human* problem more than a political one, you know? Maybe kids *can* make a beginning. Along with all the other things on all the different levels, summits and all that. So what I'm trying to say is, I'd really like to talk about it with you guys. I'd like to be part of whatever you decide."

Jordan was the first to say that that was fine with him. He sounded — to Riley — relieved as well as happy. So she made a sort of an affirmative noise herself. What else could she do? It wasn't that the night before had gone away or been forgotten; there was still a lot of heavy stuff around. But Riley, sucking in a real deep breath, discovered she felt slightly better, less encumbered. She wasn't sure she'd ever (want to) make the anger go away; that was just the way it was, it is — too bad. Pindy, she supposed, and sighed.

They stopped to do their shopping at the one public facility in Drumbee. Outside, there was just the sign: STORE — not Coors or Coca-Cola Store, no other name but STORE. Inside, there were lots of different kinds of merchandise: wool shirts and socks, and rubber boots and pants, and in a drawer some ancient whalebone corset stays. Also, tools and hardware, maps and magazines, and bottles of headache powders, and a tonic for what ailed you (or your hair). That last wasn't too bad a bug repellent, either.

And there was also almost all the kinds of food they'd put on Riley's list, including many freeze-dried items, dated 1985.

Supplied, they drove another half a mile to where there was a graveled area beside the Little Steelhead River. Riley looked around and nodded; it looked like where they'd parked before, three summers back, in August.

"The land," she said, "is that right there; all that." She gestured, one big sweep, with open hand. "From the other side of the river, and then on up" — the ground rose fairly steeply — "and all along that ridge and back of it a ways." Obviously, she wasn't talking *like-starting-here-right-back-to-the-tree-*

over-there, but more like different colors on a map.

By then it was midafternoon, and although everyone was hungry, they decided just to eat some nuts and chocolate and get started: ford the river, climb the ridge, and set up camp beside a feeder stream before they ate their meal. Jordan had a topographical map he'd picked up at the store; he showed them how it worked and how they'd go; the other four just nodded. Looking at the map, he said they ought to plan on more than one day's hike, before they reached their destination, Shangri-La. Riley nodded yes to that, as well.

She found it interesting — heck, pleasing — that Jordan Paradise, who not that long before had seemed . . . well, so naive, so out of it, almost, was now the one that everybody looked to and depended on. There were, of course, a lot of things he didn't know, that she knew, but what they were (it seemed to her) were *extras*: things like foreign languages (except he *had* done French) and labels (words — like *pragmatism*), theories, games (he'd never held a four wood in his life). *He* knew compasses and maps and how to use a lot of useful tools, and weather signs, and fire building. She envied him this knowledge, just as before she'd noticed that he envied hers.

("You know survival skills," she told him, at one point. He shook his head and laughed. "No, *you* do," he replied.)

But, either way, she thought she loved Jordan in the wilderness even more than she loved him in a car, or on a college campus. It wasn't that he acted any different, it was just he seemed to fit so perfectly, to be so relaxed, at peace. Or maybe that was just the way love *worked*: The more it lived in you, the more it grew.

They took a full day and a half to get to Shangri-La, using old logging roads when they could, but sometimes going cross-lots to save time. Jordy made them take it easy on the way: resting often, looking out for blisters — stuff like that. The scenery was gorgeous, and people had a good time, moseying along. Because they mostly walked in line, like Indians, Riley didn't have to get too close to Michael.

The last little bit, the entrance to the valley, was more than slightly hairy, though. The way they came, there was a sort of trail — it might have been a track for mountain goats, for all Riley knew — that ran along above a sheer rock face that dropped — Aieee! — *eventually*, into a boulder-bordered river. Here and there, rocks falling from above had either blocked the trail where it was wider or, in one particularly narrow place, swept it almost off the mountainside. Jordan made them rope themselves together there, showed them how to brace when one of them was on a tricky spot, taught them how to move one at a time. Riley thought that Lisa got a little pale — she certainly became real serious — but never did she hesitate, or wobble. David Gracey wiped his hands on his pants and retied his boots beforehand, and furrowed up his brow; Michael was typically quick and agile. After the first day he was quieter than usual, but eating normally again.

That last part wasn't easy, not for anyone, but when they'd made it, got into the valley, ahhh. . . .

21

CONVERSATIONS

"Uh — I guess people'll probably sleep some-where around the fire," Lisa said. She had her rolled-up sleeping bag, still in its green nylon stuff-sack, in one hand, and a couple of folded plastic tarps in the other.

After they'd chosen their campsite — by a little gravel beach, on a bend of the river — they'd col-lected a circle of sizable rocks for their fireplace, and the three guys had gone off wood collecting.

Riley smiled at her. Lisa — she was such a little actress, such a *diplomat*, standing there, looking around as if she was just getting ready to make a decision: plunk her stuff down, settle in, and homestead there, right on that very spot. She avoided Riley's eyes.

"*I* was thinking maybe we could make a little lean-to, back up there." Riley pointed away from the fireplace and away from the river, on the upstream side, where there was a nice open grove of evergreens. "That way, we'd have a decent shelter, be near the fire without getting smoked-out if the wind shifted, have at least a little privacy — *and* we could use all that area" — she gestured with a hand, upstream — "for our bathroom."

Lisa looked at her then, and had to smile herself.

"*We*," she said. "So you're not going to . . . sleep with him? I mean, I didn't know exactly what *you* guys had — you know — *planned*, as far as — "

"What I think," said Riley, cutting in, "is that the situation's still a little *stressed* — you know what I mean? — for him and me to . . . I don't know, do too much pairing up, or whatever you want to call it. Not that I wouldn't like to, needless to say. What do *you* think?"

"Yeah," said Lisa, running a hand quickly through her short hair. "I see what you mean. What a pain in the ass, though. I mean, *you* know. . . ." She chewed the corner of her lower lip. "But I'll tell you one thing: That could make *my* life a whole lot easier. Right? Not that either of them would necessarily try to . . . win my favors, as the saying goes."

Riley laughed. "You don't think so? Listen. Now it's my turn to tell *you*. I think Michael — loathsome as he is — really *was* trying to pick you up, that first day on the lawn. I know him; he has his little routines. And David, I think he's got his own ideas." She pitched her voice much deeper, hipper: " 'Let's

204

get real close to one another, man.' *If* you know what I mean."

Lisa swung the sleeping bag in her direction, looking quite outrageously delighted.

"Get outa here," she said. She shook her head. "Come on. Let's get our home sweet home set up, before the guys get back."

"Hey, lookit," David Gracey called to Michael. "How about this one here? It's about the right size, wouldn't you say?"

"It" was a sizable hardwood branch that probably had been struck by lightning a year or two before. At the thick end it was almost as big around as his thigh, and the whole thing was about twenty-five feet long.

The two of them and Jordan had made one wood-gathering trip already, returning to the campsite with armfuls of dry sticks — more the size of kindling — and now they were looking for some larger pieces, logs. ("More what people burn in a fireplace," Jordan had said, perhaps unnecessarily; but the other two had nodded cheerfully enough, and David had said, "Gotcha.") Michael was carrying one of the two Hudson's Bay axes they'd bought at the Drumbee Store.

"Looks good," said Michael, bending, peering. He rolled it over, checking for rot. "Excellent." He patted it, approvingly. "Real good firewood."

"Well, let's see," said David, slowly. "How long should the pieces be, d'you think? About like this, I guess?" He held his hands apart, at more or less shoulder width. "I probably better warn you. I never tried one of them before." He nodded at the axe.

"To tell you the truth," Michael said, "all I've ever used is a hatchet, myself. They showed us how at day camp; I was ten, I think. But this ought to be the same general principle. Let's see." He stepped back, then bent and tapped the branch with the axe edge, like a batter might tap home plate. But before he swung the axe, he straightened up again.

"Wait," he said. "It'd probably make a lot more sense to drag it back to camp in one piece and cut it up there. Don't you think? Instead of trying to carry a lot of shorter ones, right?" He pantomimed a man with an armload of logs.

"Hey, yeah." David nodded, stroked his chin, then smiled his slow, sad smile. "And maybe that way Jordan'll do the chopping for us."

"No, no, no," said Michael, shaking his head and scowling. "I'll chop it up. I want to. We can't depend on him for everything. I wasn't even thinking of that. It just suddenly struck me there was a more sensible way to. . . ." He walked to the other end of the branch and picked it up, seeing which was the best way to hold it, for dragging.

David touched him on the arm. "I know," he said. "I realize that. I was just kidding around." He paused. "Listen, there's one thing I've been wanting to ask you. How do you *really* feel about Jordan now? I was trying to figure out how *I'd* feel, if I were you. I mean, he's a great guy and all, but when there's a woman involved. . . ." He shook his head, feeling he was being very friendly, and also rather . . . philosophical. He also really wanted to know. Almost *needed* to.

206

Michael laid down the limb and looked straight up at him. "Look," he said. "You may not understand. I wouldn't blame you. Riley's an old friend of mine, just about my best friend. But we're not" — he made some swirling motions with one hand — "like, boyfriend, girl friend. We never have been." He gave a little laugh. "I guess we're not each other's type."

David shook his head again. "I guess I don't *totally* understand," he said. He laughed, too. "So what were you trying to kill him for?"

"You know, I don't exactly *know*," said Michael. "That's the other weird thing. I've always thought I was pretty good at figuring stuff out. And obviously, I've thought about this a lot. But I still don't know. I don't think I'm nuts, so maybe I was just plain jealous. Or maybe I *was* playing God, or Riley's father. Or it could be that I don't want her to get ahead of me — to have something *I* want, too, like a real, total relationship with someone. Or maybe I'm afraid of being excluded, losing my old friend. Or I can't stand how cool and — I don't know — *tuned-in* Jordy is, how goddamn *nice*, all the time. I don't think it's *that*: I really, really like the guy. But see all the possibilities? Maybe I'm a latent homosexual and I got mad at Jordy for picking Riley over me." He laughed and looked carefully at David.

"People do crazy things," David said. "Like you were saying in the car: Anybody can. It really got to me when you said that. And afterwards they *don't* always know why, exactly. In some cases. That scares me. Knowing I'm like that, and everybody else is, too."

"Yeah," Michael said. "But it also makes me realize how much *this* matters to me. And it reminds
me I have another side, too. Like the opposite of
whatever it takes to attack someone, or do some other
crazy thing. The cooperative side of a person's nature, you could call it, or — don't laugh — the *love*
side. Not like with a girl, necessarily, but just in
general. The way you feel when you're doing something right for someone — like that."

"Yeah," said David, and he looked all around, up
into the trees. In places he could see the blue sky.
"You know something? I feel like I want to do that
kind of stuff, myself. A lot. Before I fall asleep at
night, and different times. But then, you sort of say
. . . oh, what's the use? And after what happened
in that jail, I've even tried to tell myself not to care
anymore. Plus, when you're a kid . . . well, it's hard
to find good stuff to do that isn't corny. Important
stuff. Like you said, just on your own, *you* doing it,
without some adult saying — *you* know — 'You do
such-and-such.' And then, 'Good boy.' Like that.
They can make it completely different. You know
what I mean? Like it's their thing, after all, and
they've set it up for you, so you can be a good boy
by their rules."

"Yes," said Michael. "Sure. I sure do know what
you mean."

They looked at each other, and they both nodded,
took a breath.

"Well," said David, and he gestured at the branch.
They bent and lifted up the end of it, and started
dragging.

"That's very good," said Michael. "Yes. Good boy."

And David Gracey laughed out loud, the first time Michael'd heard him do that, as far as he remembered. The other time it had happened, he hadn't been listening.

"Nature's Brillo pad," said Riley, kneeling by the water's edge and rubbing a fresh handful of gravel around the bottom of the skillet.

"Hey," said Jordan Paradise. "You were talking about *me* and merit badges." He was stacking tin plates beside her on the stream bank. "Look at you, now. Are you the handiest thing since the Coleman stove, or what? Miss *Field and Stream*? Ranger Raquel?"

"I know a few things," Riley said, tossing her head toward her left arm. "Fix my sleeve, will you? Just roll it back up." Maybe she wasn't going to share sleeping quarters with him, but there could still be little touches, personal involvements.

"You're sure you understand about the lean-to?" she went on. "Why that's the way it has to be, for now?"

He nodded. "Absolutely. What you've done is perfectly clear. I hardly need a diagram." He sniffed, was acting hurt, but definitely *acting*. Riley wondered if he might have been relieved.

"My big chance to be a normal, sexually active teenager — that's what they always call us in the papers, right? 'Sexually active teenagers'? And where do I end up? Sleeping on a sandbar, five feet from a kid who tried to kill me a couple of days before. Thanks a lot, Riley."

She splashed a little water at him. "You rat — " she started.

"Though if you want to know the truth, I'm pretty relieved. Who knows what kind of lovers we might be? *I* might be. And that's just one of the scary parts about being in love. What'll you do when you find out I don't know how to bowl, and hate to dance? That scares me, too. I think about the only thing I'm *not* frightened of is the commitment. And that's what Karen's magazines all used to say that guys were scared to death of. 'Contemporary men,' *you* know. I think I'm committed *now*, if you can stand the thought of that."

Riley was quiet for a moment, her head still down, still swirling sand around in the skillet.

"I almost can't," she said, "it makes me so happy. And I know what you mean about scary. But that's okay, too. I think it's just a part of caring a whole lot. Of loving someone all that much. Like I do you."

Jordan shook his head. "Boy," he said. "Can you believe this? It must have been meant to happen, I swear. But just your *being* there — you know — right then. . . ." He shook his head again.

"Anyway," he said, taking a deep breath, "what do you think this is?" He fished something out of his pocket and held it out to her.

Riley put down the skillet on the water's edge and wiped her palms on the seat of her jeans. She took the object from his fingers; it looked like a piece of bone, though from what part of what animal, she didn't have a clue. Its thinner end was split and broken; its other end was shaped and flattened some.

"Where'd you find this?" she asked. "Do *you* know what it is?"

"Back in the woods a ways, when we were getting firewood," he said. "Yeah, it's an arrowhead; it was still on its shaft when I found it. It's been broken, of course. Probably hit a rock or something."

"Wow," said Riley. "Did you show it to any of the others? It doesn't look real old at all."

"No, I didn't," Jordan said, "and no it isn't." Back at the Drumbee Store, when he was checking out the maps, he'd heard two locals talking. One said he was sure he'd seen "the wild 'un" just at dusk, along the Little Drumbee River. "I just skedaddled," he had said. "Ain't his land, but it ain't mine, neither. Feel sorry for the bastard," he had said.

"Probably a Boy Scout made it," Jordan said to Riley, "doing some survival camping. But I don't think I'll mention it to anybody else, okay? No point getting anyone excited."

Then — surprisingly but not unpleasantly (to Riley) — he winked at her and grinned, a veritable devil.

"Except for you," he added.

And then, of course, he blushed.

"Two months ago, would you have ever guessed in a million years you'd be out here tonight, right now?" David leaned forward and tossed the stick he'd been using as a poker onto the fire.

Lisa laughed. "No *way*," she said. "Not two months, not two weeks — almost not two *days*. You know something?" she rattled on. "I still feel like I'm speeding. I know I'm really tired from the hike, getting here and all, but I couldn't possibly go to sleep yet. There's too much to *think* about, you know? But anyway — I think this is about the most surprising thing that's happened to me in my whole life, being here with you people, and for this particular set of reasons. It just blows me away. I almost can't believe it. How about you?"

"What?" he said. "How about me *what*?" Listening to her, looking at her in the flickering firelight — she had a blue scoop-necked shirt on and a darker blue bandanna knotted around her neck — had taken his mind off what he'd said.

"What you *said*," she said. "Would you have ever guessed, two months ago, that you'd be sitting out in the middle of nowhere rapping with some . . . some *totally* unpainted lady about whatever the hell it is we're talking about?" When they'd organized their packs for the hike in, Lisa's makeup had lost its place to a first-aid kit.

David smiled. "Me?" he said. "Hell, no. This is so far from anything I ever imagined *myself* being into. . . . Cripes." He mimicked himself, whiningly: "Where's the hash? Where's the tunes?" He flipped a palm toward the ground. "I am so far out of my . . . what is it they say? Natural habitat? I can't believe it. And the other thing I can't believe is how damn good I feel. I mean, this kind of shit — fresh air, good food, and exercise — is not my thing at all."

"I know," she said, nodding hard. "Same with me, more or less. And I'll tell you something else peculiar: It feels like I've known everybody here all my life, almost — like I just fit in with you and the rest of these people. And that's in spite of the fact — don't take this the wrong way, now — that when I first met you, I said, 'Twenty carat creep.' I actually did." She laughed, to underline how long ago, and how absurd, that was.

"Well, I thought that you were probably some clapped-up little groupie," David said. "So there. The sort of person whose greatest ambition in life would be to fuck a top forty group before she turned eighteen and got all fat and ugly." He stretched his legs and smiled, real pleased with that one.

Lisa laughed again, but softer. "Gee," she said, "I never knew I was that obvious. Though what I actually dig the most is elevator music, like the Maalox Symphonette. You've probably got their albums, right? *Anyway.* . . ." She took a deep breath and touched her breastbone, delicately.

"What you were saying . . . about feeling good. I know the atmosphere must help, but — I was thinking — there's got to be some head stuff, too. And what I hope is that it's more than me just being *against* something, and getting some sort of a rush from thinking I'm so bad and on the ball, while everybody else has their head up their ass. You know what I mean? How easy it is to feel great when you're agreeing with someone about how much the two of you hate all *them*? And what a cinch it is to just *love* everyone who feels the same as you?"

"Yeah," said David. "That's the way it is, all right." He made a snorting sound. "Hey" — he held up a pointing finger — "my guidance counselor, he used to have a word for that. Or two words, come to

think of it. I believe he called it 'just rebelling.' "
And he reached and patted Lisa's leg, above the
knee. Her jeans were neatly patched, right there.
"You're just rebelling, honey," he intoned.

"Could be," she said. "But seriously. You don't
think that's all we're feeling, do you? Just rebellious-
ness?"

"No," he said. "I know I'm feeling something else,
too. Do you think it'd be okay if I kissed you?" His
voice had gotten really different, fast.

"Yeah," she said, "as long as you didn't get to
thinking it meant a whole lot. Other than I'm glad
to be here, and glad that you're here, too. I don't
want to be anyone's girl friend for a while, though,
and I *do* want to keep on being everybody's friend —
if you can follow my drift."

"I think so," he said and, moving over, slid his
arm around her shoulders.

She snuggled into him and kissed him — honestly,
enthusiastically. She meant it and enjoyed it; they
both did. It was a real *kiss*-kiss, too, not just a little
what-the-hell-good-buddy. But when they moved their
mouths apart, she hopped right to her feet.

"I can sleep now, thanks," she said. "Good-night."

" 'Night, Lisa," David answered. "And thanks,
yourself. You really *are* okay. I hope you know that."

A minute later, he rose, too, went down and drank
from the brook — but didn't piss in it. After a while,
he slouched back up the bank; he almost couldn't
recollect how he had felt, before.

"One of the best and easiest ways is just to sort
of float the bait right down to them," said Jordan

214

Paradise. Expertly, he made a worm secure on the hook, hiding the barb and having the worm drip down from it, invitingly. "And when you don't have a reel or a regular fishpole, about the only way."

What they did have — he and Michael, a quarter mile downstream from the campsite — was a slender willow sapling, with the line tied on near the end of it, and a red and white bobber about a foot and a half above the hook.

"When something hits, you want to keep the line taut, but not have it break, of course," said Jordan. "And because you don't have a reel to work with, you have to use your pole to keep the tautness. The pole and your feet, that is. In other words, you run after the fish if you think the line's going to break, and away from it if the line gets slack."

Michael nodded. "And while all this is going on, you'll be . . . ?" He raised his eyebrows.

"Right here, cheering you on," said Jordan. "When you've got him tired out and near the shore, I'll kind of ease over and grab him for you, too — seeing as we *also* don't have a net, but do have a lot of appetites. And, of course, you'll probably want me in the pictures, later on."

Michael looked at him and smiled. "As a matter of fact," he said, "I would." He dropped his head and kicked at the rock and gravel buildup on that bank of the river. "You know" — he *never* mumbled, but he mumbled that — "I was saying this to David, day before yesterday, but I want to say it to you, too. I think you're about the most tuned-in, and definitely the *nicest* person I've ever met in my life." He raised his head. "Which makes what I did the other night all the weirder and all the more — I don't know — *despicable*, I guess. So I also want to tell you again, face-to-face, how sorry I am, no shit."

They stood there frozen for a moment, Michael holding the fishing pole in one hand, connected by the line to Jordan, who held it just below the bobber, with the worm on the hook swinging back and forth like a pendulum.

"Hey," said Jordan. "Really, Michael, it's okay. I really understand. I can't blame you for hating me right then. I gave you reason to." He shook his head. "That's such an incredible thing to realize. That all my life I'm going to do things that stink. No matter how hard I try, I'm going to be a jerk, from time to time. A hateful jerk."

Michael stared at him. "You really think that?" he said.

"I know it," Jordan said. "There isn't any black and white, when it comes to people. Everybody's striped. It's the same as what you said in the car — about how anyone might drop the bomb."

"So how does anybody ever love anybody else?" said Michael. He started blinking his eyes; he sounded really shook.

"I guess we have to learn to love the stripes," said Jordan Paradise. "Both colors." He dropped the fishing line and put his two hands on either side of Michael's face. He smiled.

"You see?" he said, as if the explanation, all of it, to everything, was written on his face.

Michael stood there silent, looking at Jordan Paradise, not trying to think of an answer, just listening to his heart. "I think so. Loving is accepting every-thing. And every*one*, I guess."

"That's the rule," said Jordan. "We're all in this together. I'm as sorry as you are."

Jordan dropped his hands. Michael pulled a hand-kerchief out of his pocket, and he blew his nose.

"Thanks for saying that," he said. "I'm going to try." And he blew his nose again, more loudly.

"But first," he said, in a completely different tone of voice, "I'm going to do everything right, for a while. Just watch me: not only no stripes but no spots, even. And for my initial good deed, I'm going to catch my fellow campers a nice big trout. Ac-cording to natural law, the trout is there as part of the food chain, so it isn't wrong to catch and kill and eat it — just in case you were wondering." He started to turn toward the stream.

"Try not to drown the worm," said Jordan Par-adise.

"I keep expecting to wake up, no shit," said Lisa. "I mean, two or three times today I've said to myself: This is a dream world, just a total dream world. I mean, look at this place. And look at us. Is this *Fantasy Island*, or what?"

She was lying back on an enormous round gray boulder, completely naked, by the side of a pool the river'd made by jumping down into that valley for — well — however many centuries it takes. Riley, equally undressed, lay beside her on her belly. The sun was bright; the sky was clear, pure blue; the mountains in the distance were spectacular. They'd been in the water, which was cold enough to pebble up their skins and make their bodies feel excitingly refreshed and very, very bare, and now they were almost dry, soaking up the warmth of the rock and the warmth of the sun, and getting languorous and lazy.

"I know," said Riley. She rolled over and sat up. "This is the other side of my uncle's moon. Pindy spelled backwards: *Ydnip*. Don't worry, it won't last." She waved a hand. "Believe me."

" 'Gather ye rosebuds while ye may,' " Lisa said, smiling. She looked down at her breasts. "It's hard to see both sides of things, sometimes. I guess that's good. Like, here we are, at this perfect place on this perfect day." She looked at Riley, up and down, and then herself. "So I'm a *little* pudgy. But we're feeling great, two women, digging it, together. And somewhere up the road" — she flicked her fingers toward the stream — "we've got our futures, full of God knows what. A lot of times like this, I hope, but probably — for sure, I guess — a lot of bad stuff, too. But what I was thinking, what I wanted to say was, How could anyone, any *guy* — it always is a guy when I imagine it — ever drop a bomb on *this*?" She pointed all around, then back and forth at both of them, and laughed. "Or even take away the gorgeous, naked chicks; how could they? You know, out here it just doesn't seem possible that somewhere else, probably in a city someplace, there's this bunch of guys sitting around in suits and talking about weapons and war and first strikes and retaliatory strikes, and all that gross stuff." She shook her head. "Probably in a bunch of somewhere elses."

Riley brushed her hair back, feeling the drops of water from it on her shoulders. "It *is* ridiculous," she said. "Imagine feeling you had the *right* to make a decision like that. To say, well, I guess we'll drop one there, and point to a spot on a map as if that's all it was: a spot of paper with some lines and words and colors on it. It's hard to imagine a woman doing that, you're right."

"Do you suppose that's because of the way we *are*?" Lisa scratched her belly. "Or is it just that we haven't been in the right places, most of the time? The seats of power, you might say. Look, think of the *kids* you know — that'd be a good test; none of them have any power, boys *or* girls — and ask yourself if it's only certain boys you could imagine dropping a bomb, or deciding to, or could some girls do that, too?"

Riley narrowed her eyes. "Some girls *could*," she said. "Maybe not for the exact same reasons, but they could. And you know something else? I can imagine some who'd do it with — what's the word? — with *gusto*. Like, 'That'll show those dirty rotten bastards.' And others, of course, would be sort of sad, but they'd still do it, too, saying: 'This could save a million lives' — a million *innocent* lives, it always is — 'if we kill these five or ten or fifty thousand.' I don't know. There're probably more girls who wouldn't *ever*, than boys, but some of them would just be copping out, saying: 'Who? Little *me*? Do a big, important, dreadful thing like that?' *You* know."

"Yeah," said Lisa. "I guess the reasons for doing it are always pretty much the same: fear or revenge.

219

And everybody feels *them*. Protect what you have, before it's too late, or punish someone else for being so damn wrong, or awful. According to you." She made a sort of laughing sound. "Hunh. Those really are the reasons Michael jumped on Jordy, aren't they? You could say that he had both the major motivations." Lisa waved a fly away.

"Poor Michael." Riley stood up and brushed a little sand off her bottom. She found she'd actually meant that. "I don't think he knows *what* he wants, exactly. I don't believe it really ever was me, no matter how he may have acted. Not that way, anyway, like some big romantic thing. But I've also heard that sometimes a person doesn't get really interested in someone till somebody else does, so maybe that's it. And if *that's* the case" — she looked down at Lisa, pointedly — "old David might be next on his hit list. What'd you *do*, two nights ago? And don't bother saying, 'Nothing,' either; he never looked like a . . . cocker spaniel before yesterday. Following you around, being *helpful*. I swear, Lisa."

Lisa grinned, but also shook her head. "I *definitely* did not encourage him," she said. "It's just the *situation*. He doesn't know what he wants any more than Michael does. Or, wait. Amend that. He knows what he *wants*, but he doesn't know what he *means*. We'll see. For now, I'm being cool, avoiding problems and stress, like you." She got up, too.

"Here we are, the *no pair* girls," she said, and struck a pose, her hand on Riley's shoulder. "Shit, I wish I had your legs," she added.

22

TRAILING BEHIND

Sweets hadn't gone inside the Drumbee Store, just Eric. In fact, during the time that Eric was in the store, Sweets was sitting on a fallen tree in the woods bordering the highway, less than a quarter of a mile past the store. The idea was: Eric's visit to the store would be even less memorable if there wasn't a black man with him, or even a black man sitting in a car with out-of-state plates outside the store while Eric was inside. Sweets used the time by himself constructively, paying attention to the sounds of that particular forest — birds and distant motors, mostly — and its trees. Starting to get himself tuned-in — receiving — once again, he might have said.

There were times when Eric made a particular point of being unmemorable, and this was such a time. His looks always helped, of course, in that there was never anything about his face a person *would* remember. In other words, although he wasn't handsome, he certainly wasn't ugly, either; and while he didn't smile a lot, neither did he snarl, nor slobber. His coloring wasn't light *or* dark, but medium — like his height, and his hair, and the volume and depth of his speaking voice, and the color of his clothes, and the length and condition of his fingernails. Of course he had no visible scars, no accent, no peculiar tastes (that he would ever talk about, to strangers), and no discernible breath or body odors. Eric made no impression, and so he left few tracks. In fact, if it hadn't been for the extra $23.89 that was there in the Drumbee Store cash register at the end of the day, Modecai Wilson, the store's owner, might have insisted he didn't *have* a customer that afternoon "other than some locals and that Margie May McClintock." (Margie May was visiting her uncle, Edgar Swale, the postman.) This was in spite of the fact that when he rang up the topographic map that Eric bought, old Mordecai Wilson actually remarked it was the second one of them he'd sold that week.

Other than Eric's ordinariness, the thing that maybe helped Mordecai Wilson to forget the man, the map, and the conversation was that when Margie May McClintock *had* come in, she'd been wearing a short-sleeved, silky Cowboys' jersey, number 69, no bra, no way, no fooling. That had taken him back, all right. Unlike most local people, Mordecai Wilson hadn't much minded the carfuls of hippies that used to stop by the store back in the sixties and early seventies. They had money to spend, and though he hadn't cared much for all the long-haired fellers, he *could* say, and did, about the girls: "You used to see some real fine jug-a-rums, in them days."

Sweets had to go along with Eric's logic in not wanting him to go into the store. His *spoken* logic, that is — which was that at this particular stage of this particular job it'd be good for them to be as invisible as possible. That meant never being seen together; indeed, it meant Sweets never being visible at all, if possible. There were times, Sweets knew, that Eric actually *liked* being seen with him, meaning with a black person. And in places other than dark alleys or ghettoes, or West 42nd Street, New York. Eric liked being seen with him at concerts, on college campuses, in any town where the average per capita income approached thirty thousand a year, and at private clubs in certain sections of the country.

Of course, sometimes he *didn't* like being seen with Sweets, and one such time was of Sweets's own making. They'd happened to be in a small rural store (always an iffy location, anyway) a thousand miles or more from Drumbee, and Sweets, just kidding around, had picked up a grass sickle and gone over to Eric and said loudly: "*Gorba*, tooba. Gorba, see-galaylaylay," and started to wave the thing around over his head while the storekeeper — whose eyes had never left Sweets from the moment he entered the place — turned more or less the color of the wheel of cheese on the counter there, in front of him. Eric hadn't thought that was funny at all, and even answered crossly when Sweets later asked him, "Didn't you ever want to be a local legend, man?"

Although Sweets and Eric *never* identified themselves unless they absolutely had to, Eric believed they were representing their employer at all times, and so should look and act accordingly. Kidding around did not become a nation of over two hundred million people, possessing many thousands of nuclear warheads, armed and ready to go, Eric felt. As a matter of historical fact, kidding/messing/horsing/goofing around *always* made Eric uncomfortable. Even as a kid, he didn't kid around much. He didn't even *youth* around, which, if anybody did it, would probably be about as much fun as it sounds.

It wasn't too far past the Drumbee Store that they spotted the Fiesta, parked by itself near the river. It was really in an ideal spot: *They* could set up their main camp on the other side of the road, where the wooded ground rose fairly steeply, and from there one of them could keep that car under almost constant surveillance — just in case the kids surprised them and came back to it. They wouldn't be able to see the car at night, of course, but that was okay; without a distributor cap (which Eric lifted off that very ten P.M.) there was no way it could start up anyway. Their own sedan they nosed off the highway a little ways farther on, where once upon a time there'd been a logging road.

224

By the time they'd gotten to Drumbee, Eric was really looking forward to finishing the job. That's the way he put it to himelf: "finishing the job," which was not at all like saying "getting the job over with," and not the *least* like thinking "killing those three kids."

Camping out with Sweets, however, was a different story. Eric did *not* look forward to that. For almost every satisfaction, there seemed to be a price one had to pay, he'd noticed. You had to take the bitter with the sweet — or in this case with the *Sweets*, thought Eric, with a secret, self-congratulating smile. He was lucky he could keep his sense of humor, he informed himself.

Eric's outdoor skills were pretty minimal, compared to Sweets's. He was (of course) an absolutely first-class marksman, but he wasn't what you'd call a camper, or a hiker, or a conservationist of any sort ("nature boy," to him). That meant he'd have to do a certain amount of deferring to, and asking stupid questions of, Sweets — both activities he hated. But because Sweets was such a perfect little Barry Backwoods, it might be possible (Eric thought) to divide up the things that had to be done (in order to finish the job) in such a way that the two of them didn't have to be together all that much. With Sweets somewhere else, Eric could use all the matches and paper he wanted (to get the fire lit), eat easy stuff like hot dogs and canned peaches and instant coffee and doughnuts, and not have to dig the pharaoh's tomb every time he had to take a dump. The trick was to work things out so that Sweets *would* be somewhere else . . . by first thing in the morning, say. And amazingly, that was exactly what Sweets himself suggested.

He'd looked at the topographic map for quite a while that afternoon and evening, and then had pointed out to Eric the two most likely spots on it for a place called Shangri-La to be. "Assuming they've read the book," said Sweets, and Eric nodded, wondering what book.

"My best guess'd be this one," Sweets went on, as Eric hoped he would. "What these lines mean is that there's some almost perpendicular pieces of ground right here, like cliffs or some kind of rock face maybe, and the same at the other end of this little valley, here. If you wanted to get to *it*, the easiest way might be to float in on the river, the Little Drumbee, here. But that would depend on how high the water was, and rocks, and current — all that shit. But chances are, there's probably a way to hike in, too, and if there is, I probably can find it."

Eric just kept nodding.

"So I s'pose the smartest thing might be for me to zip up there and scout around," Sweets said. "Check this one out." He tapped the map again. "And if they're not there, take a look in the other one — the other sort of secret valley, this one over here. *You* could just stay put, if you wanted to — keep the car under surveillance, like you said we ought to do. Keep the home fires burning, man." He grinned. "Once we have them pinpointed. . . ." Sweets shrugged. "If I move right along, I should probably be back before dark, providing I'm out of here before sunup. Or, we can both go, and make a two day-er out of it. That'd be good, too." Sweets smiled again. "Whatever you're in the mood for, cap'n."

Eric stroked his jaw and looked what he was pretty sure was "thoughtful," using anybody's standards. "Cap'n" he could take all right.

" 'Course if you'd rather *me* stay here and you could scout 'em up yourself, that's honky-donkey, too," said Sweets, and smiled some more. Eric wondered (naturally) about him saying "honky-donkey" so soon after "cap'n." It *could* be ignorance, or some kind of camaraderie, he guessed. Or wising-off, of course. His best guess was ignorance, though, and so he let it ride.

"That first alternative sounds best," he said, decisively. "From what the Roux girl wrote her father, it sounds as if they're just going to take it easy for a while, probably stay in one place. If I know kids" — he forced a chuckle — "they've packed in a load of dope and are lying around getting stoned out of their little skulls. So once you find out where they are — *if* you can, that is — there should still be lots of time to come back here and . . . and hand me the baton."

Eric had to smile himself. He liked that jazzy sports expression he'd just used, and his slipping in that "if you can" would supply all the extra incentive Sweets needed, if Eric knew anything at all about psychology, which he sure as hell did.

"Then I'll just take it from there," he finished.

Sweets nodded agreeably enough, and pretty soon after that they both were in their sleeping bags, and quiet. The next morning, when Eric woke up (he'd had some trouble falling asleep; air mattress or no

227

air mattress, this was *nothing* like a bed), Sweets was already dressed and finishing his breakfast. Apparently, he'd made bacon and flapjacks and brewed a pot of real coffee. ("What? No Eggs McMuffin?" Eric thought.) For a split second, actually, Eric barely recognized the guy, dressed (as he was) in patterned camouflage cloth, except for the shoes, which looked something like high-topped sneakers, but were olive green.

After watching Sweets getting organized for a minute or two, Eric thought he even *moved* a little differently in that outfit, in this setting: lighter, smoother, quieter. You could say he seemed to *belong* in the woods, almost, rather than in a complex modern civilization. That was an interesting thought, thought Eric. A new version of the old saw: "You can take the boy out of the country . . . ," et cetera. He'd have to remember to think about that some more, and maybe even discuss it some time with his next partner, who'd almost certainly be a white guy.

"Well," said Sweets, picking up a small nylon day pack, "best I be off, I guess. Like I said: With luck, I make it back by dark."

Eric gestured toward his belt. "I know you're not planning to . . . make contact," he said. "But wouldn't it be smart to carry something, anyway? I've got an extra automatic." He couldn't imagine going into a forest full of wild animals — grizzlies, maybe? — not to mention psycho Vietnam vets, without some means of self-defense, at least.

Sweets smiled. "No way," he said. "I travel light. Besides, I've got a knife in here." He shook the pack. "And these." He bared his big white teeth (again) at Eric. It could have been another grin. And then he waved and turned and left, making hardly any sound at all.

During the time that he and Eric had hung around Northfield waiting for something (like Riley's postcard) to happen, Sweets had begun to run on the high school track and lift weights at a local gym. It wasn't that he thought he was getting ready for anything — other than middle age — it was just something that he did, from time to time, partly out of boredom, but also as another conscience-stricken payback for the Kools and drinks, a more substantial one than simply washing ashtrays. He knew his workouts weren't much more than just a finger in the dike, that what he ought to do was change his whole damn life-style, but that had always seemed too . . . complicated. It was easier to just go on, and make good money, not go through the hassle of explaining why he wanted out and then — *phew!* — have to quit smoking and start again in something else, some other line of work, like God knows what. It was easier to get on a fitness kick from time to time, and see it *seem* to work (though not as well as last time, maybe). Sweets had been an athlete in school and college, and in the service he had stayed in pretty much fantastic shape — anything that might improve the odds on getting out alive, he figured — which meant he had a base to build on, you could say. A little working-out did wonders.

So, traveling light and by himself, Sweets made much, much better time than the kids had been able to make with heavy packs, together. He knew how to move in the woods, and how to read a compass and a map; those canvas boots were broken-in and lightweight; there was nothing to slow him down, not even lack of motivation. The guy was in a hurry.

Before he'd done two hours' worth of ups and downs, he'd found the kids' first campsite, where they'd spent the night on their way to the valley. He smiled when he saw it, but minutes later he was frowning. They'd camped beside a little trickle-brook, and along the edge of it he found four different sets of boot tracks — boot and running-shoe tracks — and maybe even a fifth. It was barely possible, he told himself, that someone had changed footwear for some reason, but it was much more likely that there were simply more of them. Another kid or two. Total: four or five.

Sweets didn't have to wonder if that would make a difference to Eric. He wouldn't *say*, "The more, the merrier," or even *look* delighted, but Sweets would know what he was thinking. Eric liked a challenge, and he preferred a big challenge to a regular-sized one, and a huge one most of all. Killing five people rather than one, or three, would make no moral or ethical difference to Eric, but logistically it was more of a challenge: getting the whole deal set up in such a way that the ducks were all in a row, and no one could escape. . . . When it came to digging-time, Eric always had that old disc problem of his to fall back on.

It wasn't any problem for Sweets to follow the route the kids had taken when they'd broken camp. Clearly, they were making no effort to cover their tracks, and within a quarter of a mile he came upon a place where they'd walked across soft ground. Although they'd gone in single file, he still found five distinct and separate prints, and two of them were smaller; they'd picked up another girl, it seemed. Sweets shook his head and hustled on.

The route got rougher, more big ups and downs, with rocks and windfalls to be circled. Sweets kept moving smoothly, though, snacking as he went instead of stopping for a meal, his head always swiveling, this way and that.

At one point — it was then after ten in the morning — he came out onto an open, treeless ridge, and there he did a most peculiar thing. Standing on a smooth expanse of rock — he had a lovely, sweeping view from there — he proceeded to undress, not taking off just shirt and hat and shoes (let's say), but every stitch of clothes he wore. And each time he took off some garment, he held it up and shook it. Then, when he was naked, he held his small knapsack above his head and emptied *it*, item by item, and then shook it, too, showing it was truly empty.

And finally, with his arms widespread and holding a white handkerchief in each hand, he faced first east, then south, then west, then north, pausing for a moment and bowing deeply after every quarter turn, with a big wide grin on his face. The grin was perfectly sincere; he felt good doing what he was doing; it was a crazy world, and he was part of it.

When he got back to facing east again, he dressed, put the stuff back in his knapsack, checked his map once more, and hurried on. There wasn't far to go, he reckoned.

23

THE PLEDGE

On the morning of their seventh day in the wilderness, Riley (who was given to self-analysis, anyway) took a gander at her mood, her attitudes, and her opinion of herself — and smiled. She was used to feeling energetic, but sexy was a new one, really. And self-confident? Well, she always had been that, but in a different sort of way.

From the time she'd been . . . oh, ten or twelve, Riley'd known she'd almost certainly have sufficient money and clothes, and table manners and athletic ability to get a certain level of — what? — *respect*, maybe, in the world. And that she was also plenty good enough in school to make it into college, and also into law school, if she wanted to. Even if she wasn't "lotsa fun," she'd have a friend or two, and probably marry some nice-enough-but-not-terrific guy. But she'd never thought she was good-looking, and she'd always thought there were definitely some limits to her *impact*, meaning the effect she'd ever have on numbers of people. She figured she'd be able to help a stray or two, on a small scale, but big decisions about anything were not going to be hers to make. People wouldn't ever *crave* her company, or even her opinion, except on very local matters having to do with style and decoration and bedtimes, and the hospital fund drive, and maybe (if she got to be a lawyer) their divorces or their wills.

But now she was definitely starting to feel other possibilities. She felt enlarged, somehow, and more important — and she thought she realized why that was.

She was in love, and *that* made all the difference. *Being* loved was also great, but she was used to it. Her parents had always loved her, lots, and so had Allison. (Being loved by Jordan Paradise was even better, because it had that extra spice to it.) But being *in love* was what excited her the most — about herself, about the whole wide world. About the likelihood that both of those would prosper. *In love* made her optimistic, that was it. She wasn't sure that "freaked" described her anymore.

The camp, the way they had it organized, delighted her. There was now plenty of firewood, neatly stacked, and all five of them had swung an axe and learned to make what Jordan said was called a "cow's mouth" in a log, as the proper way of chopping

233

through it. They'd dug a pit in the gravel a few feet from the stream's edge, for a place to keep stuff cool during the day, and every night they put their food supply in the middle of a tarp, tied its four corners together, and hoisted the whole thing about a dozen feet off the ground, by means of a rope thrown over a tree limb.

"Who knows if there's a bear or even a porcupine within a hundred miles?" asked Jordan Paradise, as they were rigging that all up. "And who'd really want to find out?"

"Marlin Perkins, probably," said David Gracey, putting on his sour voice. "But he's not anywhere around, thank God."

True enough, and the bears and porcupines had stayed away, as far as anyone knew. But now it was time to think about leaving, already, and to talk about the things they'd come to talk about. They were finishing their usual early lunch when Riley looked around at the other four and cleared her throat and said, "I hate to be the one to bring this up, but may I suggest we all devote a moment of our afternoon to something other than the grim struggle for survival we've been making?"

"No," said Lisa, "you may not. But you probably will anyway, so go ahead and say it, whatever it is."

"Well," said Riley, "what I was thinking was that maybe we should begin to think about this handsome sphere we're sitting on, a little more — and how to maybe save it from its own worst impulses, such as nuclear destruction and all that shit. Remember how we said we were going to talk about all that? And specifically, what kids like us might do to help?" She smiled a false, cajoling smile. "So whaddaya say, gang? A half an hour for the earth? How about twenty minutes?"

Everybody shouted no and booed and hissed, and David told her to "get stuffed," but they all shifted around a little and looked at one another, too. It was definitely time, no doubt about it.

" 'The time has come, the walrus said. . . ,' " quoted Michael. He looked at Jordan Paradise. He rubbed his hands together. "So. What I was wondering about was specifics, like a specific goal, a specific action of some sort. Last time, it was just generalities. Maybe someone said marches and rallies — I don't remember — and there isn't anything wrong with them, but they're old stuff. What I was wondering was if anyone had . . . like a first step in mind, a realistic place to start. Something we could tell a money source, for instance, that we planned to do, right off. Something potent . . . and feasible . . . but original." With Michael on a field, the ball got rolling fast.

Other people raised their eyebrows, nodded, looked around the circle.

"Wait," said David. "Before anyone answers, I'd just like to say three things. First" — with a smile and a nod toward Michael — "I'm glad we're starting on this; I'm glad you asked that question. That's the first thing. And second — my second point is — that I've been thinking . . . well, how totally impossible it probably is for five kids in the middle of a wilderness to possibly work out *anything* that would ever have the smallest effect on something as huge and complex as the arms race, for Christ's sake."

Everybody nodded, being cool. David Gracey smiled his broadest smile. "So with that in mind — and third — I promise I'll do whatever we decide, for as long as it takes to succeed, or I'm irradiated, whichever comes first. Is that right — irradiated? I'm not sure." Michael shrugged and nodded, so he did, too. "That's my opening statement."

Lisa smiled and clapped her hands a few times. "I pass on giving an opening statement," she said. "And I move that David gets the trophy, for his. I go along with everything he said, up to the promise part. Way to go, Dave." She leaned over and punched him on the upper arm.

"Me, too," said Riley. "But also I'm with Michael on his question. Good question. And it'll be a lot easier to promise once we're clear on what we want to do. And there are things, I'm sure."

Everybody looked at Jordan Paradise.

"Gulp," he said. But then he shook his head and smiled. "I didn't mean that. I've got to admit I've been thinking about this all week," he said. "And Riley and I *have* talked a little, behind everybody's back. So once again I beg you: Please, no laughter till my back is turned, at least. Here's the first thing: I think our immediate goal should be to try to get every kid in the world between the ages of twelve and sixteen to write — or at least sign, or make their mark on — a sentence on a piece of . . . anything — paper, birch bark, hide; I don't care. *This* sentence:

" 'I' — and then they fill in their name or their mark, or whatever — 'a free human being, will never willingly take part in the manufacture, transport, or use of a nuclear weapon.' "

"That's idea one. A simple pledge that any kid could make, wherever he or she lived." He looked around. "So what do you think of it?"

"Say it again," said Riley.

And Jordan Paradise repeated: " 'I' — and I thought the kids could even just put in their first names, if they thought they'd get in trouble for signing — 'I, so-and-so, a free human being, will never willingly take part in the manufacture, transport, or use of a nuclear weapon.' That's it. Short, but sweet. I hope."

David nodded. "It says it all," he said. "Really. I like it. I like it *a lot*. But maybe you ought to put in 'swear' somewhere — don't you think? Wouldn't that make it even stronger, having to swear?"

Of course they ended up going over the thing word for word, and in the end everyone agreed it was fine the way it was. Michael was particularly fond of the phrase *a free human being* and the word *willingly*.

"What I like is getting the idea across that kids are actually *people*, with rights as well as obligations," he said. "Some adults don't see that yet. On the one hand, they ask us to choose not to do drugs, or certain kinds of sex, but at the same time they want to have the power to decide whether we're going to fight or not, and with which weapons."

"And the things they claim they're *letting* us make choices about — drugs and sex, like you said — just happen to be things they know they can't control anyway," said Lisa, and everybody nodded.

"But getting back to who signs this," Riley said, "I think it's important to really try to get as many kids as possible, all over the world. Even ones who may not know exactly what a nuclear weapon is, at this point. I realize there'd be some you couldn't get to, or who wouldn't give a shit, or who wouldn't want to have anything to do with the thing, maybe; but at least you could try to give everybody a chance, you know what I mean?"

"Right," said David. "I can just imagine me heading up the old Zambezi with a dugout full of pledges." He made paddling motions. "Then, cut to frame two, and here I am" — he collected his long hair in one fist and held it straight up over his head — "drying in the sun outside the local head shop, right? But — yeah, yeah" — he waved at Riley — "I know what you mean, and you're right. Maybe we *couldn't* go everywhere. But in general, we should try."

He turned to Jordan Paradise. "So how come you decided on those ages? Twelve to sixteen. Why not older than that? Or younger?"

And Jordan explained that he thought maybe under twelve would cause some people to say that this was just a bunch of babies kicking up a fuss; kids who hadn't even reached the age of reason yet. And as far as the sixteen part went, he said he figured in most nuclear countries sixteen would still be a couple of years under the age where they could put you in the army and force you to do all sorts of things with nukes, or throw you in jail if you didn't.

"Remember, that's one of the things about this," he said. "We don't *want* people to get in trouble. What this is supposed to be is just a simple, honest statement — this is it — by one big segment of the population."

"And of course every year the numbers'd go up,"

said Riley. "As more kids got to be twelve."

"Yeah," said Lisa. "But I was thinking. How *about* adults? I bet a lot of older people'd sign that pledge."

"I think they should make their own campaign," David said. He leaned forward a little. "They're the ones with the power right now, and they've hardly done a damn thing useful — except in places like New Zealand, maybe. They could always start their own campaign, with their own pledge, if they wanted to. Then if you added together them *and* us, maybe the ones in power would listen for a change."

Michael smiled. "That's like what President Eisenhower supposedly said once, that 'people want peace so much that one of these days government better get out of the way and let them have it.' I just hope it works that way. But being realistic, doesn't everybody think that a lot of adults — even in this country, let alone Russia and places like that — would try to pressure kids *not* to sign a pledge like this? That they'd try to more or less blow kids away with so-called 'facts' and 'information' that they'd claim to have, or thought they had? I mean, face it, we're talking about *kids*, and I can imagine a lot of adults doing a pretty good job of making a kid feel stupid, or immature, or even disloyal, if he signed it. What *we're* saying is that there are some things a person of any age can know, down deep in their hearts. But I can see a kid starting to doubt that, if some grown-up that he always trusted said it was bullshit."

"Fuck *them*," said David. "Where do they get off, telling me *I'm* stupid — look how *they've* messed up — or especially what I ought to think. That's *1984*, man."

239

"Right," said Riley. "And this is 1984 plus one, so what do you expect? But of course you're both right. They'll try to make out the pledge is saying all sorts of stuff it isn't saying at all, just like they've done with the ERA. And maybe some kids would be intimidated. But I can also see a lot of them getting . . . I don't know, real *stubborn*."

And Riley smiled, imagining a lot of kids just quietly believing that they had the right to sign a pledge, and never touch a nuke — and even save the world.

24

"NEVER"

"That's just the first thing," Jordan Paradise said. "The pledge. But then there's step two, that Riley thought of. I think it's incredible." He motioned with his hand toward her.

"Well, I was thinking," she said. "The pledge is great for getting kids to really think about the problem, and where they stand on it. But there still ought to be something they can *do*, after that. A continuing sort of thing. So I was thinking we maybe could get some buttons made. That'd just say NEVER on them. Wouldn't that be neat? NEVER in all sorts of different languages? And if your parents didn't approve, you could wear the button where it wouldn't show, like on the inside of your lapel, if you had a jacket on. Or on your underwear." She laughed.

"*Great*," said David. "I can just see that. All my dates with NEVER on their underwear. Perfect." He rolled his eyes at Lisa.

"Definitely. For sure," she said, and nodded hard.

"Well, I agree that *is* a great idea," said Michael, frowning at the two of them. "But what I'm looking at is quite a bottom line. I don't want to throw any cold water, and I'm *not*, really — but just think what all of this is going to cost. It could be *millions*. Advertising, rent for office space, the cost of printing up the buttons. What do you suppose our chances are of raising that kind of money? Realistically speaking."

"I don't know," said Jordan. "Obviously. But — don't laugh, anyone — I asked the pendulum and it said yes — that we should try."

"Yeah, but did you ask it — " David started.

"Uh-uh, don't forget: It doesn't give specifics." Jordan interrupted him, and smiled. "*It* just says if it's a good idea or not. How to work it all out is up to us. And I don't just mean the *five* of us. It'd have to be kids all over, just doing it. What'd happen, maybe, is that the idea'd be big news, when it started, and so it'd get all sorts of free publicity, you know? Maybe even on the Voice of America and Radio Free Europe, that kind of thing."

"I kind of doubt *that*," Michael said. Then, smiling at Jordan, "Yet who knows? Maybe they would."

"But anyway," Jordan went on. "What the campaign is — would be — is the pledge, and vice versa. Kids could write it on their homework papers, post it on bulletin boards, send it in as letters to the editor or public service announcements — put it anywhere and everywhere it wasn't illegal or an eyesore. There'd be that, and then the buttons — that word NEVER, everywhere, in all the languages. That'd really add up to something."

"Yeah," said Lisa, "can't you just imagine everybody at a school assembly, or at a basketball game, just starting a chant like that, going, 'NEVER, NEVER, NEVER.' Wouldn't that be fantastic? I can see the teachers going bullshit. Or — actually — maybe joining in. I bet they would."

"It sounds incredible," said Riley slowly. She couldn't stop herself from smiling. "I won't be seventeen for five more months. I guess when you're seventeen, you're in another category — we could start a new one. But for the next five months — look out! What were the names of those foundations, Michael? Lisa told me what you said to that futurist guy, back in Jettison — how you told him to shove it. That was great." She smiled at him, just him, and hoped he got the message. "I bet my father might know one of those guys at a foundation — or at least know someone who knows one. If they want to put their money into arms limitation. . . ." She was babbling by then, her voice getting louder and louder.

At that point everybody got a little crazy. They all talked (exclaimed, made fun of, questioned, raved, and shouted, "Wait, wait, wait") at once. If Sweets had come out of the pines in back of Riley and Lisa's lean-to and told them there was a guy named Eric back by the highway who planned to shoot them all down in cold blood, they might very well have told him just to please be cool and park it on a log, they'd get to him in just a minute, sir.

The thing was: They really were going to do it, do something; for the first time, all of them knew that, and the knowing drove them very nearly mad.

"I bet we run into some sort of macho backlash," Michael said. He'd forgotten about money for the moment. "You know, people saying we're just chicken about the laws of nature and a bunch of sissies. How out there in the jungle you've gotta act tough, look tough, and be tough, and that if either side comes on too peaceful, like proposing a freeze or something, the other side'll start a war. That kind of thing."

"Well," said Lisa, "if that happens, we'll probably just have to come up with some bumper stickers, and fix those devils good. Let's see. . . ." She shut her eyes for a moment, pressed a fist to her forehead. "How about: 'If you think the pledge and the freeze are funny, the nuclear winter will *kill* you'?"

"Not bad," said Riley, "but the thing that'll kill *me* is when people try to put us down with the argument about how you can't change human nature. As if we didn't realize there's always going to be fighting, probably, because people are stupid." — Lisa made an idiot face — "See what I mean? All we're asking is for them not to be *so* stupid that they destroy the entire planet, right?"

"You know what?" Lisa said. "If we could just get all the *girls* between twelve and sixteen not to . . . even *date*, let's say, anybody who hadn't signed the pledge. . . ."

"It's been tried," Michael said. "Back in ancient

Greece. Or at least they wrote a play then, where that happened. It was supposed to be *all* the women, wives included, but I think they had trouble getting everyone to agree. Not to, I mean."

"Yeah, I can imagine the walls of those ancient Greek phone booths," David said. " 'For the night *before* the Day After, call Helen of T at Olympus 4–3000. Or, 'To get your missile launched by Aphrodite, just dial 867.' "

"Funny, isn't it?" said Lisa. "How easily *some* people seem to make up childish smut?"

Jordan laughed. "I wish *I* had that knack." He turned to Michael and Riley. "That was one thing I missed out on altogether, the way I was brought up: talking dirty. I'll probably have to make myself go through that stage, sometime. Karen told me it's meant to be psychologically unhealthy to miss any of the stages — like crawling, or telling on your sister, or anything. That everybody has to go through all the main ones, sometime."

Riley got to her feet. "Good grief," she said. "A delayed adolescence in your future? How loathsome. My mother says my father has some friends who have that problem. Maybe I can talk you out of it, somehow. But right now, I'm going for a walk, if we're through with all of this for the time being." She looked down at Jordan. "You want to come with me? Be part of the peace movement?" And she threw a hip in his direction.

"Yeah, look who's talking dirty now." He got up. "Sure, I'll go with you. Maybe if you say the dirty words over and over, and tell me what the different gestures mean. . . ."

"Well, there's one that stands for 'Jordan Paradise,' " said Riley. "What you have to do is make a fist and — "

Lisa whooped. They wandered off toward the pines, shoving each other's shoulder, not holding hands, intentionally.

25

IN THE FLESH

As soon as he saw Amos Goodspeed in the flesh, Sweets knew for sure that there was no way he was going to let Eric get his hands on him, let alone kill him. Of course, he told himself, he'd known that for a long time and had just put off saying it in so many words. He'd told the Rouxs' housekeeper, back in Northfield, that she didn't have to worry and she'd understood. That lady didn't need to have a picture drawn for her, or hear a thousand words. That lady, she had intuition, you might say.

But still, when he finally laid eyes on Amos for the first time, after so many years of digging, asking, waiting, guessing, being wrong, it was, beyond a doubt, a very special moment. Not only *HALLE-LUJAH!*, but relief. *Incredible* relief. Up until then, he could have been wrong, not just about Amos but about himself as well; a queasy little corner of his mind had always realized that maybe when he saw the boy he . . . wouldn't care. Not really. And that he'd shrug it off. That it'd just be "the job." And he and Eric (brothers after all) would finish it and write reports and then split up and wait for new assignments.

It hadn't happened; he'd been right — all right. In general and in particular, about the both of them. The young man — which is what he was, by then — had turned out . . . beautiful. And more. That is to say, he wasn't only surface-beautiful, but also in the stuff that lies behind the way a person looks: the way that person *is*. When Sweets saw Amos Good-speed, he could tell. Could tell that he was something special, worth preserving. And that *he* would keep him safe, somehow.

He'd first spotted the kids' camp from high above it, just before he'd started dealing with the really narrow, dangerous section of the trail into the valley. The place where you had to mountain-goat along a little ways with your breath held and your lip between your teeth because of the ledge being messed up by fallen rocks from above, and where on the open side there was a sheer, almost uninterrupted drop, straight down into the river at the bottom of the valley. Once he'd seen the camp, right on the bend of the river, and so believed the kids were there, old cautious Sweets took lots of careful time high up there on that rocky ledge. But still, when

he was done with it, he didn't lollygag around —
like, pull out his binoculars and see if he could spot
the boy. Instead, he hurried quietly along the ledge,
which angled slowly down and followed the shape
of the river, until he was well around the bend and
surely out of sight of anyone who just happened to
look up. Not too far downstream, he found a shallow
place to cross, and when he'd got his boots back on,
he headed inland, in amongst the pines, and slowly
circled up behind the camp. He overshot it by a
little, so that when he came back down, he actually
was *up*stream from it, more or less behind the Riley-
Lisa lean-to. There, he settled and relaxed at last,
stretched out on his belly, and focused his binoculars. They all were visible, all five of them together,
sitting in a circle by their fireplace.

Sweets nodded: Five it was, just as he'd expected.
He could recognize Riley Roux from the silver-framed
photograph on the side table by the couch in the
Rouxs' library, and Thalia'd told him Michael Gor-
don was a short-haired, small, intense young man.
That meant the long, lean hippie-type and the buxom
little reddish blonde were numbers four and five.
And the beautiful and central one was Amos.

He looked *a lot* the way that Sweets had oftentimes
imagined that he would (and that Thalia had said
he *did*, of course): curly black hair, large brown eyes,
and smooth tan skin. His legs, now folded tailor-
fashion, confirmed that he was tall. But what Sweets
hadn't — *couldn't* have — been prepared for was the
calm and sweetness in his face, and the fact that in
this group of five he clearly had become the central
figure.

This was something you could *see*; he didn't have to hear what they were saying. It was a combination of the way the people sat, everyone at least half turned in his direction, and the expressions on their faces when they spoke to him, or even more so when he spoke to *them*. It wasn't dazzlement, intimidation, hypnotism, any one of those. What it was was confidence, attention, trust, respect — that bunch. And even (Sweets would swear) a little l-o-v-e: love.

This sort of stuff would not go down in a report, of course; Sweets realized that. Eric would make mincemeat of it, calling it "subjective judgments" — some such jive — and Adelman, his boss, would back that up, calling him "an old romantic" and giving those words a definitely sneery twist, not quite "old queen of spades" but not that far away from it.

Perhaps that made him think of Buford — imagining Adelman looking that way, doubtful and contemptuous. Buford was the one person he'd met in all his time with the agency who he believed would simply nod and understand. Buford was amazing; he *always* understood. Not just Sweets and the other black guys, but everyone, it seemed.

Of course Sweets hadn't seen the man in years, hardly at all since his training time. He knew that Buford now was two grades over Adelman and rumored to have access to the Oval Office. But still he felt that Buford would remember him, and what he'd told him, privately, so many years before.

"Don't *ever* try to use me as a booster-rocket," he had said to Sweets. "I don't do special tricks for brothers, Charlie Brown. And you'll have to please a lot of other folks before I even *hear* of you. *But"* — he'd paused and taken off his glasses, peered at Sweets with kind, unfocused eyes — "if there ever comes a time when you *know* you're right, and no one else believes you, come to me. I'll listen."

That was all that Buford promised — that he'd listen — but then and now it was enough for Sweets. He wondered why he hadn't thought of Buford before. Probably because he hadn't *seen* Amos before, hadn't known for sure what he knew now, and what he had to do. That, and because he hadn't seen *Buford* for at least ten years, no doubt. But now he'd thought of him, so now he had a plan.

Step one would be to lie — easy enough. After stalling around for a good long time, so he wouldn't get back until well after dark, he'd simply tell Eric that he hadn't been able to find the kids. They weren't in either of the hidden valleys on the map (he'd say), and, what's more, he hadn't even come upon their tracks. To make the story even more believable, he'd act real pooped, as if he'd covered miles and miles of hard terrain. And just for extra fun he might make up some other stuff: how he'd seen a barefoot, nappy-haired wild man in frayed fatigues, and later had a warning shot from nowhere go thudding in a tree trunk just in front of him.

Telling Eric lies made more sense than trying to warn the kids did. It might be cool to just stroll up to them and say, "Guess what?"; but the trouble with that strategy was trying to think of a good next line — an explanation of why there was a guy back there who planned to kill them if he got the chance. And although sometime someone — maybe even S.C.

251

Reid — would have to tell young Amos *something*, that time was not right now.

Sweets had thought about that aspect of the case. The thing was — and this is what Buford would be asked to listen to and then believe — Sweets was now ninety-nine percent sure that Amos knew exactly zip, when it came to viruses and formulas and suicides. He'd eighty percent believed that when he'd suggested it to Eric, back at the Northfield Arms, but then he was even more interested in getting Eric talking — Eric and the House of Smirnoff. Sometime, maybe, and with Buford's blessing, he could tell the kid *almost* the truth: that his parents — doctors, scientists — had killed themselves because the Russians put some threats on them, and him. And for the past fourteen years, Russian KGBs and agents like himself had all been trying to find him. And Sweets — his group — had finally got the Russians, so the kid was safe. That was pretty close: The Russians had a lot of guys like Eric. People were the same, all over.

Of course Sweets's certainty about Amos's ignorance could be called still another example of a "subjective judgment." Or intuition, if anybody'd rather. Buford might, Sweets realized. He remembered Buford had once talked to his training class in praise of intuition, calling it, in fancy language, something he believed in. Buford had also said that much as he admired computers, he felt that an agent's intuition might often do him even better service in decision-making. Well, Sweets's intuition now suggested Amos — this young man in front of him — was ignorant of how his parents died. And for what

252

reason. The boy looked powerful and peaceful, rather than haunted and driven. There was an energy inside him, to be sure, but it was calm and cheerful, positive.

He'd tell old Buford this, the first thing in the morning. That'd be the second step of his plan. He'd go down to that Drumbee Store on some pretext or other and call up Buford from the phone booth just outside it, put all this in front of him — including how Eric planned to dispose of Amos *and* four other kids, just so there wouldn't be "loose ends." He'd ask Buford to cancel Eric's orders, and either close this case right then and there, or at the very worst let *him* pick up the boy at some point, later on, and run some tests on him. Even with that drug they had these days, perhaps. Buford would remember him (of course) and he'd think how Sweets had let some fourteen years go by before he'd taken him up on what he'd told him once ("If there ever comes a time you *know* you're right. . . .") and he'd believe, and give the order. And Sweets would pass it on to Eric, who would check on it, of course, as soon as he and Sweets split up — or probably before. Eric would be furious, but Eric would obey. The man was crazy, but he also loved his job (no contradiction there, perhaps), so Eric's number one priority was keeping his white ass completely sling-free.

Sweets focused on the five kids once again, in turn. The other four looked like the kinds of friends you'd want your kid to have. In fact, as he lay there watching all of them talk back and forth with one another, Sweets felt a strong and somewhat unexpected feeling (especially for an old black cynic like the worldly, weary Mr. S.C. Reid, he told himself). These kids looked *good* to him. Here they were, sitting around this model little camp they'd made, all of them alert and interested (nothing burning in their fingers, or going up their noses either, Eric), conversing with each other concerning God knows what. They all looked smart and friendly, positive not negative, much more *with* it than against it.

Sweets shook his head again and smiled. He was definitely getting carried away, he told himself. That probably had something to do with finding Amos at long last, and the beauty of this place he'd found him in, and yes — hell — face it: his loneliness and childlessness and being thirty-nine years old. Twenty years before — a half a lifetime now — in the gentle quiet of another summer's night, he'd had his (then uncynical) right arm around a girl, a fellow Y-camp counselor (let's see, her name was Marty), and he'd told her something soft and summery, a fantasy that he'd been working on, a sweet, sweet thing to fall asleep to, on a summer night, at camp. How about — he asked her — if some kids, some day, could make it to adulthood still unflawed — could she imagine that? — and simply turn this rotten world around. By being purely good and fair and logical, and meek and sweet (like her, he'd said). She'd murmured he was *her* sweet dreamer, and they'd got to kissing, rather than conversing.

He never had forgotten, though: not her, and not that fantasy — well, *dream* — of his. Now there were these five in front of him. Why couldn't they be it? A band of angels, you might say.

* * *

When Riley Roux got up, and then Amos Good-speed, and then the two of them started strolling, in a very leisurely way, in his general direction, Sweets backed off and got to his two feet, and beat a fast retreat.

He still had lots of time to kill, before he started back, and so he thought he'd find a sunny spot and just hang out awhile. He liked the neighborhood just fine. And when he'd first come into the valley, he'd noticed there were lots of real nice-looking places a little ways upstream from where the camp was. The river's edge was major rocks and little sandbars, both, but on this side — the side of the river where he was now — there wasn't any cliff at all, just a slope on which there were these mossy-grassy treeless patches here and there, with bare rock showing on them, too. Sweets guessed the pines grew every-where the soil was deep enough for them to get a toehold, but where it was too shallow, moss and grasses grew instead. In any case, those plots were perfect for his purposes: snacking, passing time, ad-miring the view of the river and of the cliff across the way. Possibly he'd even close his eyes for half a minute. Perhaps he'd even give up smoking.

Yessir, that sounded good to him. He liked his being — staying — sort of *with* the kids. Their in-visible, romantic, fuzzy-headed friend.

Sweets shook his head a final time. It might be that when he spoke to Buford, he also ought to ask about retirement. Thirty-nine was awful young for getting senile, but maybe old enough for wising-up.

26

SECOND THOUGHTS

After Sweets's almost noiseless parting from their campsite, Eric sighed contentedly and changed positions on his basically uncomfortable mattress. Everything (but it) was good. As usual, he thought, he'd handled Sweets effectively. *Manipulated* him? No, not really. "Manipulated" had an underhanded connotation; what he'd done was challenge, lead, arrange — all without appearing to insist, and without barking out a lot of orders. What he'd been was "masterful," thought Eric. He liked that word. Now he, the master in this case, could wait and take his ease while Sweets, the . . . *mastered*, you might say, or mustered, even *mustard* (Eric smiled: that sense of humor, again) went running off to locate their young hot dogs, if you will, their meal, their quarry.

Eric could feel his heartbeat quicken when, once again, he thought about the . . . finishing, the climax of the case. After all these months. Sweets, though, had been on it for *years*. Unproductive years, pre-Eric, to be sure, but years and years, in any case. Imagine what *he* must be feeling, Eric thought. From time to time he liked to do that: put himself in Sweets's shoes. The psychologist Carl Rogers recommended that to therapists: to put themselves inside their clients' feelings. Let's see, if he were Sweets. . . .

The next moment Eric was sitting bolt upright on his mattress with his sleeping bag unzipped, already reaching for his pants.

If he were Sweets, he wouldn't be *about* to do the sweat-work, act as bird dog, then, with tail a-wag, let Eric have the fun and hog the credit. No, what *he'd* do would be to trick his leader into staying put somewhere and then dash off and do the thing and, later claim "misunderstanding," and the honors. Years and years and years and end up in the background when it came to trophy time? No way in the world, good buddy.

Eric's heart was really pounding now. He jammed his feet into his tennis shoes.

But before he'd finished tying them, he told himself to just calm down, be cool. All of that would be if *he* were Sweets — or Sweets was him, you might say. Well, Sweets wasn't him, not even close. Completely different breed of cat. Sweets would like to rake in all the honors, sure, but he wouldn't have the . . . *subtlety* to set things up this way. He wouldn't dare to try to outsmart Eric, not after all the months they'd been together, all the talks they'd had. Sweets had a certain . . . *foxiness* to him, a sort of native shrewdness, but wouldn't that (actually) *insure* that he wouldn't dare get cute with Eric?

Eric sighed. He really didn't have a choice. This was annoying, very. *Probably* Sweets was doing nothing more than what he'd said: trekking-in and scouting-down — showing off a little for the boss. But there was always the one chance in a hundred that he wasn't — that he'd *learned enough* from Eric (you might say) to figure out a simple, and self-serving, plan.

That miserable, conniving, son-of-a-bitch (thought Eric), as he headed for the car.

Mordecai Wilson rose at five A.M., summer and winter — he was always in bed by nine — and opened up the store between six and six-thirty, although the sign on the door read: HOURS, MON. THRU SAT., 7 to 7. As a general rule, he did a lot of business during the first hour and a half of any given day: fellas going to work (or even fishing) and needing milk or doughnuts, gloves, a six-pack, half a pound of bologna, antifreeze, whatever. That day, a fella with a hat and glasses on bought a quart of orange juice and a half a dozen Reese's Peanut Butter Cups. Old Mordecai'd never seen that guy before, far as he remembered. He also didn't see him steal the topo map right off the rack beside the one that had the comic books. Or the compass, either. Eric had waited till the proprietor's back was turned, and he was reaching for the pack of Winston Lights somebody wanted.

Once he'd parked his car well off the road again, Eric opened up its trunk and carefully, almost adoringly, unwrapped the rifle that he had back there. He also took a jacket out and put it on, stuffed the candy in its pockets; then, swigging from the o.j., he was off, the rifle in the other hand. For the first bit, he didn't need the map: He had to cross the river, climb that ridge, for openers. Once he got up there, he'd stop and study the darn thing. He could do it. He wouldn't be dealing from an established strength, but he could do it. People who knew Eric really well knew that Eric knew most people could do a lot more than they thought they could. It was mostly a matter of their making up their minds. Well, Eric's mind was made up this time, and so, it knew, he could accomplish almost anything; he was sure of that. If Sweets was playing games with *him*, he was in for a big surprise. Eric had it all figured out, as usual.

It was not totally beyond the realm of possibility (thought Eric) that Sweets would also have to "disappear."

27

SERIOUS BLUE JEANS

As soon as Riley and Jordan were out of visual range of the people still sitting by the fireplace, they stopped goofing around and just stood still for a moment, looking at each other.

"This'll be all right, right?" said Jordan Paradise. "Our going off like this? Nobody'll mind, do you think?" Once away from the others, he seemed to have gotten a lot more serious.

Riley shrugged her shoulders. "Meaning Michael? I don't think so," she said. "We've done it before. And, frankly, I don't care." She leered and changed her voice to throaty, older — overacting, like in the soaps. "I have my needs, Jordan. Michael may succeed in killing you next time, but I'm prepared to take that risk. My chromosomes insist on it, I guess. Now kiss me." She closed her eyes and shoved her lips at him in an outrageous pucker.

He stepped right up and, feet together, bobbed his face toward hers, looking like a chicken pecking seed. Their lips met and made a noisy, smacking sound. That made them laugh, and they grabbed each other's hand and started strolling farther away from the camp, along the edge of the pines.

"But seriously," Riley said. "I'm sure Michael's okay. And anyway, that was so great back there, I just had to be alone with you a little while. Partly just to tell you how I felt. I *made* you get up and come with me just now, you realize that? Sheer willpower, on my part." She shook her head. "It's pretty amazing what the human will can accomplish."

It was easy walking, where they were — not along the river's edge but paralleling it, angling closer to it all the time. The river, much larger long ago, had made that valley and Riley liked to think the valley still belonged to it, and she and other people were just visitors. You could hear its rushing sound wherever you were, and nothing else when you were close to it.

Now, she and Jordan Paradise wandered in its direction, walking like three-legged racers for a while, with their near legs moving in step, together, and then their outer ones. They both wore running shoes, no socks, and in spite of the difference in their heights, Riley's bare, tan legs weren't that much shorter than his. She thought their legs looked great, moving ɔgether, and for a second imagined the two of them completely naked, just walking in the dappled shade like that, together. They'd look real good, she thought: Adam and Eve, a-saunter in the G. of E. Pretty foxy couple, no mistake.

Actually, they both had on blue running shorts, his much darker than hers; he wore a gray T-shirt and she, a soft lavender polo shirt that (wonder of wonders) was totally devoid of alligator, kangaroo, fox, bobcat, great horned toad, or tuna. Lisa had approved that shirt, when Riley'd put it on. "Nobody advertises on *my* tits," she'd said, "unless they pay me for the privilege." Riley liked the way the shirt felt *on* — so soft — as well as how it looked. She was very much alert to all sensations (she believed), walking hand-in-hand with Jordan Paradise.

"Well, it *was* amazing," he said, "and it really felt good, listening to everybody get into it, like that. The more I think about those NEVER buttons. . . . But I want to ask you. Do you really think it can work? The whole campaign, I mean."

"You bet I do," she said. "That's one of the things I wanted to tell you. When we were talking back there, this time, I got a whole new feeling about this idea. And you know something? It really *can* work. Things really *do* spread all over the world, nowadays — in no time at all. Just think of blue jeans. And Coca-Cola. Rock 'n' roll. This could be, like, serious blue jeans. I mean it."

"Well, that's good," he said. He had sort of a wan smile on his face. "I guess I think that, too, but I don't know. I'm such a dope I go around and round in circles. Like back there, a little before we left

. . . I don't know." He seemed to try to wave the thought away, whatever he was thinking.

But then he said, "It's ironic. Before, when I didn't even *have* a future, I just assumed there'd be one. But then I met you, which on the one hand gave me the best future I could ever imagine, but on the other hand got me thinking — *you* got me thinking — about all this nuclear stuff. So now, when I think about 1990, or 1995, or the year 2000, it's not just in terms of me — what maybe I'll be doing when I get to it, or even *us* — but in terms of them, those years. That was what was going through my mind, part of the time, back there.

"Are there going to be any such years as 1990, 1995, 2000?" he asked her. "It's like that old question about whether the tree that falls down in the middle of the forest when there's nobody within a hundred miles of it — whether that falling tree makes any sound or not. Well, if there isn't anyone around — alive — in 1995, is there a year called that?"

Riley stopped dead again. She looked at the ground, and for a moment she didn't say anything.

"This is funny" — her head gradually came up as she spoke — "what you're saying is you think this idea had *better* be serious blue jeans, or we've had it. Everyone, including us." She looked serious, more than serious: dazed.

"I shouldn't even have said that," Jordan said. "I know I'm not telling you anything you didn't tell me first. I didn't mean to upset you. It was just — kind of — like something that passed through my mind, and it seemed so bizarre I felt like saying it to someone. Sort of like David's dream — so maybe

I wouldn't have to think about it anymore. I'm sorry."

Riley looked at him, and he saw she wasn't sad so much as thinking hard. "Oh, that's all right," she said. "What's funny — crazy, really — is how we've almost changed places, in a way, in just about three weeks. Here *I've* been thinking, worrying, blabbing about the future of the planet since junior high, and making fun of the kids who couldn't see any farther than Saturday night, or the backseat of some scuzz-ball's father's plushmobile . . . " She smirked. "And then you come along, and in a few weeks' time most of what I think about is mush and moonlight nights and . . . dirty words."

She waved a hand. "Let the world out there take care of itself," she said. "The only land-based missile I'm interested in is . . . forget it. And while I'm thinking about all that, *you*, who's the real cause of my thinking that way, *you're* having bad dreams about. . . ." She sighed.

"Damn it, Jordy" — he thought she was laughing, then — "I'm sorry." She reached and put both hands around his neck.

"I guess I'm sorry we can't just live like normal human beings," she said, "and mess around and never have to think about anything but . . . but what my mother calls the facts of life — still. Boy, it must have been a dream to be a kid when she was, back in those days."

"I'm the one that's sorry," Jordan said, again. "There wasn't any need to bring it up — what I was think-ing of. I really am a jerk."

He had both hands spread open on her shoulder blades, and was talking at her upturned face. Of course they kissed each other then. And pretty soon they felt a whole parade of other feelings (other than regret and sorrow) marching through their bodies.

"Mmmm," said Jordan Paradise. "I love you — that *and* you. And there's our future. That and other . . . shall we say, *activities?*" He leered.

"You'd *better* think that," Riley said. She took a deep breath and shook herself a little. He was trying to shift his mood, and she would, too. "But we'll see, soon enough. When we get back to my parents' house, we'll see how serious you really are, and how . . . *active*, did you say? You probably won't dare come anywhere near me — oops — unless my mom and dad decide to go to Europe or something, and take Allison with them. I'll be wanting to take baths together, and all sort of other neat . . . activities, and you'll be making up excuses, and holding the door open for my mother, and going 'Abso*lute*ly, sir' to everything my father says — acting like the perfect little guest-wimp."

"Back to your parents' house?" he asked. "Is that where you want to go from here?"

"I don't know." She smiled. "I was just saying that. We'll probably get there eventually, don't you think?" She looked down at the sandbar they were walking on, at that point. "I guess I was hoping you'd . . . live with us," she said quickly. "That it'd be your place — home — too." She forced a little laugh.

"Wow," he said. She looked at him. He was smiling enormously, from ear to ear. "You think that's possible? I mean, do you think your parents would ever let me? Hey!" He held up a forefinger. "I could pay my own room and board, if that'd help."

Riley reached across her body and stroked his arm.

"You know something?" she said. "You are so *cute*. I swear. I just *love* you, Jordy, I really do. But room and board wouldn't enter into it, I don't think. My parents are weird — I mean, they do a lot of weird things, like going to that fat farm — but they're also pretty great about some stuff. Like letting me make a lot of my own decisions."

"They trust you," Jordan said.

Riley stopped again. She picked up a flat stone and bounced it up and down in her palm.

"I guess they do," she said. "Not to be perfect, but to think about the alternatives. To try to make good decisions, taking everything into considera-tion." She bent at the waist, and stepped, and threw the stone, sidearm, at the water. It took one giant skip and landed in the middle of the river, just about.

There were a couple of huge boulders just in front of them, part of the bank, not loose and wobbly, and on the edge of a small pool. Jordan Paradise bounded up the side of the nearest one, and Riley came quickly, lightly, after him. They stood there next to each other, looking at the dark, still pool formed by an even larger boulder on the other side, and at the rushing river beyond it, and at the little gravelly beach down beside the rock they were on.

"I guess a lot of things come up," Jordan said, "that a person has to decide . . . sort of from the gut. Or with the help of a pendulum."

"The *gut*," Riley said. She was smiling. "Or other organs."

He gave her shoulder a push; she teetered on the rock.

She pointed at the pool. "This is where Lisa and I go swimming all the time," she said. "Skinny-dipping."

He didn't seem to react to that information at all, and when she peeked at his face, she could see he was still thinking hard about something — possibly the gut, she thought.

"You know," he said. "I guess you *do* know — or you've probably *assumed*, but still I want to tell it to you straight, so if I do get to live with you. . . . You say *you're* inexperienced. Well, so am I. Like, totally. You realize that, don't you? I wouldn't want to present myself under false pretenses, or whatever it is they say." He sounded rather stiff and formal, ill-at-ease, to Riley. "I haven't been anybody's lover in my whole life, if you know what I mean."

Riley nodded solemnly. "I think I do," she said. "Well, me neither."

That information didn't seem to cheer him up, excessively, and so she added, "Does it make you feel . . . I don't know, *retarded*, or something, being a boy and all?"

"What does being a boy have to do with it?" he asked. And it occurred to Riley that Jordan Paradise had had possibly the least sexist and most isolated-from-society (did the two go together?) upbringing of any guy she'd ever met. "Isn't everybody the same as far as wanting-to goes?"

"I don't know," she said, truthfully. "You hear different things. But I'd say probably everybody wants to get the first time out of the way, in a way. I know I do. In a way."

Jordan raised his eyebrows, then he looked at her and smiled.

"Really?" he said. "That's a pretty general thing, you think?" She shrugged and nodded, so he nodded, too. "I can see that." Suddenly, he seemed to have relaxed a lot. "Probably some day they'll have machines for that, then — robots. Attractive-looking ones, of course — heated and all, with little computers and everything. They could make them to look like different actors and actresses and rock stars — and athletes and models and stuff." He grinned. "That way, people wouldn't have to take a chance and do it without any birth control. You know, just because they had this real good opportunity to get their first time out of the way. I bet that happens a lot, people taking a chance, just so they get it . . . on the record books."

Riley laughed. "You're *gross*," she said. "You know that? Talk about a dirty mind." She looked around the area. "Here he is, folks — the Edison of intercourse. Inventor of the micro-chippie. The Japanese could probably produce them by the millions. But the trouble is, people'd still know they hadn't *really* done it." She shook her head.

"But while we're on the subject," she went on, "I'll tell you something else." She could barely believe that they'd actually gotten on the subject she'd had in mind from the beginning, and sort of by evolution, you could say. "When I was talking about *activities* just now, like, if you lived at my house . . . well, I was just more or less joking around. I wasn't talking about us having to start doing it right away, or anything like that. You know how I just said I'd like to get the first time over with, and then I said 'in a way'?"

He nodded.

"Well," she said, and she could feel her heart starting to pound a little, "the strange part is that's the way I *did* feel before . . . well, before we really got together. But now — now that we have, and there's a specific guy I really *want* to do it with sometime, it's like the person's gotten more important than the act. Now all I know is that it'll happen when it should, when no one could possibly get hurt by it, on some perfect warm, but not actually hot — "

"When you're ready," Jordan said, and smiled again.

"Right," she said. "When both of us are — which isn't, *obviously*, just when . . . *you* know, it's possible, and all. Boy!" She shook her head some more. "It's hard to know what's mature or immature, or natural or unnatural, don't you think? Or to know what 'being ready' really involves, or whether it makes the slightest difference whether you are, or not. . . ."

"Nothing major is easy," said Jordan Paradise, as he'd said before.

"I guess that's good," she said. "Isn't it?"

"I think so," he said.

"I hope so." She smiled.

"Loving someone seems pretty easy, at first," he said, "but then you get into things, and you see it isn't — that it's hard. To do it right, I mean." He scratched the side of his head.

"But you know something?" he went on. "I just figured this out. The hardness is part of the fun. No, don't laugh." She'd stuck her tongue out, giggled. "You know what I mean. If loving someone was easy, it wouldn't be such a big deal, so important. And when you figure every person has a body *and* a mind *and* a whole bunch of emotions. . . . Getting to know all that — *would* take time. Not to mention energy." And then *he* panted.

"Well, what it is is a process — it just goes on and on," Riley said. "You probably never do totally get it. Or get *there*, or however you want to say it."

"It's like a big, long, never-ending chain of things," he said.

"A chain of flowers," Riley said, "And every link makes the whole thing sweeter. And stronger."

"I bet even this talk is a link," he said. And she just smiled and threw her arms around him, and they gave each other such a hug they spun around on top of the boulder, until they had to break it off, before they lost their balance.

"I'm going in the water," Riley said. "I feel so great I can't believe it."

She jumped off the rock, down onto the little beach, where she peeled off the polo shirt and pushed down her running shorts, and stepped on the heels of her shoes, so as to slide her feet out. That left her with her underpants, a very brief white cotton pair, which once they got wet would pretty much be see-through anyway, she realized. So she dragged them down and off and waved with them at Jordan, standing on the rock, still. She wasn't going to have any secrets from him, or act any way she didn't feel.

But as she turned to run into the water, she thought she hadn't done that — taken off her clothes — for him (to turn him on, to please or show him) as much as for herself. Swimming naked was the way she liked to swim — that was the simple truth — to feel the water all around her body everywhere, and the good part was she could *do* that, by herself, with him around. Loving someone gave you that prerogative, that *duty* you could say — to be yourself.

She leaped and dove beneath the surface of the water and, with arms extended, wriggled fishlike toward the bottom. Loving someone is a lot like being by yourself, she thought, but better. She was wearing one huge underwater smile.

28

CHALLENGED

Moving really rather smoothly, Eric trekked along a route that he believed would take him to the mountain valley on the map that Sweets had pointed to and named most likely to be Shangri-La. From time to time, he told himself that he was "lookin' good" and "right on target." And he was even reasonably sure he was telling himself the truth.

He'd pushed it from the first, really forced the pace. His idea was to take advantage of the time that he was fresh — fresh*est* — to get where he was going, check the situation out. He could always make it back, somehow. And, of course (he told himself a time or two), the chances really *were* that Sweets and he'd be coming back together. Sweets would be, like, totally surprised to see him, sure — surprised that he had changed his mind and followed after him, surprised that Eric had that sort of savvy. But he'd accept it, recognize it, and respect it, too, as being . . . well, another master, unexpected stroke on Eric's part. The sort of thing a guy like *Eric* could bring off.

Following the map was difficult, but Eric figured he was doing it. Whenever he could, he'd check himself — the place he thought he was — against the higher elevations on the map: If he was *here*, that mountain should be *there*, like that. Then, too, there was the sun, which gave him some help on directions — it and the compass he'd picked up at the store. He didn't altogether trust that compass, having never used one in his life before, but still he pulled it out from time to time, and when it seemed to agree with what he thought, that gave him quite a little rush. Here he was, a navigator: Eric the Red (White and Blue). Sailing not toward Vinland (did they call it?), but to Shangri-fuckin'-La. No, Eric didn't use that sort of language much, out loud, but now he felt completely right in thinking it. And winking as he did so. At certain times, the cool, poised agent-analyst became the bold young rakehell blade. . . .

By the time Eric reached the path that also was a ledge that ran along the cliffside, it was 3:18 P.M. His digital watch told him that; it didn't have a face but *he* made one; this better be the valley he was looking for. If it was, he — everything — was golden.

As long as the kids were there — alive or dead — he was in good shape. If they were alive, he'd finish the job. If they were dead, it'd mean that Sweets was double-crossing him, but Sweets would also still be in there, too; he wouldn't have had time to kill the kids *and* bury them *and* their equipment. In that case, Eric would *really* finish the job. The bad part'd be if it was the wrong valley, then he'd be up the creek: "screwed, blued, and tattooed," as he would think of it, sometimes. The kids might get away; Sweets would write him up in any case, for leaving his location, ruining their trap. Either way would be, like, borderline disastrous. This better be the valley; he went forward.

But before he'd gone a hundred feet, he stopped. Right there, bang in the middle of the trail, was what looked (to him) very much like a half a boot print. It was certainly a mark that something like a boot could make; he got down on his hands and knees to study it. Doubtless there were deer or elk or mountain goats or big-horned sheep (or *grizzlies?*) around, so maybe one of them had made this mark, but it looked to Eric like the mark a boot would make if someone, walking, just tripped up a little. He rose, backed up a little ways, and then came forward once again, deliberately catching his toe just after where this other mark was. The test was inconclusive. The mark he made was something like the first one, but nowhere near identical. Eric narrowed his eyes. He was the sort of guy who played his hunches, sometimes, and his hunch was he was getting closer — on a right warm trail — and he kept going on it.

The track got narrower, hugging the cliffside; it yielded no more footprints, animal or human or unknown. Eric could see that all along, this trail was being attacked by the elements, and by erosion. Heavy rains or melting snows had started rockslides high above; he could see a place ahead where there wasn't much ledge at all, and what ledge there *was* was covered by a pile of rocks of different sizes. There was like a gouge or gully cut into the hillside, running up and down; it was dry right then and full of stones, some of them quite huge. Eric checked the clear blue sky. The next big storm would mean another rush of water down that gully, he believed, with another major rockslide as a consequence. That might be the end of access to the valley, at least by that route, anyway. Though he couldn't see any great distance ahead — the trail bent fairly sharply left, around the mountainside — this was much the most unstable — make that *dangerous* — place he'd come across so far. A person who slipped off at this point would go shooting down another gully (this below the trail, of course), which was also very close to being perpendicular, and then, from it, drop straight down to the boulder-bordered river.

Eric bobbed his head just once; one downward glance was plenty. He was *not* the sort of guy who dwells on negatives (and he *was* the sort of guy who can't stand heights).

He hated this. His hands, his pits, his *sides* were soaking wet. To calm himself he sent his eyes on a field trip, checking out the view. They followed down the river — lovely sight — to where it started bending, and there he saw . . . their camp!

Eric felt his heart start pounding differently. He'd found them, no mistake. Three tents — or two and a lean-to, actually — or one shelter per kid. A fireplace. This *was* their camp. He didn't see a kid around, but hey! — that didn't matter. They were somewhere in the area, alive or dead. Probably alive, or Sweets would be in sight, taking down the tents, et cetera. Eric had a thought: Maybe Sweets had lost his way, screwed up the map and compass work. Would that be comical, or what?

He took a breath and started forward — slowly, slowly, testing every step, respecting the terrain, his eyes riveted on the pile of rocks ahead of him, the ones he had to cross.

And then he saw. . . .

At first, it didn't register as strange, or out of place. Eric, after all, was basically a city guy, and what he saw was just a tiny edge of what, on any city street, would be a little bit of litter: a tiny, sparkling little bit, just sticking out from underneath a stone.

Very slowly, he sank down again, this time to one knee. He reached and moved the stone and plucked the bit of litter up. It certainly was not an unfamiliar item, this small piece of cellophane, the kind they use to wrap a mentholyptus coughdrop in.

Eric smiled, but not as if he'd heard a joke, or met a friend (if any), or got the news of a promotion. His smile was more like a gourmet's, when faced with caviar and toast points. For a moment, he didn't move at all, just stayed there frozen, with that crinkly little paper in his fingers. Then he nodded as the

276

pieces fell in place, inside his mind, his memory. Elementary, my dear Sweetwater.

He began a close examination of the area around him, and there, about a foot ahead of where he was, he saw what he had (just) expected he would see. It was a piece of nylon filament, the thin but very sturdy stuff you use for flying kites, or certain kinds of fishing. It was taut and mostly covered up by stones, and it ran across the path in front of him.

Eric craned his neck and leaned way forward, to see if he could see exactly how the trigger worked. It *looked* as if the stones over the trip-wire were placed in such a way that wherever a person stepped, around there, the stones would shift, and one or more of them would drop down on the wire and give it a little jerk. Then God only knew what would happen. Eric couldn't see, but his best guess was that the lower end of the wire was tied securely around a solid, major rock, and that the upper end was tethered on a little keystone, maybe, which, when it was yanked on out of place, would make a major rock-slide start. A slide that'd surely sweep the trail completely clear of guys who liked a challenge.

Of course, there could be explosives involved, too. Eric wasn't an authority, but he knew you could get a lot of power in a real small package, nowadays.

He scratched his head. He wasn't about to try to cut the filament, or otherwise disarm the trap. Liking challenges was one thing, sure, but Bomb Squad wasn't him, no way. Not when there were easier and safer routes to follow. It'd be a real long step to go right over that unstable section, and on to a nice large flat rock on the other side. But Eric had long legs, and he was limber. One giant step for Eric-kind, he thought.

And took it.

At once, the world quick-tilted and flew out from under him. He didn't hear the little snap made by the small dry stick that Sweets (not all that long before) had stood up underneath that nice large rock, to make it look so flat and stable (instead of like the surfboard he had planned for it to be). Eric also didn't feel his flailing hand (the one without the rifle in it), clawing for a handhold, seize that piece of nylon filament and pull it loose, quite easily. It wasn't tied on either end, in fact.

He only heard the clatter of his fall and felt himself go speeding down the gully on his back, spreading out his arms and legs to try and stop himself, but thinking — even as he did these things — that he had (quite unfairly) had it.

29

OLD UNCLE
PEEPING TOM

When Sweets's eyes came open, he gave a little start. It wasn't that he'd tried to keep from falling asleep; as a matter of fact, he'd stretched his body out on the nice soft grassy patch and wadded up his little knapsack for a pillow. But there was always the fear of oversleeping, and that was what produced the little start. He quickly checked the sun's position, and then relaxed again. No problem. Just the briefest catnap it had been — nothing more than that.

He sat up, stretched, breathed deeply, happily, as what he planned came back to him. Then, very much by chance — although perhaps their movement, their arrival caught his eye — he looked downstream, below him to the right, and there was Amos Goodspeed standing on a rock, with Riley Roux beside him.

Sweets quickly lay back down again. The kids were looking at the river, but that didn't mean they had to keep doing that. He rolled over onto his belly and wriggled through the grass toward a little thicket to his right. Once he was behind it, he sat up again. Perfect. No way in the world they'd spot him there, behind a bush and — what? — most likely a half mile away. He took out his binoculars.

They made, Sweets thought, a mighty fine young couple. He liked the style of that Roux girl — just one of those first impressions you can get of a kid, sometimes. Her parents had real major money — he knew that — and her father had an attitude to match it, certain ways; but she looked unaffected, natural, in shape. Plus, she very clearly had a thing for Amos, there. And vice-surely-versa, he would say. Just the way they stood there with each other, you could tell; they had an easiness, the way they talked and smiled. And then — look there — the two of them were hugging, spinning 'round and 'round on the rock. Sweets had to smile, himself. It was a kick to see young people as happy as that. Amos, he *deserved* that kind of happiness; he had it coming to him. Nothing in the past was *his* fault, anyway.

The girl — Miss Riley Roux — jumped off the rock and down to the little beach beside it. Sweets's glasses followed her, and — whoa! — young lady seemed to have a swim in mind. A swim or something else you didn't need a top for. Sweets checked old Amos back up on the rock, but he's just standing there, and looking down, and smiling.

Sweets swung back down to Riley. Hey — certainly a sight to smile about, all right. He'd been quite correct in calling her "in shape" — oh, yes, indeed. There wasn't a single part of her that wasn't, he could swear that on a Bible, now; this kid had done some workouts in her life. But still, she also looked real womanish, he thought, not like those hipless darts of things you'd see on some balance beam, on ABC-TV.

Sweets followed Riley's naked body into the water. *And* caught himself, *and* felt his face go hot. Old Uncle Peeping Tom, he thought, and chuckled; then sternly: not *your* girl friend, buddy. Quite deliberately, he took the binoculars away from his eyes. The situation seemed to require . . . not name-calling, but a bit of, like, mature reflection. Was there anything so wrong with watching this young couple . . . in a state of nature, so to speak? After all, he *did* have what might be called a rather special relationship with the boy. And the girl, too, in a way. Saving a person's life *created* a relationship, he'd have to say. And his motives . . . well, weren't they, in fact, *most* like a connoisseur's, examining a gorgeous painting, say? A Botticelli maybe?

All this time, as he carefully refrained from looking down at the river, Sweets let his (naked) eyeballs wander carelessly around the lovely landscape that surrounded him. Now, they swept along the cliffside, more or less across the way from where he was, and —

Sweets yanked the glasses up again. Dear God.

What he was looking at was Eric, Eric jammed into the gully — this crevasse or chimney, would that be? — this washed-out space between the cliffs. Eric with a rifle in his lap. Eric looking down into the river, just where Amos Goodspeed and the girl were.

Sweets moved the binoculars up the gully to the path, the ledge, the trail into the valley. Obviously, his trap had worked — his just-in-case-the-mother-gets-real-cute trap. Eric had fallen down the cliff-side, sure enough, but what he managed to do was brake himself, somehow, before he flew out of the gully and down the last long drop into the river — or its rocky border. The guy looked pretty badly scuffed, but not so much that he couldn't shoot that rifle, and the shot he had, though on a downhill angle, would be a piece of cake for Eric.

Sweets jumped up, dropping the binoculars. He knew quite a number of things, even as he started running, screaming at the top of his lungs, down across the grassy space in front of him, heading for the river. He knew, if Eric was about to shoot, he couldn't make it there in time to save those kids — get them *down*, at least, behind a boulder. He knew they couldn't hear his hollering, where they were; the river's noise would drown him out, completely. He knew the chances were, like, *minimal* that either of them would chance to look in his direction, and see this madman, waving arms and pointing, with his mouth wide open, running straight down toward them. Hell, if *he* had Riley Roux to look at, he'd hardly get the urge to do a survey of the scenery behind him.

But there were some other possibilities. *Eric* could,

conceivably, hear him; sound does funny tricks on mountainsides, and both of them were well above the river's roar. Also, Eric might just *see* him; unexpected motion always catches eyes. And in both those cases Eric would have to decide whether to shoot him first, or not.

That'd take a moment, that decision. Because if Eric didn't shoot him first, he'd know that Sweets would hear the shots he used on those two kids, and would (once he heard them) dive for cover. Which'd mean Eric would still have Sweets to deal with, in a setting — on terrain — which clearly didn't favor Eric. And conversely, if he *did* shoot Sweets first, the kids would hear *that* shot and be alerted, probably get down themselves. Once they knew that they were being hunted, they'd be a different, and a greater, kind of problem.

It never occurred to Sweets that he didn't have to do what he was doing.

30

ACTIONS AND REACTIONS — 2

Jordan never heard Michael coming. That had partly to do with the sound the river's current made, and partly to do with how deeply he'd gotten into looking at Riley in the pool, and thinking how beautiful she was, how much he loved her. She was the first naked girl he'd ever looked at, not counting Karen Archibald, and he guessed that was part of the reason he found her so . . . exceptional, but he also had the feeling there was something else involved in it. The thing was that all the different parts of her, and especially the ones he wasn't used to seeing — her small breasts, her butt, her patch of pubic hair — they seemed so *perfect* for her, so adorably and absolutely *Riley-ish*. He couldn't imagine wanting her any other way or, indeed, liking any way more than the way she was. He couldn't imagine being more excited — and this was weird — more *touched* by any other kind of beauty. Jordan Paradise couldn't believe it, and couldn't understand it — and also didn't worry about it — but in addition to feeling himself get very much turned-on by watching Riley, he also felt like crying.

The other reason he didn't hear him coming was that as he got closer, Micheal had stopped yelling and was putting every ounce of energy he had into his all-out, pell-mell, red-dog sprint.

So, before Jordan even knew he'd left camp, Michael had his arms locked tight around him, and the two of them had tumbled, rolled — oh, two, three times — along the gravel beach.

31

DISAPPEARED
FOR GOOD

It's hard to run, yell as loud as you can, wave your arms (*and* point); and also look (a) where you're going, and (b) at a man with a rifle in a gully on a cliffside up and way ahead of you, and (c) at two kids, one in, one by a river, down and to the right, in front of you. Sweets would have known all that even if he hadn't been trying to do it, but the experience got the point across with a special and immediate authority. At any moment, he expected he'd be going ass over teakettle down that gentle hillside, whether he got shot, or not.

What he found himself doing was darting real quick glances at each of the three major points of interest (a, b, and c), bouncing from one to the next, more or less in sequence.

First he'd find old Eric — oh-oh, picking up the rifle: trouble.

Then he'd check the kids — Riley standing waist deep in the river, beckoning to Amos, now.

> "Come on Jordy," Riley said and smiled seductively. "I promise you, the water's really warm today. You'll love it."
>
> But he still shook his head. "I just don't feel like it, right now." He made a prissy face. "And anyway, I didn't bring a suit, and some of us . . ."
>
> "Oh, sure," she hollered, "*chicken*. That's what you are, nothing but a big chicken. I'm going to give you three to start undressing, fowl, and if you don't. . . ."

And last he'd look to see where he was heading — better veer to miss that 'chuck hole, over there.

Next time around, it seemed that things had gotten worse, and also weirder. Eric had the gun up to his shoulder, and down there by the river Amos wasn't standing on the rock but rolling on the beach, fighting — from the looks of it — with someone; who, he couldn't tell, just then. And Riley, she was running toward the two of them, and almost out of water, making just about the perfect target — for a person who could shoot a naked girl at all.

"Michael! Cut it out! Have you gone crazy?" Riley screamed, but when she'd gotten close enough to hear what he was saying, she dropped down in a knee-bend sort of crouch and started turning toward the cliff across the way. She'd never felt so vulnerable, *exposed*, in all her life.

". . . quick, behind the rock, he's got a gun . . . 'way up on the other side . . . he's going to shoot . . . hey, Riley, come on — quick!"

And then all three of them were scrambling to get behind the boulder, and when they got there, Jordan put his body over Riley's cold and bare and wet one, and Michael tried to cover parts of both of them with his.

"He was looking right this way," he panted, "directly at you guys. He must have slipped and fallen, to get down to where he is, but he'd still held onto this big rifle and — *I* don't know — somehow I *knew* that he was going to. . . ."

Even as he thought all that, a shot tore at the slope one step in front of him — before Sweets heard the sound of it, of course. He pushed off with the foot he'd landed on, trying to jerk his body to the left, begin the zig-zig-zag that he'd been told (one time was all it took) was best when under sniper fire. This time, though, the foot he pushed with slipped, and he went tumbling — instead of either zig- or zagging — down that grassy hill. He didn't hear, or feel, another shot, and wondered (while he rolled) if maybe Eric thought he'd gotten him.

Then — bump, turn, somersault — he found his feet were under him again, and he was up. His eyes, by reflex, jerked back up to Eric, just in time to see him disappear, for good.

Of course it wasn't until much later that he used that exact expression, talking with Buford, actually, in Buford's own apartment, holding golden sherry in a goblet in his hand. "I knew he'd disappeared for good," was what he said; there wasn't any better way to say it.

Eric disappeared behind a thunderous waterfall of rock — of rocks and boulders, dust and gravel, tons and tons that poured on down that cliff face, starting up above the ledge they'd all come in on. It swept those gullies bare of everything: loose stuff and anything that might have rooted there (including Eric), and it left a fresh, new, deeper gouge into the cliffside. Clearly, what there'd been was like a vertical fault line in the solid rock, that had started to erode before, but this time suddenly gave way and cleaned itself out altogether. Eric had been under it, so he had gone on down with it, and now was buried in a huge new heap of real old rubble, piled against the bottom of the cliff and even spilling half into the riverbed.

Sweets thudded to a stop in four more steps, eyes wide, heart pounding. He looked next for the kids, and there they were all right (*all right!*), the three of them, standing side by side, with one (Sweets now could see that it was Michael Gordon) pointing to the spot where Eric just had been. And then the three of them were looking at each other. Suddenly, the girl ran off, put on her shirt and shorts, and as Sweets watched, they wrapped their arms around each other, sort of huddled, with their heads together.

The three were talking, all at once, at first.

"Michael," Jordan finally said, a little louder. And he waited. They shut up. "You risked your life for us. If he'd started shooting . . ."

"Yes," said Riley. "Michael, you're our savior, you know that? If it wasn't for you — "

"No. You guys," said Michael. "No, it wasn't anything like that. Face it, he never even shot the gun. He probably was just a hunter. . . ."

"Shut up," said Jordan. "That's not it. There isn't a hunting season now. That guy was going to kill us. You saved our lives." He moved his head. "*He* saved our lives," he said to Riley.

"I know," she said. "I know. He absolutely did. Oh, Michael." And she laughed, almost hysterically, and rubbed his head as if her fingers, in that way, could tell him all the joyful, grateful things she couldn't put in sentences.

"I almost can't believe you did it," Jordan said, nodding up and down for emphasis. "No, what I mean is that of course

I can believe *you* did, but just that *I* could never have. You saved us, Michael, you're a hero, and I'll never, ever. . . ."

"Stop it, Jordy," Michael said. "Believe me, it was just a reflex. Really. You would have done the same, or better."

They straightened up, but stood there in a circle still, now holding hands.

"Jordy," Michael said. "That guy. You think he could have had — *you* know — like, anything to do with. . . ." He sort of jerked his head and shoulder toward . . . the world, back there, where they had come from.

"Hunh," said Jordan. "I don't know. I guess he could have." Then he shook his head some more. "I really doubt it. No. There must be . . . well, some other explana — hey, wait!" He turned to Riley. "Remember that arrowhead I found?" He switched to Michael. "I found an arrowhead, first day we were here" — he was talking faster now — "a pretty newly-made one. And before, back at the Drumbee Store, I heard these two guys talking. About some 'wild man', this guy said, who lived somewhere along the Little Drumbee. The guy telling the story said he 'skedaddled' when he saw him, so he must have thought he was dangerous. I probably should have told you guys what I heard, but — well — I just wanted to get out here so much."

Now he looked at both of them, in turn. "I'll bet *that* was who that person with the gun was. The wild man. Some crazy paranoid hermit who thought we'd come to spy on him, or settle on his land, or something."

The other two were letting that sink in. It was . . . conceivable. There'd been some stories in the papers: killings, kidnappings by different wild survivalists and mountain men. One story'd even gotten in *Sports Illustrated*.

"That'd be amazing," Michael said. "A paranoid afraid of us." He shook his head and made a little bitter laughing sound.

"I'm pretty sure that's it," said Jordan, nodding, talking softly, almost to himself. "No one's after me, not anymore. I have a new life now, like Karen said I would. That's over with. I'm sure it is."

They stood there for a moment longer. Riley and Michael looked over at the cliff and at each other, and then the two of them were nodding, too.

Sweets made his eyes go back on up the cliff again, starting at the immense rock pile at the bottom and then climbing up the fault line to the top. It seemed, already, much less like a wound in the rock than the place from which an old infection finally had been cut away. It was like a miracle, he thought, to have had the thing let go like that, just at the perfect —

make that *necessary* — moment. Sweets didn't *dis*believe in miracles, but agents were advised to look for other explanations. And maybe keep on walking, on the day they didn't find one. He wondered if, perhaps, that shot — the sound of it — could possibly have started something going, way up high. . . .

And then he saw the figure standing at the top, but back a ways, not at the edge; he wouldn't have been visible from where the kids were. He was simply standing there and looking at the big raw notch in front of him, it seemed to Sweets. Lacking his binoculars, he couldn't see his face or other details clearly; what he saw was just a slender man with nappy hair, a black man he was pretty sure, with nothing but a pair of low-slung, tattered trousers on. He was holding what appeared to be a heavy wooden staff, about as tall as he was. It was heavy enough and tall enough to be a crowbar, heavy and long enough to pry a big old boulder from the top there, send it tumbling. And one is all it takes, sometimes, to start a major rockslide.

In an old western movie, this guy . . . he would have been an Indian, the chief, the guy whose place this *was* (thought Sweets), whose ancestors were buried there, who hunted buffalo out on the range, and hid out in these mountains, where his spirits lived.

But now, in 1985, the buffalo were gone, and so were chiefs and Indians, from there. According to the Census Bureau, no one lived in these parts anymore. But Sweets knew this guy did, and understood the reasons why. Maybe they had ancestors in common; for sure they'd shared some similar experience, and feelings. And luckily, some instincts, too.

Before he'd thought what he was doing, Sweets put his palms together near his chest, and bowed. When he straightened up and looked again; the figure had disappeared, and the three kids had been joined by the other two, and all five were picking their way along the edge of the river, heading downstream toward their camp.

> The five of them had wrapped their arms around each other, as if they had no thought of letting go. Not for a good long time.

So, pretty soon, it was just Sweets by himself. But there was still a lot of sunlight left.

ABOUT THE AUTHOR

JULIAN F. THOMPSON never drove a cab or worked as a lumberjack, but he did coach a football team that lost only one game in five seasons, and later was a speechwriter for a U.S. Senate candidate who also lost just once. He and his wife, Polly, who is a painter, printmaker, and designer, live happily in northern Vermont in the winter and southern Vermont in the summer, for reasons that he swears make sense. His previous novels are *The Grounding of Group 6*, *Facing It*, *A Question of Survival*, and *Discontinued*.

DATE DUE